"This is Savage's third novel about the big lake and it is his best."

—Don Boxmeyer, Columnist Ret.
St. Paul Pioneer Press

"...the plot is intelligent and nicely complicated, the characters interesting, and the dialogue frequently quick-witted.

Among the many imaginative features of the book, however, is his astonishing characterization of Lake Superior."

—Lois Roney, Ripsaw News

"All in all, 'Lake Effect' is a good summer read that'll teach you something about the preciousness of the Great Lakes."

—Mary Ann Grossmann, Book Critic
St. Paul Pioneer Press

"Savage makes you want to believe it all in this his third and best-yet Lake Superior Mystery."

—Marshall J. Cook, Creativity Connection

"Another 'Superior' read from Mike Savage, pun intended."

—Amanda Parker, Manager
J.W. Beecroft Books & Coffee

"Fast action and crisp writing. Terrifically accurate hometown Duluth, MN/Superior, WI (and surrounding area) settings. It rips."

—Andy Goldfine

"The characters are interesting, the plot clever and the sense of place satisfying."

—Mike Nardine, Reader Weekly

Lake Superior holds almost 3,000 cubic MILES of water, enough to contain four Lake Eries, Lake Michigan, Lake Ontario and Lake Huron combined.

It takes 191 years to cycle all of the water in Lake Superior. Lake Erie cycles the entirety of its water in 2.6 years.

The Great Lakes hold about 18 percent of all the world's fresh water.

French explorers referred to Lake Superior as "le lac superieur," meaning "Upper Lake" a reference to the lake "above" Lake Huron. Lake Superior is also called Kitchi-gummi or the Great Gitche Gumee, derivatives of a Chippewa Indian term meaning "great water."

Lake
Effect

A Lake Superior Murder Mystery

PRESS

Box 115, Superior, WI 54880 (715) 394-9513

First Edition

ISBN Number 1-886028-44-3

Library of Congress Catalog Card Number: 99-91342

Published by:

Savage Press
P.O. Box 115
Superior, WI 54880

Phone: 715-394-9513

E-mail: mail@savpress.com

Web Site: www.savpress.com

Printed in the USA

Lake Effect

A Lake Superior Murder Mystery

by

Mike Savage

Dedicated

To

Cornucopia

Acknowledgments

I acknowledge my debt of gratitude to Molly Martens, Tish Stewart, Bob and Mary Brooks, Chuck and Beth Johnson, Debbie Zime, Jessica Radzak, Don Garner-Gerhardt, Kevin Ahlstrom, Susan Gleason, Dave Walker, Julia Voelker, Bob Ledin Jr., Pam Christman, and all my relatives and friends who have each in their unique and specific ways made vital contributions to my life and this work.

1

The lake is a big blue doom, being without personality—un-beginning
in its basalt bed in the heart of the continent.

—Jeff Lewis, in "Lake Superior"
from his book *Treasures from*
The Beginning of the World

The great gray lake trembled in the cool morning air. A giant shudder crawled across thirty-two thousand square miles of surface like goose bumps marching across cold, tight skin. The largest body of fresh water in the world was waking up.

The huge, strange behemoth shivered all along its silver spine. Three hundred and sixty-five miles long from its head in Superior, Wisconsin—to the rapids and shipping locks of the Sault St. Marie in the east, the lake rolled and pitched itself to a higher level of consciousness.

Not one entity on the planet understood the watery being. The Rocky Mountains had an inkling. They were big too. But soooo pretentious. They posture and pose for countless pictures. They give up the royalties on countless post cards and calendars. They accept the admiration of millions of visitors a year. The only thing they haven't figured out yet, is how to autograph the flashy coffee table books. On the other side of the planet, Everest understood somewhat, being the singular mountain on the orb. The massive mountain identified with the immensity of the lake. But still, all the great deserts, all the vast plains, the great seas—all were noted, distinctive; either being hated or loved or singled out for particularly reasonable reasons. Lake Superior's greatness, on the other hand, was basically ignored by National Geographic and the rest of the nature publications.

This lack of respect made the Big Lake generally cranky. This grumpiness came out in the spring when the lake, in direct opposition to the surrounding geography, refused to warm up to summer.

For all of June and most of July the lake fussed and mussed and exhibited antisocial behaviors such as raining on parades and spoiling golf tournaments. It was like that one aunt or uncle who sublimated their hostility by being unpleasant at family picnics. However, by the time midsummer rolled around, the lake, like the disturbed auntie melting when she's handed the newest newborn baby, warmed to the music festivals, sporting extravaganzas, and other celebrations that people insisted on celebrating on its shores. The exposure to all of the good vibes helped the lake's self image improve to the point where it almost always granted a genuinely sublime Indian Summer of warm days and balmy nights smelling of fruit and berries and luscious humid decay.

With the fall departure of its fair weather friends, the Big Lake started to feel lonely again. The rejection helped it get in touch with its dark side. November is always an iffy month around the beast. Sometimes the dark side can turn downright mean, as was the case on 10 November, 1975. Woe to the ship caught in a monster November storm. Beyond woe, worse things are perpetrated by an angry Lake Superior. The mighty Edmund Fitzgerald and the 29 crew aboard met their sorry fates in one of the lake's most monumental tempests.

By mid-January the Big Lake's mood turns frigid. Everyone still populating her shores is treated to the cold shoulder. The on-again/off-again indifference of November and December hardens into the unmitigated hostility of icy winter. Hunkering down into its basin, pulling huge blankets of white snow over its shoulders, the Big Lake throws off glacial winds of, sometimes, pure brutal cold.

During these atrocious times, oddly, the lake can be the most beautiful. On the ice, fishermen dropping lines through the thick skin, hear the lake's somatic breathing. Deep rumbles and thunks of ice expanding and contracting telegraph the deepest dreams of the sleeping giant. The rumpled sheets of ice stretching off for miles to the horizon project a certain singular uniformity and solitude that does not exist in civilization or the soul of mankind.

When a single small man, standing alone and tiny in the middle of such unquestioned grandiosity perceives the truly immense nature of this gigantic beauty, true humility is the only response. While mankind grapples with the severe beauty of the lake's primal nap, the creature takes its great rest.

And thus, the cycle of life continues for the Big Lake. Year-in, year-out, it coped with being the ungainly cousin at the Natural Wonder family reunion. Shunted to the periphery of ecological family gatherings precisely because of its colossal enormity, the Big Lake had come to terms with its invisibility. It had learned patience over the eons. Learned that all good things happen in their own good time. Learned that, even bad events, when given time, will always work out for the best.

On this particular June morning, the Big Lake woke up shuddering. It sighed crosswinds of remorse and spit up petulant waves of irritability. The far western shore, with its thirty miles of pristine sandy beach, absorbed the ill-tempered waves with good grace and compassion. The entire lake sagged heavily—so heavily, it bent the very crust of the earth, despite being firmly held by the oldest solid basalt basin on the planet.

The Big Lake was conflicted. Unusually conflicted. Big changes were foreshadowed. The feeling in the air was reminiscent of those few eons ago when the lake was even larger. The shores were wider, the depths deeper. Back then, the waves on the western end lapped up against the crests of the bluffs twelve miles distant. Back then, the Big Lake discharged its overflow to the south. It's northern shoreline was defined by the edge of the receding glacier, last of its kind, first to gouge the future Hudson's Bay. To the east, a solid sheet of water rippled to within sight of the Appalachians.

Then, after centuries of stability, something snapped geologically. With a roar, the miles-thick black basalt granite that had held the enormous lake, shifted. Billions and billions of gallons of water exploded to the south. The flood destroyed three highly developed civilizations. Wiped them out without a trace. The entire planet reeled from the atmospheric effects. Tiny tribes in the Middle East experienced rain the likes of which had never been recorded.

One tribal chief, in order to save his family, built an ark larger than the biggest ore boat to endure the unending downpour.

The last of the dinosaurs south of the equator learned to swim again—before they drowned for the very last time. The event was so cataclysmic that the great granite bed in which the Big Lake slept, tilted eastward. The Niagara Escarpment was formed and the flow of water to the south ceased. The prehistoric body of water cascaded to the east over the Niagara Escarpment eventually forming a great falls that ate away at the earth and formed the largest river by volume on the planet.

Before long the water level lowered enough to form Sault of the St. Mary's River. Lakes Michigan, Huron, Erie and Ontario were born.

Something akin to those long-ago events was happening now. There was a familiar foreboding, a mild premonition of great events about to unfold. And yet, as the lake awoke, it knew that the events about to occur were not on the seismic scale. No, this morning it was a still small voice whispering in the wilderness that said there was change afoot.

As with all change, there was a vague feeling of doom. Sensations of imminent calamity fogged around the bays and beaches of the primal beast. At a fundamental level of awareness, the Great Blue Doom knew that its essence was once again flowing south and west. The new flow southwest felt odd to the lake. The siphoning stung with a real feeling of diminishment. It felt angry. It felt exploited. It felt abused by the men responsible. Something had to be done.

The Lake looked around. There wasn't a human soul awake for miles. It was safe to act. Slowly a slender spout of shimmering, silver water rose up out of the waves. It rose and rose like a snake charmer's cobra. It towered high above the tall red clay cliff that bordered the sandy beach. Then the Big Lake sneezed. A precise blast of water sailed through the air and showered a man sitting on the lip of the bluff. The water finger retracted instantly.

"Dave" Davecki awoke with a start. He rubbed his face, looked around. Peered up and down the beach in the soft gloom of the early morning light. "What the?" he said.

2

Some things have to be believed to be seen.

—Ralph Hodgson

lphonse "Dave" Davecki scanned his surroundings. He was seated on the crest of a tall clay bank that overlooked the wide beach of Wisconsin Point, on the eastern edge of Superior, Wisconsin's beautiful natural harbor. There was enough light to see clearly. But it was not yet dawn. He looked over his shoulder and to his left and right. There was nothing in evidence to suggest a solution to the water problem he'd just encountered. He looked at his wet palm again. The water was beaded up. It glistened softly in the early morning light. *Where the hell did that come from?* He shrugged his shoulders and scrubbed the wetness into the dense, ballistic fabric of his red Aerostich riding suit. He rubbed his face again and then rubbed his hands together. "Weird," he muttered. He massaged both his thighs, "Man it's chilly," he said.

His voice reverberating in the lucid air surrounding him brought his vision back to the water in front of and below him. He gazed far across the seeming infinity of Lake Superior. He leaned his long nose into the east wind. The breeze brushed gently the fragrant scent of pureness across his angular face.

The eastern sky lightened even more. When he'd arrived an hour ago, the cloak of velvet blackness above made the silver stars seem close enough to touch. In the dark, the only sure evidence that there was a body of water before him was the sound of waves washing ashore and the immense blackness that flowed like a river of dark from the radiating ambient light of Superior and Duluth on the left.

As the light grew in the east, the black above had given way to gray. A faint horizon appeared. The black below had evolved into dull blue, the color of glacier run-off. Far, far in the distance, a thin break in the blackness began to bisect the scene like a line across an Etch-O-Sketch. The horizon was opening its eye. Custard white clouds oozed outward from the line across the panorama like delicious eyebrows. The feather edges of the eyebrow cloud flared magenta. Swiftly the magenta bled inward turning the eyebrow into flames shooting out in all directions. The cool blue indifference of predawn was being heated by the red hotness of sunrise.

Suddenly a sliver of intense yellow erupted from the watery horizon. All the water around the intense flame boiled. The sliver grew. The deep velvet retreated hastily. The gray of dawn ran away from the fullness of day. Lively pale-blue sky surged westward like a stampede of life. Behind the pale blue, an intense, rich, blue blossomed with power. The rapidly expanding web of light, color and life swept across the sky in a furious explosion.

In the fullness of light, Davecki looked at his left hand again. He looked across the sand to the waves.

The lake played dumb.

There was nothing but relatively smooth water all the way to Minnesota. He gazed across the waves for a long time, fixated on a nearly invisible point of land thirty miles distant. He looked left to Duluth. Two miles away, flashes of brilliant golden sunlight reflected off triple glazed windows of million dollar houses perched on the crest of Duluth's Central Hillside. Almost in the middle of the Duluth backdrop, Davecki saw the piercing green light of the Superior Entry blink mechanically atop the squat red-roofed lighthouse at the end of the east pier.

Then he looked back right where the water, the land and the horizon met. *That's about where Canada starts*, he thought. He looked back left. *There's downtown Duluth.* He looked a few degrees to the right. *That's gotta be about Lester River*. He looked further right. He shielded his eyes with his right hand, squinted. *That's about Two Harbors*. Looking back to where his attention had been drawn, he stared some more. *That's gotta be about Silver Bay*. He shook his head. "Get a grip, Alphonse," he admonished himself out loud.

He got up and scanned the immediate area again. The only sound was the waves nudging the sand far below. They sounded like little laughs, the kind of laughs people use when sharing an inside joke and the object of their tittering is nearby.

The long strand of sand curved away to the right and left of Davecki. To the west, the ponderous clay bank withered into sawgrass, subsided, and eventually gave way to sand dunes that humped their way silently toward the water. Large chunks of weathered driftwood blemished the dunes here and there. On the right, the elegant clay banks undulated to the east. Balsam and poplar trees growing on the tops of the banks watched over the entire scene. Davecki looked up. *Blue sky... nothing but blue sky do I see.*

Davecki looked out at the lake again. He rubbed the trace of wetness from his skin again. Or maybe he was rubbing it in more deeply. "Something strange is going on," he muttered, and he turned from the huge, strange, weirdness that Lake Superior is and did what everyone who ever connects with the lake at subliminal levels always ends up doing. He walked away.

Ambling through the tall grass that swayed in the offshore wind, Davecki crested a slight rise in the field that was once the City of Superior's dump. He breathed deeply.

The smell of fresh water, fresh wind and the intangible scent of wide-open spaces accented with the aroma of freedom filtered through his lungs and into his soul.

He looked westward, looked across the slough of Superior Bay at the tall taconite silos of the Burlington Northern Santa Fe loading facility. Just beyond were the huge, decommissioned ore docks. Two ducks sped across the surface of the still water between the industrial site and the marsh grasses across the road. In the marsh, fifty yards from the road, a great blue heron stood on long spindly legs. At the side of the road a brilliant red Honda VFR motorcycle was parked.

Shards of morning light reflected off the bike's chrome. The stabs of light pierced Davecki's eyes. He pinched the bridge of his nose with his thumb and forefinger. He stopped walking. He glanced back toward Silver Bay. Song lyrics popped into his head. *Something's happening here. What it is ain't exactly clear.* Davecki scratched the back of his head, ruffled the loose brown hair hanging there. He eyed the Honda waiting at the side of the road. The piercing light shards cut his retinas again. Shaking the stabbing pain in his eyes away, he resumed walking and thought, *Something tells me this summer is going to be very strange.*

He jumped the fence, walked up to his trusty motorcycle mount and threw his left leg over. He twisted the key that he'd left in the ignition, and thumbed the starter button. The YokoOno custom carbon fiber mufflers blatted throaty echoes of exhaust across the water toward the BNSF facility.

The blue heron took flight. It tucked its long neck into a tight ess. The long legs trailed behind the graceful bird as its powerful wings flapped slowly. Water dripped from the bird's toes.

Davecki donned his helmet. The curly cord attached to the helmet bounded and rebounded between the man and machine. He thumbed the Push To Talk trigger on the handlebar and said, "Headquarters" into the helmet mic. Listening to the cell phone dial the police desk, Davecki thought, *Strange or not, a man's gotta eat. Time for a little breakfast.*

"Police department," a woman's voice answered.

"Connie!" Davecki yelled. He revved the bike's engine higher. "I'm coming in from Wisconsin Point." He banked the bike hard left into the on camber and uphill corner rising from the flats to the top of the clay bank. "No, I didn't see any sign of underage drinking. I scoured the beach from one end to another and then I established a covert observation site. Didn't see a thing." *No way am I going to mention that it rained on me and there isn't a cloud in the sky.* The right turn at Moccasin Mike road approached. Davecki shifted down two gears. The engine whined. The exhaust rapped. "I can hardly hear you!" He twisted the throttle and got the weight off the front tire for the ninety-degree right turn. Exiting the apex of the turn, he yelled, "Tell the Chief I'll be a little late. I gotta get some breakfast!"

Davecki torqued all the throttle he could find, shifted up, and yelled, "I can't hear you. I'll call later!" He thumbed the PTT button, toed the shifter up again and rocketed for Julie's Restaurant, home of the best and cheapest breakfast in town.

3

An answer is always a form of death.

—John Fowles, The Magus

Far across the lake from Davecki, five miles north of Silver Bay, Minnesota, Little Willie Horton's classic, black Harley sailed awkwardly into the pristine morning air. The big bike's V-Twin shovelhead engine howled as it over-revved. The bellow of the slash-cut Screaming Mimi exhaust pipes echoed up and down the rocky coast for miles. Hundreds of ring-billed gulls were frightened awake from their early morning dreams of french fry handouts. One huge gull, the bully of the Palisade Head pecking order cocked its head, following with beady, orange-ringed eyes, the aerodynamically challenged Milwaukee iron's attempt at flight.

The 1977 FLH, elegant while harumphing down the highway, behaved badly in midair. It had as much lift as a four hundred pound rock. It fell. It fell like the proverbial ton of bricks. The machine dropped its nose in surrender and plummeted toward the profane boulders below.

The better to follow the motorcycle's fall, the gull launched itself into the air. It wheeled about on the strong updrafts of cool air that shot up from the lake's relatively placid surface.

The updrafts were whooshing up the granite face of Palisade Head. It was a long face, over two hundred feet from the water to the brush-covered top. Following the downward spiral of Willie Horton's entire earthly economy, the bird knew that food of some type always accompanied human folly.

At the back of the Hog, the many silver studs and flashy conches of two large leather saddlebags reflected compound shards of dawn sunlight. The covers of the oversized bags flapped crookedly like the crippled wings of a car-hit crow. Fluttering from the bags, hundred dollar bills created a green stream of cash that looked like the contrail of a Grand Forks, North Dakota B-52 high in the jet stream.

The lake was calm here, calm as an open sea can be. Long sweeping swells rose and fell as they shrugged toward shore. Then the indifferent waves slurped ashore like gigantic gulps trying to swallow the huge boulders strewn about the cliff's base.

The motorcycle shrieked its last and crashed horribly. Chunks of metal and gleaming chrome parts exploded in every direction. Hundred dollar bills poofed into the air like the WTC dust cloud.

The gull was about to swoop down to inspect for food, but movement on the mountain brow distracted it. Rising quickly on the brisk updraft, the gull got to the top in time to see a man running from the cliff edge.

Something was happening here. What it was wasn't exactly clear. The running man was tall and broad of frame. A slight paunch, hairy and gleaming white in the strengthening light, bounced up and down between the lapels of a dirty denim vest hanging loosely on the strong looking shoulders.

The running man darted into the bushes. He stretched his muscular arms out in front of him to ward off the limbs of sumac, balsam, birch and aspen. Multiple tattoos, some faded, some bright and new, garnished the hairy arms. Bulky, black engineer boots thunked dully on the solid granite as he scuttled up the cliff's rocky scalp. Long brown hair flowed straight down like a horse's tail between his shoulder blades. The hair obscured the matted club logo embroidery that festooned the back panel of the vest.

As the man's back vanished into the bushes, a silver Thunderbird careened over the crest of the narrow roadway that curved down into the small parking lot. The car skidded to a stop at the rock wall between the blacktop and the cliff edge.

The seagull carved another turn in the pure air.

The car door opened sharply. A snakeskin cowboy boot heel thunked down. A lanky man emerged from the car. As he rose, the lanky man swept a large Stetson cowboy hat onto his head. The ivory colored hat stood in stark contrast to the man's black hair and deeply tanned face. It was an angular face. A sharp, aquiline nose heightened the intensity of the dark brown eyes that scanned the parking lot. "Damn it!" the man said.

"AILLL," the gull squawled.

"The name's not Al buddy," the man answered. Scanning the

area again, he said, "I could have sworn he would be up here."

The gull squawled again. Glancing up Lanky Man said, "Well, he couldn't have gotten far. I'll find him." The door-ajar alarm bonged its mild calamity. The lanky man started to lower his slender frame to fold himself back into the driver's seat when he stopped abruptly.

The man lifted his head and twitched his knife-like nose upward. He sniffed, turned his head and sniffed again. He said, "I knew he was up here."

The man slammed the car door. He jumped like a cat to the top of the stone balustrade fronting the parking lot and reached inside the soft suede cream colored blazer he wore. From under his arm the man's bony hand extracted a pistol. The menacing black gun looked small in the big bony mitt that wrapped around the carbon fiber weapon. The man pushed up on the brim of his ivory Stetson with the gun's muzzle. He turned his head sniffing all the while. He jumped down and hustled nimbly downward toward the ledge.

Five feet from the dizzying precipice, the man slowed and bent his long frame to the ground. His knees cracked loudly as he stooped. He reached down with the gnarled fingers of his left hand and pinched up a small pile of black powder. This he raised to his nose. "Still warm," the man muttered after smelling. He stood and whispered, "I got you, you bastard."

The lanky man moved to the edge of the cliff and lowered himself to his belly. He crawled to the very edge of the cliff. Looking over, he sighed. "What a loser," he announced to the wind.

He pushed back from the edge and trotted uphill across the granite. At the edge of the bushes the man stopped and yelled, "Come on out asshole!"

The only reply was the wind whispering through the leaves.

The man scratched his forehead with the muzzle of his pistol. He looked around, glanced at the inlet to the parking lot. He looked at the fence that kept only the lazy off the towering orange antenna that rose like a needle from the rock. The man sighed loudly. He looked back into the bushes. "Son of a bitch. Now I'm going to have to go in there and get him." The man glanced toward the parking lot entry. "Make it fast, Nevada," he said.

The gull watched as the lanky man named Nevada strode into the bushes. The ivory hat bobbed and weaved around the clumps of vegetation. The hat had only gone a few yards when Little Willie Horton bolted from the brush running full tilt for the parking lot. Horton's big boots thunked loudly on the granite.

From a clump of sumac a loud curse echoed.

The gull watched as the ivory hat turned abruptly and sped through the bushes toward the parking lot.

Little Willie pumped hard in his big boots toward the car.

The ivory hat broke out of the brush as Willie was halfway across the lot.

The lanky man raised his weapon. He did not fire. "Give it up asshole! I got you dead to rights!"

Little Willie kept running.

"Stupid. Stupid. Stupid," the man said.

The malicious black pistol flexed its slender shoulder unquestioningly.

A ten-millimeter shell casing jumped from the breech.

Instantly, Little Willie jumped into the air like he had catapulted off a trampoline.

"I'll be damned!" the lanky man said. He looked at the gun. "Useless piece of Austrian crap," he said. And he took off running.

When Little Willie came down from his adrenaline-enhanced vault the thick heel on his left boot caught the surface and tumbled him. Just as he started to rise, the lanky man advanced with gun drawn.

"I told you to stop, knucklehead. What's the matter with you? You got shit for brains?"

Little Willie uncoiled from his crouching tiger position and hurled himself into the midsection of his enemy.

The lanky man dodged Horton's charge like a matador and grabbed the biker by the flapping vest in passing. "So it's going to be like McDonalds, hey? HAVE IT YOUR WAY," he barked. The lanky man tugged Horton around in an arc and smashed the bulky biker into the back of the Thunderchicken.

Horton was a solid man. Instead of crumpling to the ground in a heap he bounced off the car. A bright stream of blood gushed down Willie's forehead. Without hesitation he charged Lanky Man like a water buffalo. "Have it your way is Burger King, you creep," Little Willie yelled.

Lanky Man pirouetted again, jumped into the air like Bruce Lee and, using the heel of his inordinately expensive rattlesnakeskin boot, kicked the rampaging biker into unconsciousness.

"Burger King, McDonalds, they're all the same ya loser," Lanky Man said. He placed his gun in the underarm holster. He glanced at the entry to the parking lot. "Move it, Henderson," he muttered.

He tugged his Stetson down on his head and grabbed Little Willie by the arm.

Rolling the big, bad biker over, Little Willie's vest flapped aside. There above his left breast was a strikingly beautiful tattoo. It was a tall waterfall that cascaded onto huge boulders. Emerging from the frothy bottom of the splashing water, gigantic rocks transmogrified into big block letters that spelled the word FALSIES in red. The lanky man coughed out, "That explains everything."

Hauling Little Willie forward powerfully, Lanky Man stooped low and executed a swift fireman's pickup. Two bundles of hundred dollar bills fell from the pockets of Little Willie's vest. The man hardly glanced at the money. Instead he humped Little Willie toward the cliff edge like it was a rescue competition. At the cliff, the lanky man launched Little Willie into the air. As Little Willie's arm flew by, it knocked the Stetson free.

"Damn it!" the man said. He ignored Little Willie's falling body and watched the hat tumble downward. Then he turned and sprinted toward the bushes again. He scanned the ground briefly and suddenly bent to pick up the spent shell casing. He hustled to the rear of the T-Bird. He stooped and picked up the bundles of money. Stuffing the money into the inside pocket of his suede blazer, Lanky Man scrubbed at a small splash of blood with his boot toe.

The gull, floating effortless about ten feet above Lanky Man's head, screeched again.

The man looked up and told the gull, "The love of other people's money is the root of all evil." He jumped into his car and burned rubber exiting.

4

Mighty in diction and contradiction the Big Lake never apologizes, explains or justifies. It just speaks, sometimes loudly, sometimes in a whisper. Regardless of tone or dialect, it is always speaking, speaking, speaking to those who have ears to hear.

—Rev. Emil Meitzernen
at commercial fisherman
Chunky Cadot's funeral.

The gull wasn't interested in the car's rapid departure. It swooped down to examine the red spot on the blacktop. It pecked at the blood twice and took off again. It dove over the edge of the cliff and sped toward the blue water below.

Little Willie's body had rebounded off the boulders and skipped like a stone into the water.

Today the Big Lake was accepting donations as it had done so many times before.

Usually the contributions came in the form of sinking ships, swallowed greedily during gigantic storms. Little Willie's battered body was received with a small, shallow splash. Willie's carcass settled into the rhythm of the waves and bobbed like a fisherman's bobber signaling a bluegill nibbling below. Horton's soul was off the hook now.

The alpha gull did not hesitate. It swooped down and plunged through the swarm of cousins that were circling for the feast. The bossy gull landed on the biker's beer belly. Horton's header into the boulders had partially scalped him. His twenty inches of light brown hair swirled in the water like detached sea kelp. The gull waddled up the undulating torso. Orange webbed feet stepped on various tattoos; a naked lady, a cannabis leaf, the fresh FALSIES waterfall. Various sized yin and yang symbols artfully graced the skin.

Horton's long tresses entangled themselves in the frayed vest.

The muscular frame rolled gently in the two-foot swell that swept shoreward. Like a log birler at the Lumberjack Championship at the Hayward Musky Festival, the seagull walked across the buoyant body. Cautious in the way of all animals that court civilization, the bird jerked its head nervously about, wary, too familiar with the diabolic nature of humanity. It leaned its beak toward Horton's death-glazed eyes. It's a law of nature. Every carrion eater goes for the eyes first. If there is no defense of the eyes, there will be no trickery.

And so the seagull supped. It feasted on the eyes of a man who had seen too much, lived too hard and taken one too many chances. The price of that hard living having been exacted by the feathered debt collector, the lake heaved up a sudden swell that pitched the gull from the corpse. The still-hungry bird flapped into the air with a shrill cry. Apparently breakfast was over.

Calming down instantly, Lake Superior wrapped its wave arms around the mortal remains of Little Willie Horton. Had anyone been watching, they would have seen a miracle, the suspension of the natural laws of wave motion and water hydraulics. Rocking the body gently, the Big Lake guided Little Willie away from shore instead of into the nearby rocks. At the same time, tiny little finger-waves began herding all the packets of floating hundred dollar bills and shooed them into a line like little ducklings following in the wake of Little Willie Horton.

The swarm of gulls followed the body away from shore. Every time one of the flock tried to land for snacking, a wave would squirt up and frighten the devourer off. Eventually they all, even the bossy bird, tired of the pursuit and returned to the parking lot to wait for negligible nibbles held skyward on the tender fingers of timid tourists.

The fabled saying, "Lake Superior doesn't give up her dead," was going to be untrue in Little Willie's case. But for now, there were miles to go before Little Willie truly slept.

5

But they deliberately forgot that long ago by God's word the heavens existed and the earth was formed out of water and with water. By these waters also the world of that time was deluged and destroyed.

—2 Peter 3:5-6 NIV

r. Don Cameroon, senior professor of geology and theology at the University of Wisconsin–Superior, was honoring his commitment to his employer by actually holding class on the cool summer morning. He stood at the front of a dozen dozy students in the cavernous Old Main classroom. His sturdy physique was accentuated by the green chalkboard directly to his rear. For his seventy-some years, the professor possessed a surprisingly youthful frame with broad shoulders hinting at rugged virility. His dark, piercing eyes scanned the room.

Cameroon cleared his throat. "The Lake Superior Rift Valley at one time—several thousand years ago, at least—contained five times more water than it does today. Modern geologists call this ancient body of water Glacial Lake Duluth. At that time, a tall barrier of solid basalt existed between Bardon's Peak at the western end of the Duluth escarpment and Big Manitou Falls at Pattison State Park south of Superior. A gigantic waterfall, far larger than Niagara, cascaded southward. There are evidentiary water marks in the Thompson Dam area and Jay Cooke State Park that indicate a reverse course of the flowage on the waterway that is now known as the St. Louis River. It is *this* waterway that was the original source of the Mississippi river." He unbuttoned his tattered Ecuadorian sweater. "Any questions so far?"

The brown-haired beauty in the front row fluttered her ivory hand gently and asked, "Why did it stop?"

He glanced at her. The look lasted longer than normal. "Beauty, my dear Ms. Shyness, does not excuse one from coherence. Why did what stop what?"

The young woman's nostrils flared. She narrowed her eyes, "Why did the flow to the south stop? Was it too old?"

Cameroon snorted loudly. His laugh echoed heartily around the room. Two students woke up. He rocked on his heels, grinning. "Ahhhh the exuberance of youth," Cameroon said. He moved across the room to the east and gazed out the tall window that admitted more light than the school admitted mistakes or students. "Before I answer your question directly, Ms. Shyness, I'd like to remind you and your youthful cohorts herein," at the word herein he turned and swept his large hairy hand in a wide arc to describe the entire room, "that old age and treachery overcomes youth and exuberance in every instance." Cameroon chuckled.

"In the absence of a more specific question about geology as opposed to my biology, I presume you are asking why the water stopped flowing south? Or why Lake Superior water levels dropped? Or is it why the outflow changed from the western outlet to the Mississippi, to the outflow into the St. Mary's River at Sault Sainte Marie. Or perhaps all three?" He raised his eyebrows.

Miss Shyness nodded mutely.

"All three then," Cameroon said. He left the window, stalked to the chalkboard and snatched an eraser from the tray. He slammed the eraser against the chalkboard. The chalk in the aluminum tray rattled. White chalk dust exploded. "FORCE," he bellowed. He craned his neck back to examine his flock. "Force," he repeated, "not the sudden, catastrophic force of, say, a volcanic eruption, but equally powerful."

He tossed the eraser into the air. Obediently the felt pad slunk into the narrow tray like a chastised dog returning to the kennel. He grabbed a chalk and scrawled EROSION high-wide-and--handsome as he said, "EROSION."

He chucked the chalk into the kennel with the eraser and paced the room. Sweeping his arm toward the tall windows, Cameroon said, "Seven thousand years ago, these windows, this building, that campus out there, were all under one hundred and sixty feet of water. What changed all that?

"What probably happened was this. The relentless FORCE of the cascading waterfall ERODED the basalt the same way the Niagara river is channeling through the escarpment it falls over. Eventually the natural dam burst. The resulting outflow of water was cataclysmic. It created the Sea of the Great Plains that at one time kept all of Nebraska, Kansas, Texas, Oklahoma and parts of South Dakota underwater for decades."

An eager-looking blonde boy spoke up. "That means that, way back when, the Black Hills were beach-front property."

Cameroon looked startled at signs of other intelligent life in the room. "Precisely, Mr. Fleming. Very good."

The boy beamed, his toothy smile actually diverting Cameroon's attention from his girlfriend in the front row.

Warming to his subject, now that more than one person in the audience had actually displayed some interest, the professor pulled off his sweater. A fine burst of talcum-like powder mushroomed into the atmosphere when he tossed it across the back of the chair tucked under the oak desk that centered the front of the room. Turning, he hooked his thumbs into the waistband of his khakis and continued. "The shores of Glacial Lake Duluth receded as the water rushed southward."

"What happened to the Great Plains Sea?" Mr. Fleming interrupted.

Cameroon scowled. He paced three steps in silence. He glanced at Fleming, then said, "It sank."

"HUH? How can a lake sink? Things sink in lakes, not the other way around," Fleming said.

Cameroon grinned. "You're right, of course, Mr. Fleming. I suppose it would be more accurate to say the land absorbed the water. By and large, the entire freshwater Sea of the Great Plains was sucked up by the earth, creating what hydrologists call the Missouri aquifer. There was a certain amount of evaporation and some flowage to the Gulf of Mexico of course, but the greatest volume of water soaked into the arid desert that is now the Great Plains thus forming the Missouri aquifer, one of the greatest underground pools of freshwater on the planet."

"Nebraska and those other states were a desert?" asked a young woman with frizzy, red hair that erupted in wild strands like solar flares. She was tall and sitting splay-legged at her desk wearing a tan GIVE ISLAM A CHANCE T-shirt. Her supple legs emerged from dark brown cotton shorts.

"They were. And they will be again."

"No way!" Fleming exclaimed.

"Way, Mr. Fleming. Way," Cameroon replied. "The Missouri aquifer has been pumped dry. The water has been virtually depleted, at least compared to levels of one hundred and fifty years ago. This depletion has been accomplished by crop irrigation, the irresponsible watering of lawns and golf courses, too many showers by too many people on too many days, too much laundry, the unconscionable waste of water in industrial processes, too many swimming pools, and on and on and on."

"Wow!" Fleming said.

"Wow indeed," Cameroon mimicked. He folded his arms and half-leaned, half-sat on his desk. "Much remains to be seen. No one knows the consequences of global warming, overpopulation, and natural resource gluttony. It is my view that a water Jihad is inevitable. Perhaps not in my lifetime, but certainly in yours."

He paused and again surveyed the students before him.

"Lake Superior will one day be the focal point in national and global politics. When this happens, first the cash will flow as quickly and forcefully as a flood of water. But, eventually—and unfortunately, blood, if history is any indication—will flow just as freely.

"I don't think so," the redhead said. She crossed her lovely alabaster legs.

Cameroon smiled. He casually reached to his left and picked up a manila folder. "Maybe. Maybe not. It's difficult to say what starving, thirsty people will or won't do. As we've seen at the WTC and the Near East, things can get ugly and uncivilized in a hurry." Opening the folder Cameroon said, "I'm going to quote a Texan as he was quoted by the *Chicago Tribune* of March 25, 2001. The title of the article is: TIME BOMB TICKING AT EARTH'S ARID EDGES. The specific issue was water for the city of El Paso. I quote: The growing population is thirsty. About 90 miles to the south of El Paso is an area known as the Valley of Hidden Waters. This valley has a self-sustaining aquifer."

Cameroon unfolded a large piece of yellowed-looking newsprint from the folder. He continued, "The city wants the water. The farmers say it's theirs for irrigation. An anonymous Texan from El Paso says, 'If 2 million people need the water, then 75 farmers can go to hell,' and I end quote our articulate Texan friend."

"Wow," the redhead said. She uncrossed her legs, leaned forward. "Those Texans sure are a bunch of gunslingers."

Cameroon arched his back and looked at the ceiling. He shook his head. "Wow. What vocabulary you people have," he said.

Then he said, "As the mentality of Texans is not our main focus here, I'd like to inform you all that water diversion has always been an issue, not just in Texas and the arid parts of our globe.

"Back around 1965, after Jeno Palucci—the pizza roll king from Duluth—had made his fortune selling junk food to the masses, he proposed building what he called The Missing Link Canal from Superior to St. Paul. This waterway would have enabled commercial barge traffic to inexpensively transport grain from the northern Midwest states and Canada to one of the world's great milling centers. It would also have provided cheap transportation of European manufactured goods even further into the heartland than the St. Lawrence Seaway was providing. Those cargoes could have gone all the way to New Orleans and the Gulf of Mexico far more efficiently than going around Florida. What wasn't discussed openly was the fact that the canal would have also, each and every day, provided millions and millions of cubic feet of clean, fresh water for our southern neighbors to continue building their empires of agriculture, manufacturing, and luxury.

"So what happened?" Ms. Shyness asked. "Imagine this kind of intrigue happening right here in the Twin Ports!"

Cameroon chuckled. "Poor old Jeno. His fingers were soundly slapped by scoffers and, if I may quote Spiro Agnew, the ever present 'nattering nabobs of negativism.' After the idea was dismissed, Palucci packed up all his toys and moved to Florida."

"Wow, what a story," Red said.

"Wow indeed. And there's more," Cameroon said. He snatched up a book from the desk. "According to Albert Marshall in his book, *Brule Country*," Cameroon held the blue book aloft, "and I'm summarizing here, U.S. Engineers, spelled with a capital E, prepared a map of a proposed canal to connect Lake Superior with the Mississippi after a n1895 survey." Cameroon put the book down, picked up a sheaf of papers and said, "Ms. Shyness, would you dispense these copies of the proposed canal route to your fellow truth seekers?"

Shyness stood silently and accepted the task.

"SO," Cameroon boomed, "The canal idea wasn't original with Jeno."

"Amazing," Fleming said.

"I'm so happy you didn't say wow," Cameroon said. "And, there's more. In the nineteen sixties there was some discussion of building a water pipeline from Duluth to Arizona to provide the masses in the deserts there, and in Mexico, with water."

Cameroon's brow furrowed, he lowered his voice, "Even today, some people say that Great Lakes water should be used to refill the Missouri aquifer, that the pipeline should in fact be built. That the poor of Mexico and the millions of our fellow American citizens roasting thirstily in the Valley of the Sun should have access to OUR water. What say you to that, Mr. Fleming?"

"No way! If they want our water, let 'em come up here and live."

"So you're saying you'd be willing to have half of Phoenix, Arizona, roughly 2 million people move to Superior?" Cameroon scratched his chin.

Fleming did not answer.

"You remind me of a deer in headlights, Mr. Fleming," Cameroon said.

"We don't want all that riff-raff up here. We should send the water down there," Miss Shyness contributed. "They've got farms and families to think of." She was a pixie of a girl with pearly white teeth and cobalt blue eyes under curly brown bangs and long hair falling loosely to her shoulders.

"And what happens when their demand for our water exceeds what we can responsibly give? Do you, or anyone," Cameroon swept his arm in front of him to indicate the rest of the apparent zombies before him were welcome to speak, "know when the diversion of fresh water from the Great Lakes becomes an ecological disaster?"

The redhead raised her hand.

"Yes, Rebecca," Cameroon said.

"We've got all kinds of water. I mean, look at Lake Superior alone. It's huge. And there are four more lakes. No way would it hurt to send water south. Plus, think of the money it would bring in. I mean, we wouldn't just give it away would we?"

"Some people are advocating that it is our moral obligation to provide… how do they cast that particular proposition… to provide a cup of cold water in Christ's name, is how I think they phrase it."

"No way. That would be wrong. You can't sell water. Water belongs to everybody," Fleming said.

Red said, "It would be wrong to keep it from them, but they should pay for it."

Cameroon glanced at the clock. Papers began to rustle. Feet scuffed. "Not so fast!" he shouted. "Your assignment: by Friday I want a two thousand word essay on the pros and cons of diverting Great Lakes water. Good day to you," he shouted just as the bell clanged loudly.

He grinned, "Still with the great timing, Don," he mumbled. He stood and began gathering the folders, papers, and books on his desk. Into his peripheral vision a pair of thick, black shoe-toes stopped before the desk. He raised his eyes. Miss Shyness stood before him.

"Are you mad at me?" she asked. Her hands were rutting around the inside of her book bag as she spoke.

"On the contrary, Ms. Shyness. I'm entirely too pleased with you," Cameroon answered.

"Earlier you seemed irked with my question about the water flow."

"Oh well, chalk that up to persnicketyness," Cameroon said continuing to organize his documents.

"Persnickity. Wow! I haven't heard that word for a while."

"Ah the lexicon of the young. Entirely too mundane," Cameroon muttered.

"I was thinking, maybe you could read this," Shyness said. She extended a comb bound booklet toward the professor.

"What is it?" Cameroon asked.

"Poetry."

"I'm not a professor of literature."

"This is theological in nature."

Cameroon glanced in her direction. "Hmmmm," he said. He took the work and read aloud from the title page. "A Treatise of the Song of Solomon." He glanced at the girl.

She, hopeful of face and stature, smiled.

He, suspicious of hope and enthusiasm, didn't. He read more, "This thy stature is like to a palm tree, and thy breasts to clusters of grapes." He sighed and stuck the poetry into the Duluth Pack valise of green canvas and brown leather.

"When can we talk about it?"

"I prefer to have my one-on-one student sessions in the mornings, before classes. Call Phoebe the secretary and she'll schedule an appointment."

As he picked up the valise, one of the leather handles slipped from his grip. A thick blue folder slipped out. Written in bold print across the width of the folder was the word FALSIES. Cameroon grabbed the packet quickly and stuffed it back in the bag.

"FALSIES? What's that?" Shyness asked wrinkling her cute nose.

"If I told you, I'd have to kill you."

She eyed him without blinking. Her blue eyes softened.

Cameroon laughed out loud. "I wouldn't have to kill you. It's a joke. Seriously, falsies can be purchased from Victoria's Secret. You obviously..."

"Why don't you like me?" she asked in a low voice.

"Oh I like you, Ms. Shyness."

"Why don't you call me Linda?"

"I do beg your pardon. Linda it is."

She swung the book bag to her back and said, "Seriously, what's falsies?"

Cameroon glanced at the open door. "It's an acronym. Well, come to think of it, actually it's more of an oxymoron. I have a theology class in,"—he checked his watch—"seven minutes." He started walking toward the door.

Shyness walked with him. "Do you always use big words when you get nervous?"

"No," was all he said.

"Oh. I just thought you might be mad at me for asking dumb questions."

"There are no dumb questions, only stupid answers."

She nodded. "What's the acronym stand for?"

"It stands for Finns Against Lake Superior Import Export Schemes."

"So you really are against water diversion! Can I come to a meeting?"

Cameroon said, "Well, actually, the group is patterned after the secret societies of the old days. Groups like the FALSIES were closed to outsiders and infiltrators. Newcomers aren't exactly welcomed with open arms."

"That sounds fun. Can I come?"

"Oh, I'm sure you can," Cameroon said as he stopped at the doorway and bade the girl through with yet another sweep of his arm.

"When?" Shyness asked.

Eyes lowered, he followed her through the door. In the hall he raised his eyes from the coed's behind to see a woman leaning against the door frame. "FRAN!" Cameroon said.

"Don," the woman of fortyish answered. She had short black hair, thick eyebrows with a deep worry-V between. "Are you flirting?" the woman asked.

"I'm too old to flirt," he said.

The woman joined the duo in walking down the hallway. "The Chancellor will be very displeased. You certainly do seem to want to make a Marder of yourself." She extended her hand to Ms. Shyness. "I'm Fran Hansen. Biology."

"Linda Shyness," Linda said as she shook the offered hand. "I heard Professor Cameroon was an atheist. How can he teach theology and be a martyr if he doesn't believe in God?"

"That's because he's blind as a bat emotionally and has a remarkable facility to embrace double standards without hesitation. And, when I said martyr I meant Marder as in our most famous defrocked professor of recent history," Hansen answered. She laughed.

"Excuse me ladies, but your victim here is still alive. Could you at least kill me and wait for my carcass to stop quivering before you start eviscerating me in public? Besides, they would never fire me. Hell they can't even get me to retire at the normal age. And, for all here gathered, please let it be known that I'm agnostic."

"Whatever," Shyness said.

"Whatever indeed," Hansen said.

"I've got a computer class down here," Shyness indicated a hallway to her right. "So, can I come to a Falsies meeting Dr.?"

Hansen arched her eyebrows.

Cameroon said, "I believe in theology, not God. Theology is comprehensible. God, if there is a god, is not."

"I hate when men don't answer direct questions," Shyness said looking at Hansen.

Hansen grinned. "Yes. They are rude that way, aren't they? What about it Don? Can she come to a meeting?"

"You're a Falsie too?" Shyness asked.

Hansen giggled. "Well of course. It's all the rage right now. So secretive. So intense. No, more than that. I'd have to say passionate."

"Oh that sounds sooo cool. I'd love to be a part of a passionate group." Shyness looked at Cameroon.

Hansen looked at Cameroon.

After a long pause he said, "I'll think about it and give you a direct answer at the appointment you're going to schedule."

"I gotta go. Don't forget to read my poetry!" she said over her shoulder.

"Don. Don. Don," Fran said. "You are the biggest fool."

The two resumed their walk down the hallowed hall of learning. "I have two words for you Professor Frantastic…"

"I know… Mind your own business."

"That's three, and a far cry from the two I was thinking of. Besides, you know I've always been a fool for love."

"Love? COME ON! You are soooo cliché!"

Cameroon waved his free hand. "Keep your judgmentalism and your shame to yourself, young lady," he commanded. "Not to worry. Ms. Shyness will never attend a FALSIES meeting."

"Why? You going to keep her at home, barefoot, pregnant, and tied to the wood stove in the kitchen; tied there by frilly apron strings?"

"That's not a bad idea, but no. She won't be there, because I respect the group conscience about inviting outsiders in willy nilly."

Hansen laughed. "Willy nilly. I haven't heard that one in a while."

Cameroon huffed. The professorial duo stopped at a Y in the hallway.

"Oh Don, you are so dear." Fran said. She reached up and pinched his cheek.

He swatted Hansen's hand away.

"I'm so looking forward to the media circus. It will be a welcome change from the war news constantly. You'll be doing the public a real favor. The drama of it all. The PASSION. You could take her on a field trip to New York. We'll get to read about her first visit with the Chancellor. Someone from his office could accidently release the video tapes she made. We'll all be witness to your final greatest battle for a pension. Won't that be sweet?"

Cameroon scowled. "Yes, that would be sweet. Thanks for the prognostication. I can think of something even sweeter."

"And that would be?"

"Your funding for exotic species research getting cut-off because the Office of Homeland Security followed the money trail to Dubai. It would be nice to see your free ride come screeching to a halt."

"Don," Fran said over her shoulder as she sashayed away, "the only dismal thing I can see right at this time is your grandiosity." Hansen laughed a high, tittering laugh that echoed like a dozen sparrows singing in the deserted hallway.

"You wish," Cameroon muttered to himself as he strode toward his class in Erlanson Hall.

6

...Water will gush forth in the wilderness and streams in the desert.

—Isaiah 5:6-b NIV

Three thousand and some odd miles from the watery consciousness of Lake Superior, the inbred world of UW-Superior, and the muddled wanderings of Detective Dave Davecki, a gray gecko scurried from under a buckskin-colored rock and skuttered in a circle on stubby legs. Sand scattered from the animal's feet. The tiny lizard trembled, each of its beady black eyes rotating on an independent axis simultaneously. A pink tongue darted out. Something was wrong in the Valley of the Sun. Something was very, very wrong.

The animal could smell, taste, hear, feel, but not yet see, the danger. It scurried atop a fifteen-pound rock and rotated again in a nervous frenzy. Then it stopped, hypnotized. An onrushing tidal wave instantaneously ended its every dry instinct.

Seventy-five feet away and thirty feet above the lizard's last contact with dry land stood a tall, gaunt man. He wore an ivory Stetson, a tan, pearl-buttoned work shirt and boots made from the gecko's cousin. Around the waist of his faded blue jeans, a wide leather belt seemed to circle endlessly behind a large silver buckle in the shape of a bucking bronco. The man's face was sharp-featured, with deep lines radiating like ravines from intense deep brown eyes. His brown skin was burnished. The wrinkles that softened the harshness of the visage gave the appearance of soft, supple leather. This was a face that had spent decades outdoors.

Next to the gaunt, leathery man stood a person shorter than the cowboy by a full foot. This face was pale. Its complexion was buttery smooth. The face was almost as big as a dinner plate. This face was surrounded by fine white hair that wafted in the gentle breeze rising up from the small valley below them. The man's girth was

Sumo-like. Hung on the immense frame was an expensive western cut sport coat. The man's stomach bulged like a ship's bow from between the lapels of the three thousand dollar suede sport coat. Across the expansive belly, a taut, silvery silk shirt of blue stretched. From the ends of the sport coat's sleeves hung meaty hands, sparkling with diamond-studded gold rings.

The view from their perch was panoramic. "You know Nevada, I don't think I've seen such a beautiful sight since being in Vegas last week."

"How's that, Mr. Albertson?"

"I won six hundred grand in five hours," the fat man replied. He gleefully rubbed his large hands together.

"And tell me Isak, how is that beauty and this beauty similar?" the gaunt Nevada asked.

Isak Albertson scowled. He said, "Because they are both rivers of cash you damndable fool!"

"Oh. Now I understand, Mr. Albertson."

"Drop the Mr. Albertson crap Nevada. I know you're tired from flying down here. You always get snippy with me when you're tired."

"Sure thing, boss."

"Christ you are a pain sometimes."

"And what's so painful about agreeing with you?"

"It's your tone. Your damndable tone of superiority."

"I'm just answering you directly, boss."

"Don't go all innocent on me, Henderson. I know when you're trying to piss me off."

"Whatever," Henderson said.

"Well, screw you, Nevada. I brought you out here to see personally our moment of triumph. I'm not going to let your pissy attitude spoil the glory of this moment."

"And what would I be celebrating? You're the one who is going to make all the money."

"And that's as it should be. After all, I risked it. What you should be celebrating is the fact that you are an absolute frigging genius. Your mechanical genius and your pipeline connections are a technological wonder. How you got them pipeline boys to cooperate is beyond even me, Nevada."

"Thank you," Henderson replied. "It might behoove you to know that those pipeline boys might not exactly know entirely what's happening inside their tube at all times."

Albertson eyed Henderson. "I don't even want to know, Nevada. All I want to know is that the water is flowing. And, for that, I'm thankful."

"You're welcome. And thanks for the new hat."

Albertson turned his attention quickly to the rising water. "Yessir," he gloated, "before long the whole damn lake will be covered with half-naked women sunning themselves on the decks of hundred thousand dollar boats."

"Most of them bought from Albertson Marine," Henderson said staring straight ahead.

"That's a no-brainer," Albertson said. "What I'm waiting for," waving his arms in a large circle, "is the big marble statue with the bronze plaque that says: ISAK ALBERTSON: THE MAN WHO MADE THE DESERT BLOOM! Won't THAT be beautiful? Think of it Nevada, we're building a goddamned LAKE in a DESERT. This is a victory! You should be basking in the glory of it all for Christ's sake!"

"I didn't do it for the Lord."

Albertson stared at his companion. "You are such a pain," he said. Then he turned and watched the water surge and swirl across the desert floor.

Henderson lifted his Stetson, wiped sweat from his forehead with the upper part of his arm. The moisture darkened the light cotton of his shirt. Below them, the water rose. All around them, Tempe, Arizona sprawled out like a comfortable dog soaking up the sun.

Albertson groused, "And furthermore, if anyone should be worrying around here, it's me. I've got millions tied up in this deal." He waved his immense, pudgy hands in the arid air.

Henderson continued to gaze across the coulee. Dirty eddies of water swirled violently around the bottom of the swale. "Millions your daddy left you. Millions you made buying and selling WTC scrap steel."

"Hey, the media over-blew that. By a long way. Those liberal bastards at the networks just get jealous when somebody's making more money than them off that tragedy. They think they got exclusive rights to that deal. Hell, I don't see them doing an exposé on selling ads for WTC TV specials.

"Besides, the money doesn't matter. What's important is, I'm creating a lake in the desert that will make me go down in history as a great man."

His pudgy paw carved another wide arc in the hot air. "What's important now is that statue. If I lose my ass on this deal, I'll be a laughingstock. This whole lake thing will just turn into a big sewage ditch."

Henderson pulled his Sphinx-like gaze away from the water covering the desert. He fixed Albertson with a glacial stare. "Vanity, vanity, all is vanity," he said.

Albertson stood silently for a few seconds. "Well, anyway, the statue thing is no matter of yours. What does concern you is that biker. What about him? Is he going to be trouble for us?"

Henderson shook his head slowly. "No way is he ever going to be trouble for you. For me maybe. But your ass is in the clear if that's what you really want to know."

"You sure of that, Nevada? You seem awfully distracted. Or is it something else?"

"It's nothing else. The biker got what was coming to him. I wish to hell I could have rid the world of him sooner. I wish to hell he'd had the sense to simply fuck your daughter and take the money. But no, he was a Falsie, and that means they're planning something that requires the kind of money he got from the safe."

"Leave Dolly out of this. You didn't tell me he was a Falsie."

"I didn't have the chance with you blathering on about your damn statue."

"Did they get any of the money?"

"No. The loser launched his bike off a cliff and tried to hide in the bushes. Probably thought he could come back and pick up all the money once he got away from me. Now it's all going to end up in the Sheriff's coffers as recovered drug money."

"What was he? Stupid? Nobody gets away from you, Nevada."

"Some have."

"GOD! Would you lighten up? I'm just trying to pay you a compliment and you get nitpicky. Anyway, what do we do about the Falsies? What are they up to?"

Henderson put his hat back on. "Well, on the first point WE don't do anything. I do it. On the second point, I have no idea what they're up to. They're probably planning to buy a whole lot of 20/10/30 and fuel oil."

"Oh you can't be serious. With all the loss of civil liberties thanks to Homeland Security they can't possibly think they can buy enough fertilizer and fuel oil to do a McVeigh on the pipe?"

"Hey, they're farmers. Fertilizer and fuel oil are staples of their diet."

"I can't believe it. You actually think that's what they're planning?"

"It's what I'd do. That's what terrorists do, Isak."

"They're not terrorists. They're just backwoods conservationists."

"If you say so, Boss. Anyway… when I'm done down here, I'll go back and snoop around. If I can find out what they're planning, I'll put a stop to it."

"That's what I like about you, Nevada. You like taking care of the dirty work. Me? I like bribing the politicians and strong-arming the bureaucracy."

"Far as I'm concerned, Isak, your contribution is about as useless as tits on a boar. The U.N. has got it all fixed up already. Only thing all your money is accomplishing is speeding up the process, and making out-and-out thievery look like economic development. Those people up there are so far out of the money, they'll do anything to get a few bucks spent in their town."

"Yeah, like build a friggin' maximum security prison right in their backyard. Friggin' idiots." Albertson laughed. He straightened his spine, pulled his coat over his belly. Albertson reached up and clapped a meaty paw on the tall man's shoulder. "Just remember, Nevada. It's not a crime to divert water. It's already legal to take millions of gallons a day thanks to GATT and NAFTA. The only difference between us and those damn fool Canadians is, we had more sense than to go right out in front of God and all the people and try to do it from a giant tanker on the middle of a big lake and in broad daylight. Sure what we're doing may be pushing the envelope of legality a bit. But hey, I don't recall it being all that legal to throw people off cliffs."

Henderson snorted. He flicked a look at the sausage fingers on his shoulder. Albertson pulled away. "Isak, those people up there aren't stupid. At least some of them. They'd just as soon let the entire Valley of the Sun die of thirst before sending so much as one drop of their precious water down here."

"Obviously, everyone up there isn't in agreement. My money has convinced at least some people otherwise." Albertson fanned himself. "It's too hot to stand out here, especially when we're arguing. Let's go get some breakfast." He spun on the high heel of his boot and lumbered toward a large white Continental twenty yards away. Albertson paused at the passenger door and watched Henderson walk directly to the driver's side door.

"I'm not your damn doorman," Henderson said. He doffed his hat and dropped into the Conti.

Albertson muttered something unintelligible, opened his own door and dropped his considerable carcass into the passenger seat. "Who's the boss around here, anyway?" he grumbled.

Henderson put the car in gear, staring straight ahead. "You are, Isak."

"Damn straight." Albertson picked up a faded newspaper and rattled it loudly. "Now let's get over to Pishkey's and chow down. I'll read this to you while we go."

"Like Ross Perot, I'm all ears," Henderson said. He steered away from the lake birthing. He pointed the car's nose down an embankment toward the blacktop and the road to Scottsdale.

As the white car rolled through heavy traffic, Albertson read, "It's from The Business Journal. Guy named Mike Padgett wrote it. Headline says: 'NEW LAKE FOR TEMPE.'" Albertson cleared his throat and read, "In about a month, one of the most unusual man-made lakes in Arizona will start forming in Tempe.

"The lake, with a capacity of 980 million gallons, is designed to promote water recreation and economic development in Tempe, said Mary Fowler, marketing coordinator for the Rio Salado Project in Tempe.

"The lake will be filled with Colorado River water diverted from a series of canals. Later, treated effluent could be used to keep the lake filled."

From behind the wheel, Henderson said, "Where's that from?"

"From right here in Phoenix. Ain't that the damndest?"

"You sure know how to get good PR, Isak."

"You call that GOOD? Hell. The guy didn't even mention my name! The ingrate. I practically spoon fed him the story."

Henderson turned off the street and pulled into an angled parking spot in front of Pishkey's Palace. He shut the car off. "You never asked how much he got out of the safe."

"Who cares? A few thousand here or there is decimal dust. Besides, it was all Dolly's. For spending sprees." The big man reached for the door latch.

Henderson put out his hand. Rested it on Albertson's forearm.

Albertson twisted abruptly toward Henderson. "What now?"

"He got almost two million."

Albertson bounced agitatedly in his seat. "WHAT? You never told me that!"

"You never asked."

"Why in the name of God's green earth would I HAVE to ask about something like that. That's some pretty good money, Henderson. What the hell was that much cash doing up there in the safe anyway? I never put it there."

Henderson reached into the back seat and fetched his hat. "Dolly must have been building up a stash for some reason."

"That's a helluva stash. Where'd she get that kind of money."

"You tell me," Henderson asked.

"SHIT! The fucking United Nations I can handle. State legislatures I can handle. Hell, even a negative public opinion's a snap. Even the frigging FALSIES I can handle, because I got you. But these young people—they're too weird for me. What the hell was she thinking?"

Henderson narrowed his eyes. "I have no idea whatsoever."

"God damn it!" Albertson rubbed his belly. "Now my gut's acting up. Thank you very much for ruining my breakfast."

"You're entirely welcome."

"Don't get smart with me, young man. Take me back to the office. I got no desire for food now. Besides, I'm taking Talia to Hawaii tomorrow—she's been acting weird lately. Cranky. I figure she needs a romantic getaway."

Henderson grimaced. He tossed his hat back into the backseat and twisted the ignition key.

Albertson continued, "You've got to get back up to Wisconsin right away. See if you can stop those goofballs from whatever in good god damn they're planning."

Henderson backed the Continental out into traffic.

"Two million god damn bucks," Albertson muttered.

Henderson said, "But I just got down here. I thought you wanted me to supervise the outflow rates and erosion coefficients?"

"Forget that. I want you up there right now, yesterday in fact. I don't care if you just flew down. Get back up there and find out what the hell they're up to. Didn't you hear me the first time? Besides I want you riding herd on my daughter. Find out what she's up to at the same time. Take the Cirrus back up there and check it out before those crazies blow up the goddamned pipe."

"Anything you say, boss."

7

Fortune brings in some boats that are not steered.

—William Shakespeare, Cymbeline

A year before, a vengeful arsonist, who was still at large, had torched Davecki's last domicile. It was a fine place to live, atop the old ore dock in Superior's East End. The view of the lake was spectacular, though the near constant wind tested his patience often.

Since the big fire, he'd been living in a Toyota mini-camper. The little tin can of a home was perfect for his paranoia. He could move it around at will and avoid being burned alive.

As the months of living inside the tin can progressed, his longing to live in a place more permanent but just as unlikely to catch fire grew. After a year of basic vagrancy it seemed reasonable to assume that the real threat of immolation had passed. Then, while waiting for his yearly DRE at the St. Mary's/Duluth Clinic, he read an article in *Modern Maturity* about the tax benefits of living on a houseboat.

All the lights in his head went on at once. It made perfect sense. Live on the water. If the thing ever did get flamed, he could just dive into the natural fire extinguisher beneath him and be saved.

Charmed Davecki's life was. Less than a week later a For Sale by Owner ad appeared in the Superior *Daily Telegram*. Davecki was aboard said houseboat along with the builder/owner who was pitching the merits of the watercraft. Said owner was a stocky man whose iron grip felt crushing when Davecki shook it at the Barker's Island public landing. "I'm Nikos," the man said.

"Dave Davecki."

"Nice to meet you, Mr. Daytecky," the short man with the wrestler's body said. He hustled his powerful frame to the mooring lines and cast off saying, "Let's take 'er for a spin."

Davecki was impressed by the sound when the engines fired up. Nikos, seeing Davecki's eyebrows raise, said, "Not only is it entirely hand built from scratch, I put two supercharged Chevy big block 454s in. It goes like a raped ape."

Davecki considered asking how an ape got raped in the first place, and if so, how it went afterward, but he let it pass, not wanting the sales pitch to be interrupted by disturbing visions of simian violation and haste thereafter.

"What I can't figure out is, why in heck did you waste two gorgeous big blocks on a house boat, and why on earth you went to the trouble of supercharging them Mr. Ahhhm... Mr... ahhm?"

"Just call me Nikos, Mr. Daytecky. I'm like the artist formerly known as Prince," the swarthy man explained cheerfully. "Going by one name is much simpler."

This doesn't look good. Guy's an arteest. Probably asking a million bucks for his work of art.

"As to your questioning the use of rare and valuable Chevy big blocks for a mere boat, this thing is built to withstand everything short of a nuclear blast. Remember that movie *Storm of the Century*? Hell, this thing would bust those waves right in two! I mean, it weighs twenty-three thousand pounds dry. Get some big storm on Lake Superior and... BAMMO! This baby will carve right through the worst of it. But, the trouble is, it's so damn heavy, if you want to get any sort of speed up, you need all the available horsepower that can be coaxed out of every cubic inch."

When he had boarded, Davecki noted that everything about the vessel seemed perfect. *This appears to be a very high-class operation.*

Davecki settled on the comfortable cushions that wrapped around the stern. The Artist Known As Nikos chattered happily about the boat's construction. "Picked out the keel myself. Searched high and low. Tramped the woods from Embarrass, Minnesota to Crandon, Wisconsin. You know what?" Nikos asked. He turned from the instrument panel and large wooden wheel and stared at Davecki.

Davecki was suddenly aware an answer was expected. "No. No I don't."

"Finally found the perfect hard maple tree being cut down by a City crew on Elm Street. Can you believe that? I put thousands of miles on looking for the perfect keel-tree and there it was practically in my back yard," Nikos said.

"Imagine that, a perfect maple growing on Elm," Davecki said.

"Yeah. I thought about that too," Nikos said as the boat rumbled past the channel marker. Nikos heaved the heavy wheel hard to starboard and yelled, "I gotta show you what this baby'll do!" and he jammed the two chrome throttle levers forward.

The deck of the houseboat seemed to come alive below his feet. Davecki grabbed onto the railing as he was thrust backward by the acceleration. The boat seemed to rise out of the water. Once it got up on plane, the thirty-five foot craft behaved more like Michael Johnson complete with steroids. It fairly sprinted across Superior Bay toward the Superior Entry and a grand exit onto the Big Lake. There was no talking. The engines roared. The wind whistled. The men absorbed the powerful exultations of the happy internal combustion engines below their feet. Their legs flexed as the hull pounded the waves.

For a full ten minutes, Nikos pounded the boat across the waves. Then he cut the throttles. The boat sank into the rolling swells like a big chunk of concrete and Nikos yelled, "Don't want to give OPEC a heart attack. This baby really sucks fuel." The high-speed cruise had brought Davecki and companion to a spot about a mile due north from the red-roofed lighthouse. Nikos said, "Go forward and toss out that sea anchor will you? I'll get us some beer… if you want."

"Beer's good," Davecki said, "but it gives me terrible headaches. Unless, of course, you happen to be the one person in Wisconsin who stocks Stella Artois." He didn't wait to see Niko's face as he headed for the bow.

Back on the salon deck Nikos handed Davecki a bottle of Stella Artois.

"Where the hell did you get Stella?" Davecki exclaimed.

"Oh that? That's impossible to get around here. I got friends in Hamilton, Ontario. They mail it to me." Nikos gestured toward the rail seat, "Sit. Sit." He sucked down a long gulp of beer and launched his pitch.

"There's five different kinds of native Wisconsin wood in the cockpit alone. Plus, I used Honduran rosewood, Sitka spruce and Brazilian mahogany too. See that?"

Nikos pointed to the highly polished dashboard that displayed a glistening array of brass instrumentation. "That's teak. Very durable. Very expensive."

"And take this compass bollard." Nikos patted his calloused hand on a stand-alone pedestal between the wheel and the dash. It looked like the trunk of a small tree, except there was no bark. The smooth surface, the color of a palomino horse's coat, glistened in the softening light. "You're not going to believe this, Mr. Daytecky, but this here is a real live, honest-to-goodness spaulted maple tree trunk." Nikos beamed. He plunked his bottle down and squatted next to the bollard. He ran both his hands up and down the lustrous column like it was his wife's thigh.

Davecki felt his eyes glazing over. *"Spaulted?" And what the hell's a bollard?*

Nikos gushed, "The entire hull is white oak from the Penokee Mountains south of Sanborn."

Davecki looked around. *Should I swim for shore? It's only a mile or so. I could call a cab from Sky Harbor or hijack that Cirrus Design SR-20 parked there.*

As Nikos talked, Davecki watched the Duluth hillside growing purple. The sun was setting in the west. The available light on the hillside facing the harbor and lake was diminishing.

"See these cushions, Mr. Daytecky?" Nikos thumped the thick vinyl pads that formed a U-shape around the rear of the boat. "They're hand crafted by Rosslynn's Custom Upholstery of Billing's Park. That sea anchor? Custom crafted by Mirlee the Sail Maker from Oulu."

Davecki gave the purpling hillside one last, longing glance. "It's *Davecki*."

"Oh man, I'm really sorry. I'm terrible with names. Anyway. See that rail?"

"Handmade, right?"

"Exactly!" Nikos said. "But, what's more important is, that baby's made from a hundred year-old tamarack."

"That's old. You counted the rings?"

"Of course. Doesn't everyone?"

Davecki focused on the pink hue the rail had acquired from the setting sun. He looked west. The sun was huge and vanishing behind Bardon's Peak out by West Duluth. *Red sky at night, sailor's delight; red sky at morning, sailors take warning*, he thought.

Just like when he'd read the houseboat article at SMDC, a light went on in Davecki's head. *I could name this thing Steak Warning.*

Davecki bounced heavily on the transom cushions. Nikos described taking the tamarack from a place called Muskeg Swamp.

Suddenly Davecki didn't care. He drained the last of his Stella. He was tired of hearing about wood. Tired of listening. All that mattered was, it floated, it felt safe, and it was available. "How much?"

Nikos had the body of a rugby player but, at the question of money, his eyes flickered and narrowed. Davecki recalled Michael Douglas playing a junk bond king from Wall Street.

Moment of truth, Davecki thought.

"I really need the money," Nikos said. "I've been trying to sell this all spring. I've got to send my son to college in the fall."

That's good, a motivated seller.

"I've been asking a hundred and fifty grand."

Davecki didn't flinch. He did, however, stand up. "That's out of my league. Sorry."

Nikos held up his hand. "Hold on a second. If you're really a serious buyer, I'd take less."

"How much less?"

"Cash?" Nikos asked.

Davecki's fatigue lifted. "I have some savings. But not that much." Davecki walked over to the helm and twisted the wheel. "Feels good under the hand," he said. "If the price is right, we could get the money tomorrow if necessary."

"Seventy-five thousand," Nikos said without hesitation.

Half off instantly. I'm feeling much better. "Ummmm," Davecki said. He caressed the bollard with the palm of his left hand. *He's gotta take less.*

Nikos beat him to the punch. "I'm not going to take any less. That's a giveaway price. In fact, I wish I hadn't said it. But if you want it for seventy-five grand, you've got it, but you have to take it now."

"I haven't even been below decks," Davecki said.

"So that's in your price range?" Nikos asked.

Davecki scanned the boat. *Beats the camper.* He turned in a circle. *Pretty fancy-schmancy for me.* "It's in the range, but I'm not convinced," he said.

"I figured you had potential Mr. Daytecky. Otherwise I wouldn't have given you the Stella. You'd have gotten that skunk piss from

Chippewa Falls. I'll show you below decks and we can get another Stella."

"Best news I've heard all day," Davecki said.

"Holy mackerel this is nice," Davecki said as he turned around in the cabin.

"It's small, but you can't deny this is a fully functional, floating, two bedroom mansion for only seventy-five G's," Nikos said.

"What about the bathroom? It got a shower?"

Nikos took a swig of beer, said, "Hey, you wanna be a sailor, you gotta use the proper terminology. Out here it's the head and it's right behind that door."

Davecki grabbed the door handle.

"Solid birch, that door. No goddamned veneer."

Davecki opened the door. "I guessed as much," Davecki answered. He stuck his head in the head. A low whistle echoed out. "Man, this is fantastic. Is that marble?"

"From Italy. But first it was in the old City Hall. I got a bunch of it before they razed her. Looks awesome, doesn't it, Mr. Daytecky."

Is he trying to irritate me? Okay Dave, focus. He already came down seventy-five grand instantly. He's gotta be hurting. I'll offer him sixty. Davecki scanned the interior. Stove, fridge, cupboards, curtains, the whole nine yards was present and accounted for. *All I'd have to do is haul my junk from the camper into here.* He drained his Stella. *He'll take fifty grand. No he'll get pissed if I low-ball him.*

"You're thinking way too hard. I need some air," Nikos said. He bounded up the three steps to the salon deck.

Davecki followed. *He who hesitates is lost.* "I'll give you fifty grand cash tomorrow."

"You just like being an asshole? Or didn't you hear me earlier?" Nikos asked.

"Come on, Nikos. Lighten up," Davecki answered. "You and I both know you need to sell this thing. I'm not interested in getting in a pissing match here. I'm just interested in paying a price I can live with."

"I'm interested in getting a price my wife can live with. You throw that bone in front of her, she's likely to become rabid."

"Hey, I've never been married so I wouldn't know about that. But I do know, you aren't going to get cash offers every day or even every month. Hell, not in a year. You hold out, you might get more, but your wifey will be waiting all summer for the financing to be approved."

"Hey, cash is the same whether it comes from you or the mortgage company. I'm not going a penny below sixty," Nikos said.

Davecki stood considering his future. The soft evening light was as consoling as light can be. A gentle wind had picked up. "Doesn't that air feel good?" Davecki asked.

"Yeah, it's really nice. Usually it's cold out here on the water," Nikos said.

Davecki listened. In the far distance he could hear the drone of the BNSF taconite facility. There were little waves rippling against the white oak sides of the boat. He was sure the waves were, each and every one, murmuring: *Yes, yes, yes. Buy it. Yesssss.*

Who was he to argue with the largest freshwater lake in the world? Davecki said, "You know, if I hadn't gone in to get my prostate drained, I wouldn't be here."

"Huh?" Nikos said. "What the hell are you talking about?"

Davecki chuckled. He looked Nikos up and down. "Oh yeah. You're too young yet. Plus you're married. Your pipes get cleaned out regularly. Just wait. You've got a real treat ahead of you... getting all clogged up and having to get the old prostate drained is a truly unique experience."

"You're telling me prostate surgery might sell my boat?"

"Not surgery. That's old technology. Nowadays they're going back to even older technology, the infamous DRE and manual manipulation..."

"You are weirding me out man. We got a deal or don't we?" Nikos asked.

Davecki rubbed his chin. He listened. The waves were still saying, "Yes, yes, yesss. Buy it."

"Oh, don't mind me. I tend to get a little flaky during times of stress," Davecki said. He extended his hand, said, "Deal."

"Hot damn!" Nikos said, and they shook hands. "I'll get the anchor. As the proud new owner, you get to pilot it back. You ever been a helmsman before?"

"Many times," Davecki said to Nikos' broad back departing for the bow.

As Davecki stood before the instrument panel, decoding the gauges, switches and instructions, he heard Nikos yell, "HOLY MOTHER OF GOD!"

Probably a huge hole in the hull, Davecki thought. "What?" he called.

"There's a dead body tangled up in the sea anchor!"

"Oh for cripe's sake!" Davecki said. He jumped around the helm, pivoted past the bollard and careened alongside the cabin to the foredeck. Joining Nikos at the bowsprit he bellied down on the deck and peered over the edge. There, floating in the dark water and tangled in the rope was Little Willie Horton.

"What the hell happened to his eyes?"

Davecki snorted. "Probably a damn seagull."

"You know, technically, they're not seagulls," Nikos said. "They're actually Ring Billed Gulls."

"So I've been told," Davecki said.

"I thought it was a pretty hard pull at first," Nikos said. "Then I figured the wind had picked up. But this. This is not good."

"Why's that?" Davecki asked.

"Because now we gotta call the Coast Guard and they'll call the cops and there'll be a big investigation and you'll welch on your deal because you'll think the boat is cursed because it trolled a dead body in. My wife is going to raise hell now. CRAP!"

Davecki backed away from the edge of the boat. He looked out at the waves forming a vee behind the transom. "Sort of gives a double meaning to the term wake doesn't it?" he said.

Niko stared at Davecki. "Are you nuts man? This is serious shit." He looked at the rope he was clutching between both powerful hands. "There's a dead body at the end of this rope."

"Oh, yeah. I forgot. Civilians forget about the gallows humor of cops."

"What's that mean?"

Davecki considered Nikos' rattled condition and considered trying to get the price down another ten thousand. *Naw. A deal's a deal.*

"That means you've already got one of the three complications out of the way. And it means I'm not going to back out of the deal."

Nikos looked at Davecki. "What are you babbling about?"

"Well, you can call the Coast Guard easily enough with all that radio equipment mounted in the teakwood dash right?"

"Right," Nikos replied.

"Well then, the hard part's done, because the cops are already here." Davecki pulled out his wallet and flashed his badge.

"Oh man, what a relief!" Nikos said. "You're a cop?"

"Detective Dave Davecki, Superior Police Force at your service." Davecki grinned. "I've always wanted to say that."

"Oh man, what luck. Aren't you the guy who found Thurber Gronsby floating off Wisconsin Point?"

"He wasn't floating when I got to him. He was doing the old dirt nap on the beach sand. But, yes, the very."

"What luck. You saw the whole thing right? You know there's no foul play, right?"

"Oh there's foul play alright Mr. Nikos, just not on your part as far as I can see."

"What's all that stuff floating nearby?" Nikos pointed toward the water.

Davecki reached down and grabbed at one of the objects bobbing on the surface in the shadowy light. He pulled a packet of hundreds out of the watery deep. "I'd say this here is twenty-thousand dollars," he said.

"Holy mackerel," Nikos said. "No wonder you cops can pay cash for everything."

"Very funny. I wish it was so easy. Last cop from Duluth that bought an expensive boat for cash went to prison for a long long time."

"No kidding? What happened?"

"He went to Korea and bought a big boat for three hundred thousand cash, had it sailed back to Duluth and, for some odd reason, couldn't explain his wealth when the IRS started asking questions."

"Drug money huh," Nikos said.

"Nope. Pull tabs. But that's another story. Right now you better call the Coast Guard. Then we'll have to secure the body and gather up the money."

"Will do," Nikos said. Before he pushed away from the bow, he asked. "Don't you think it's kinda strange how all that money is floating around him?"

"I never classify anything as strange in this business. Especially when it comes to Lake Superior," Davecki said. "Now go call the Coast Guard, Mr. Nikos."

"It's just Nikos. None of that Mr. stuff for me. I'll call the Coasties."

"That more official nautical talk?"

"You betcha Officer Daytecki," Nikos said as he tied the rope off on a large chrome cleat at the bow. Corpse secured, he bounded toward the rear of the boat.

Davecki looked westward. It would be dark in an hour. It would be midnight before this was all booked in and he could get some sleep. He looked eastward. The first edges of darkness were looming up out of Ontario. "No rest for the wicked, Alphonse," he mumbled.

As iron sharpens iron so one man sharpens another.

—Proverbs 27:17 NIV

 Callahan… years and years ago the Milwaukee Journal had dubbed the larger than life figure, THE RICHEST POLICE CHIEF IN THE NATION. Right now he was probably the unhappiest cop in the county. As always, the perfectly tailored, expensive suit gave him more the appearance of a Mafia don than the chief law enforcement officer of the City of Superior. Not a silver hair on his large head was out of place. His pencil moustache was trimmed straight as a ruler. At the sound of his office door opening he said, without looking up, "You got a lot of nerve keeping me here this late."

"I got here as fast as I could, B.D.," Davecki said. He tugged on the rugged nylon zipper of his Aerostich suit and took a seat in front of his boss's desk.

"So I heard on the scanner." He nodded toward the black box in the corner of the room. Red LED lights zipped across the face of the low profile electronic ear. "Have you ever considered observing the speed limit? You're setting a bad example for the rookies."

"Hey, if they're so concerned, tell one of your rookies to arrest me instead of gossiping about it on the airwaves."

"Arresting a fellow officer is always trouble, nothing but trouble. Wouldn't be prudent." Callahan stood. He was a stout man, with a belly artfully concealed by the tailor-made suit and the massive width of his broad shoulders. His tipping waddle across the room hinted at obvious physical power, or at least, past physical strength. He crossed the room and lifted a carafe of water from his credenza. Ignoring the three glasses on the tray, Callahan drank directly from the carafe. And drank. And drank.

Davecki watched incredulously as Callahan patiently gulped down the entire contents with methodical repeated swallows, then placed it gently back down on the credenza. "Ahhhhh," he said. He pulled a monogrammed, pressed handkerchief from his breast pocket and dabbed at his lips. "Nothing like good old Lake Superior whiskey to quench a man's thirst. People don't drink enough water."

"What are you, a camel?"

"No," answered Callahan. "I've never had much of a taste for sand. But I read recently that most people are dehydrated." He returned to his desk. "Now, kindly tell me just how in the hell you managed to get into trouble even on your day off. If you had come in earlier to talk with Mothers Against Police Abuse like I asked, you wouldn't be in this mess."

Davecki shifted in the green fiberglass chair. "Why don't you get some comfortable chairs in here, B.D.?"

"Because I don't want the people sitting in them to become too relaxed."

"Not likely."

Callahan grinned. "What's the situation with your dead body?"

"Ugly, as usual." Davecki shifted again. "Guy's scalp was partially detached. Eyes pecked out. Damn flying-rat seagulls. He was all smashed up. And the Coast Guard told me it was my problem."

Callahan's eyebrows rose. "How did they reach that brilliant conclusion?"

"According to them we were in Wisconsin water. Just over the state line they said. Because the deceased was a resident of Superior, they said they would transport the body, but that's where their responsibility ended. Said it was local jurisdiction."

"And you believed them?"

"I think it was just convenient for them to have a Superior cop at the scene. What was I supposed to do?"

Callahan leaned back in his leather chair and steepled his manicured fingers. "You could have gotten the hell out of there and let the damn thing float into someone else's life. You always lack judgment, Davecki."

Davecki scowled. "I love you too, B.D. Wouldn't that have made a rather bad impression on Mr. Nikos?"

"Since when have the Superior Police been concerned about what the public thinks?"

"If that's true why did you want me to chitchat with MAPA?" Davecki asked.

Callahan eyed his Dick, "Because PR is PR and police work is police work. When the bad guys are bashing heads I want cops tougher than the MAPA ladies kicking ass. You used to be a tough guy before Detective."

"You're right as usual. Back then, this Dick followed his... way too much. Oh well, you know the story. But, I agree, I'm glad the piss and vinegar guys are working graveyard."

"And don't you forget it."

"Forget what Chief."

"That I'm right as usual." Callahan groaned. He bent his backwards. The sound of bones crunching echoed in the cavernous office. The big man returned to his desk. "So, it's no big deal anyway. The dead guy's from Superior? It would have eventually landed at our doorstep anyway. What's the name?"

"Little Willie Horton."

Callahan blinked. "No."

"Honest. I could hardly believe it myself at first."

"His old biker friends must have caught up with him."

"You're probably right. It had to be some old vendetta or something. Too bad."

"Why's that? I'd say it's good news. One less dirt bag biker to deal with."

Davecki rubbed his chin. "Not really, I heard Willie had straightened out." Davecki stood.

"Yeah right. Once a dirt bag, always a dirt bag. You know the difference between a Harley and a Hoover?" Callahan asked.

"No," Davecki answered.

"One sucks and one is a vacuum cleaner. I've never known a dirt bag to straighten out," the Chief answered. He stood up also. "Anything else?"

"There was a lot of cash present at the scene."

Callahan raised his eyebrows. "Excuse me?"

"There was a whole bunch of cash on him too. "

"I love your detective-like accuracy."

"If it's accuracy you want. Technically, the cash wasn't on him."

"What the hell are you talking about?"

"Well, it was more just floating around him. Like fall leaves crowding around a piece of driftwood."

"Don't start with the artsy fartsy metaphorical crap. Just how much cash we talking about?" Callahan strutted over to the window, half-sat on the marble ledge that made up the sill.

Davecki said, "There were two dozen bundles of Franklins hovering in the water nearby and five more stuffed down his jeans."

Callahan snorted, "Down his jeans? Don't even begin to tell me how you found them. What's twenty-nine times twenty?"

"I calculated it on the way here. Five hundred and eighty thousand."

"Sounds more like a drug deal than a vendetta."

"When the news of a body loaded with cash floating in Lake Superior gets out, I'm predicting there'll be a huge boom in fishing charters," Davecki said. "Just think of the tourism benefits. Treasure hunters will scour the shorelines. It'll be just like smelting used to be."

Callahan snorted, "Hey, if people will eat worms and drink blood on TV for cash, they'll certainly cruise Lake Superior with dip nets looking for floating twenty thousand dollar packets of hundred dollar bills." The stocky man walked back to his desk and sat.

"You seem antsy, B.D.," Davecki said.

"I am. I need to get going."

"Got a big date?"

"No, a small date. I'm taking my daughter to the WWF tonight. Now that Governor Ventura has been sent back to the ring where he belongs, she can't get enough. So, what else do you want to bother me with?"

"Why didn't the bad guys take the money? It's not like them to let that much cash get away," Davecki asked.

"Who knows? They probably got most of it," Callahan said. "Something you probably didn't do."

"What's that supposed to mean?" Davecki rose from his relaxed position.

"Don't get defensive. All I meant was, you and the Coast Guard probably didn't sweep up all the money. Cash will be washing ashore all over the place all summer."

"That's what I like. A lake filled with money," Davecki said.

"I suppose we'll have to alert the media to tell people the money is evidence and that they should turn it in."

"What do you mean WE, Kemosabe? You're the Media Relations guy, Chief."

"Don't give me any more of your lip. You're probably going house shopping first thing tomorrow. If I hear you went out and bought a new house, I'll have to start an internal investigation."

"Well, isn't that a coincidence," Davecki said.

"What?"

Davecki rose and walked toward the door. "It just so happens that I just bought an unbelievably beautiful house boat for sixty grand this very night."

Callahan stared at Davecki "You're kidding right?"

"No I'm not. That's why I was out there in the first place. We were testing out the boat."

"We?"

"Me and the seller. Nikos."

"Nikos is selling his boat? The one he hand built? The one with the twin six-hundred horsepower big block Chevy 454s? He said he was going to give me first chance at it."

"The very," Davecki said. "He obviously judged you well."

"What's that mean?"

"It means he probably knew you would have chiseled his price way too low."

"Up yours Davecki." Callahan looked thoughtful. "Nikos can verify all this?"

"Of course."

"It's going to look awful fishy to a lot of people, Dave. Maybe you should decline the purchase."

"I don't welch on a deal. Besides, it's a good buy. And another besides, I don't want you to buy it out from under me."

Callahan rose abruptly. He placed his palms on the desk. "I was merely waiting for him to become a motivated seller."

"Well, you waited too long, Chief."

Callahan snorted. He added, "Do you plan to contact the next of kin tonight?"

Davecki, standing by the door, grinned. "Nope. As Chief Public Relations Officer for the department, that's *your* job. *I'm* going to the Anchor for a burger."

Callahan glared.

Davecki stared back. Then he laughed. "Lighten up, B.D. There is no family."

"How do you know that?"

"I knew Willie from high school. He lived way out in the boonies. We used to go grouse hunting together on his old man's Harley trike. When he was thirteen, his whole family died in a house fire."

"What became of him after that?"

"Not that I've kept real close tabs on him, but, hey, it's a small town. Social Services couldn't find any living relatives so they placed him in a couple of foster homes. Marines. Vietnam. Drugs. Ascended to the right hand of the throne of the Lost Tribe and, when El Commandante for Life Sonja Bergeron died, he took over as President. Got religion and died at an early age by drowning in Lake Superior."

"You'd make a great obit writer," Callahan said. "I thought the president of the Lost Tribe was a guy. Sonny something, wasn't it?"

"It was. He was. Er, she was," Davecki said. "But she had a sex change operation and the club booted her."

"And those esteemed club associates? Should we notify them?"

"Like I said, best I know, he hasn't been affiliated for years." Davecki reached for the doorknob, then paused. "But there is one group who might want to know. I'll check it out."

"Do that," Callahan called after him. "Check out everything. That money came from somewhere, and I sincerely doubt it was from his savings account."

9

*You can find your way across the country using burger joints
the way a navigator uses stars.*

—Charles Kuralt

fter the arson fire destroyed his home on top of the old Great Northern ore dock, and after buying the Toyota mini-camper, and considerably prior to buying his first houseboat, Davecki bought himself a brand new 2002 Honda VFR Interceptor.

It was not, as some said, a mid-life crisis purchase. Davecki's love of motorcycles started early. His first scooter provided many thrills. His first Honda, a 305 Dream, provided a way to meet girls. Davecki and Little Willie went grouse hunting on the old 1948 45-cubic-inch Harley Servi-Car. After the fire and before his body fell into decrepitude, Davecki knew it was time. Time to get back into motorcycling. The VFR was the best machine for the job. At a hundred and thirty horsepower to the rear wheel—after modifications, of course— it was fast. It wasn't as rad as a Suzuki GSXR or a mean, green, Kawasucky crotch rocket, but it would still do excellent roll-on wheelies. And, with Heli Bars added, it made sport-touring down-right pleasant.

Another great attribute of the VFR was its ability to exit Davecki from the cares of the world. All he had to do was get on, get going, and let the cares of the world fall away in the slipstream behind him. Pulling wheelies could heighten these momentary escapes.

Which is exactly what Davecki did a lot of. Leaving Headquarters, he pulled a long second gear wheelie down Broadway toward Tower. After a reasonable "stop" at the red light he turned right and cranked the throttle as far as he could without setting a bad example for the rookies. He rolled past the Gentleman's Club on his right. *No gents there-in*, Davecki thought. Across the street, in front of the "Limplifter," as the beat cops called the strip joint, a lone woman stood holding a sign. *BE GOOD*, the sign implored. *Good for you,* Davecki thought at her. He thumbed the Push To Talk button of his integral cell phone and chanted seven numbers into the voice-activated dialer.

"Anchor Bar," echoed in his earpiece.

"Hiya, Bean. It's Davecki. I'm heading your way. Wanna have Paula throw together a Mexi-burger for me?" He listened and said, "Yep. Thanks." Listened some more. "Yes. I will. See you in a few." He thumbed PTT and opened the throttle.

A fast bridge circuit was another balm to Davecki's oft-tormented psyche. Speed always got Davecki in touch with his true self. The rush of shifting-twisting-leaning-being alert, and significantly ratcheting up the adrenaline content in his bloodstream always flushed the crud out of his soiled soul.

The speedometer registered 80 as he sped north on Tower. Another common phenomenon that Davecki most always experienced in the morning upon waking also tended to happen when riding the VFR at speed. Songs began playing in the left rear quadrant of his brain. As he set the bike up for the entry into the cozy sweeper that turned Tower Avenue into Highbridge Boulevard, *Whooooo are you, who-who who-who...* blasted out of his in-brain stereo and reverberated between his ears. Picking the apex of the turn, Davecki opened throttle slightly farther. He loved transferring weight from the front to the rear tire and sticking the suspension into the physics of a pleasantly on-camber corner. The law of inertia raised his angle of incline as he accelerated out of the corner. The right side of Davecki's brain proclaimed, *it's so nice when a body in motion tends to stay in motion!* His left brain answered with the, *deedle la deeee... deedle dul laa dah dah...* of Bach's toccata in D-minor for organ, his right brain chimed in, *centrifugal force is standing me up... standing me up... standing me up! My fair lady!*

To express his pleasure even more, he twisted the throttle hard and pulled a smooth acceleration wheelie that rocketed him toward the foot of the Highbridge. As the bike's front wheel danced above the ground, the singing in his head was accompanied by the music of the exhaust note rumbling from the YokoOno carbon fiber muffler.

Tipping the bike to the right for the Highbridge on-ramp dumped all the melodious echoes in his noggin out his right ear. The lean angle and g-force focused his attention on carving the line of the corner. The whine of the valve train chain and the hum of the tire blistering rubber became his new music. Cranking 5,000 rpms and building, the engine sang. No worries in the world could keep up.

Taking the Superior/Duluth Highbridge at speed was for love, or lust.

Surging past 100 mph up the Wisconsin side of the bridge, the go-fast virus infused all of Davecki. The mysterious joy that comes from weaving through traffic at triple digit speed began to crescendo as he streaked under the huge center span of the bridge's arches.

Rice's Point Flats at 142 mph was better than sex. Duluth's working water front of the DM&IR docks area, and the long, long Wisconsin exit to the Bong Bridge, along with the dash under the second set of blue center span arches was sublime.

The roll-on wheelie up the Belknap Street viaduct, the refusal to shift up between Globe News and the National Bank of Commerce produced nearly window breaking booms from the YokoOno pipe.

Better than dopamine.

He downshifted when a Talon's front end poked from behind CC's Tap. The car didn't pull out. He sped up.

Better than Welbutrin.

His gullet, now fully prepared for one of the world's best burgers at the certifiably tenth best tavern in Wisconsin, Davecki got off the throttle. He slowed as he crossed the railroad tracks by Sweeney's Flooring and Sanding. Decelerating past the strip clubs, Davecki noted that the picketer had moved from the Limplifter to the Gentlemen's Club.

That's a strange duck I'll bet.

By the Tyomies Building, Davecki shifted down and prepared to grab some front brake. Directly in front of the Anchor Bar on his left, he squeezed the lever. The VFR's rear wheel lofted in a perfect stoppie, the body of the bike pivoted smartly on the hinge of the front end's neck bearings and clomped back down to earth.

Davecki let the clutch back out and, with the throttle at something just over a high idle, he maneuvered the bike around and backed it into a parking spot right in front of the Anchor's door.

He dismounted, took off his helmet, plopped it over the upside mirror, draped the cell phone's curly cord across the gas tank, and entered the "best dive in the Twin Ports" as owner Tom Anderson described the Anchor.

Davecki walked in. As expected, occupying the first stool was Luke the Lucky, the Anchor's afternoon anchor. Luke was widely known as the best stream fisherman in the area. He caught steelhead when steelhead weren't supposed to be caught.

"Dave," Luke said.

"Luke," Davecki replied, and waited.

Luke didn't disappoint. He delivered his standard line. "You know, we gotta go fishing together some day."

"That we do, Luke. That we do," was Davecki's equally standard response, and he ventured on in, deeper and deeper into the musty-trusty womb that the Anchor is.

The nautical ambience wrapped around Davecki like a warm hug. The dusty USS Fleet flag drooping from the ceiling, the unpolished brass fixtures, the thick mooring ropes, the smell of frying burgers, and the sound of fresh raw fries crackling in the deep fat fryer all sounded, felt, and smelled good. He plunked his arse down on a stool about halfway to the solitaire machine.

"Hiya Bean," Davecki greeted the bartender.

"Hey Dave," Bean answered. Bean had been in the business a long time. "Too long," as she'd said many times. Davecki had witnessed Bean's tough and quick mind completely deflate testoster-one-pumped and malicious drunks with only sharpness of tongue. Now she was ringing up a sale at the cash register. A mean-looking six-inch-long sap hung from the ceiling above her. The braided leather head of the weapon was a work of art. A shorter bludgeon, the size of a child's fist, hung beside it. A brass scorpion dangled upside down next to the second sap. "Your Mexi will be right up. What can I get you?"

"Water."

She eyed him suspiciously. "No Leinnies? What's with you?"

"Most people are walking around dehydrated. I'm not going to be one of them."

Bean's eyebrows rose. "O-kayyyy…" She turned and picked up a glass and the water gun. "So, what's new?" She pulled the trigger. Water spewed into the glass.

Davecki glanced at the TV at the end of the bar, above and in front of Luke. CNN was broadcasting the weekly school shooting. He turned toward the Cyclops at the other end of the bar. Another terrorism expert blabbed. He was about to answer her when she said, "You and I should have a fling. It'd be fun."

"Sure, Bean," he replied.

She plunked the glass down hard on the bar in front of him. "You could at least laugh."

"Sorry." He shook his head. "I'm distracted."

"What's bugging you now?'

"Little Willie's dead."

Her eyes widened. "You're kidding!"

"Nope. Found him in the lake myself."

"I can't believe it."

"Too true," he said.

She said, "I just can't believe it. He was in here just last night."

"Really?"

"Would I lie?"

"Never known you to." Davecki rubbed his chin. "Anything unusual happen?"

"Nothing unusual for Willie. Left with some chickie girl. I just can't believe it," she repeated.

"You know this woman's name?"

"How should I?"

"Why shouldn't you?"

"Because I got a job to do, and it's not fooling around memorizing names of little size-six's wearing lycra," Bean said.

"She been around here much?"

Bean looked toward the grill. "Hey, hey Paula," she yelled.

Paula poked her pretty face out of the cubicle kitchen and smiled. "What?"

Bean beckoned. Paula walked over, wiping her hands on the white flour sack towel tied around her tiny waist.

"What's up?"

"Little Willie's dead," Bean told her.

"Oh my God!" Paula looked at Davecki. "Really?"

"It's true," he confirmed. "Any idea how I could get in touch with the girl he was with last night?"

Bean said, "Your best bet would be to show up after midnight tonight. I think she comes in with the Duluth rush."

"I hate staying up that late," he complained.

Bean frowned. "And you're a cop?"

"I think that woman worked at a coffee shop," Paula offered. "That new one up on Tower."

"Little Willie's dead," Bean said slowly. Davecki and Paula looked at her. "I'm trying to make it real. It sounds so strange. Little Willie's dead."

"What?" Luke called from the end of the bar.

"Little Willie's dead," Bean yelled.

"Oh, my god!" exclaimed a voice behind Davecki.

He turned and saw Rose, frozen in the act of clearing a table.

"He was in here just last night," Rose said.

"That's what I told him," Bean said.

Paula roused herself. "I've got to get your Mexi."

"Wait—the coffee shop on Tower... Which one? The one by Community Bank, or the one in the Nottingham Building?" Davecki asked.

"Nottingham, I think." Paula about-faced and headed for the kitchen. Knowing it was way too good a view, Davecki refused to watch her departure. Instead he fixated on the large brass pressure gauge that was permanently stuck on 400 PSI.

"I still can't believe it," Bean murmured.

Conversation ceased. Everyone sunk into a hypnotic state. On the juke box, Accidental Porn's hit, *Refusing to Rock Like a Rolling Stone* played. The two carved wooden busts of ancient mariners on either side of the cash register looked stunned also. Paula emerged from the kitchen with the Mexican burger. Despite his malaise, Davecki ravished the tall beauty. It was anchored by a hefty hand-patted slab of lean ground beef. Lettuce was stacked high atop a thick slice of onion. Salsa oozed down the sides. Teetering on top was a golden brown, East End Bakery bun.

Rose turned the corner by Luke the Lucky and trundled down the bar-way. Her hands and arms were loaded with dirty glasses, half full mugs, and catsup stained paper plates with crumpled napkins. Unloading her restaurant debris, she turned to Davecki and said, "I seem to recall that girl being a stripper or something."

In mid-chomp, Davecki recalled the protester in front of the Limplifter. Something clicked inside. *That's a lead.* He chewed hard.

Spoke around the food, "You know anything else about her?"

"She had a tattoo."

Davecki swallowed too fast, and before drinking his water chaser, asked, "Where? What kind?"

"It was one of those arm bracelet tattoos, like the kind all those NFL linemen have." Rose replied with a smile. Her eyes twinkled, revealing the kindness therein.

Davecki pushed back from the bar and stood. He unzipped the slash-cut pocket on his Aerostich and pulled out folding money. He threw five bucks on the bar and said, "Gotta run."

"Aren't you going to finish your burger?" Paula asked.

"Thanks for all your hard work Paula, but when it comes to a clue, food can wait," Davecki said.

"Don't be a stranger," Bean called.

"He can't help it," Luke remarked. "He was born strange."

"Good one, Luke," Davecki said clapping the fisherman on the shoulder in passing. He pushed open the board and batten door and fled.

He sped up Tower Avenue, and there she was, still picketing. Smack dab in the middle of Superior's seediest section of town, parading forth and back with her BE GOOD sign.

Johnny B. Goode, thought Davecki. Getting off his bike, he looked around. The urban landscape had changed greatly from the old days. Gone was the Saratoga Hotel where he'd worked waiting tables as a college student. Burned to the ground. Gone were the window tappers sitting behind glass like human confectionery for sale. Gone were the pimps, the moonshiners peddling corn whiskey, and the cops walking the beat. Gone were the thousands of sailors, foreign and domestic, all spilling pocket-loads of cash to grease the social machinery of the once bustling North End. All that was left of Superior's famed red light district were two derelict strip joints and one odd looking woman with a picket sign.

As he doffed his cranium can, out of the corner of his eye, he observed that she was observing him.

10

The message is: Water is not for sale. Water is a common good.
Let's not make it a commodity.

—Siegfried Kleinau, Lion's Head, Ontario.
Testifying at an International Joint Commission
hearing. From a story by Milwaukee Journal/
Sentinel reporter Don Behm. Published in the
Duluth News Tribune on Monday Sept. 27, 1999

orthwoods Coffee is a hangout. The brightest and best hooligan illuminati of Superior, Wisconsin gather there to emit the brilliance of their cognitions, shine the light of their profound thinking upon the gathered masses and keep their delicate caffeine-to-bloodstream ratio balanced.

"LTV Steel will never be closed," Don Cameroon suddenly asserted from the depths of his overstuffed chair.

Fran Hansen and Simon Jensen, seated on the sofa, looked at him, then at each other.

Simon worked for Fran as a deck hand/lab assistant on the L.L. Bean freshwater research vessel. A veteran of decades of sailing the various Great Lakes fleets, Jensen called the L.L. Bean a "freshsquatter" vessel. He carried out the orders of the day involving turbidity testing, current measurements and algae mapping, chemical analysis, non-native species acquisition, and the host of projects Fran's research created. Jensen was also the best diver in the Twin Ports. In that capacity, he worked with area law enforcement on artifact recovery jobs, more commonly known as fishing bodies out of the bay. For additional fun and income he contracted with shipping companies for below the water line vessel repairs. Jensen smirked at Hansen. They both hoisted their coffee urns to silently drink.

When his companions didn't respond, Cameroon continued. "Okay, so the fish aren't biting today. I'll just have to give you the hook. Of course it's already closed down. But it will reopen. That ore isn't going anywhere, and the greedy individuals who own it will come back for more. Like in *Poltergeist*."

Fran stared blankly.

Jensen said, "Don. Poltergeist was about a subdivision built over a graveyard. What does that have to do with iron ore? And what does iron ore have to do with... anything? Let alone water diversion."

Cameroon smiled. "At last, a fish to play! It has to do with the grand picture, the big picture. One day the papers will have big bold headlines, *THEY'RE BAAAAACK!* announcing the return of taconite mining in Hoyt Lakes."

Fran raised her eyebrows. "I question your simile, Don. Anyway, who exactly are these greedy individuals?"

"The super-wealthy. Ever since time began the rich have exploited resources. Rich cave men chased entire herds of wooly mammoths over cliffs just so they could eat a few pounds of fresh meat for a few days before it all rotted.

"Nowadays they run plants 24/7 with minimal maintenance. All they want is the ore out of the ground for the least amount of cost. For decades they've dug up the ore, crammed it through the machinery—pounded the entire plant into virtual uselessness—and shipped it east. Luckily they employ hard working, resourceful Iron Rangers who pride themselves in being able to fix anything and keep any worn-out piece of junk machinery running. The only money the super-wealthy put back into the place is what is absolutely necessary to keep it cranking out the taconite."

Cameroon leaned back into his chair and beamed.

"You're comparing wooly mammoths to LTV Steel?" Fran looked at Jensen.

Jensen shrugged and grinned. "I remember sailing with one captain who would always say, 'Any metaphor in a storm.'"

Cameroon, scowling, leaned forward, kicking the low table between him and his audience. Fran's latte sloshed onto the table.

"Don!" She grabbed her napkin. Wiped up the precious liquid.

"Rich cave men?" Simon said.

Without acknowledging his hecklers, Cameroon continued. "Here's how it happens. Some hung-over CEO realizes he's spent too much on the new Gulfstream III corporate jet or his golden parachute. He recognizes that the plant's efficiency is declining due to his failure to reinvest some of the profits on modernization. But, it doesn't occur to him to redirect a few hundred million of his own stock options into modernization. NOOOOO. He announces that the plant is beyond salvation and says, 'Turn out the lights the party's over!'"

"That doesn't sound like greed to me. It sounds like he's just facing facts. The plant's eating up the profit margin," Jensen said.

"That's exactly what they WANT you to think," Cameroon answered. He clapped a hairy hand on his knee. "What's really going on is, last weekend on the company yacht, Mr. CEO heard from his pal running mining operations in Brazil that they increased their profits by a zillion percent by shooting all the high paid workers and hiring children whom they chained to their work stations."

"Get real, Don," Fran said.

"Hey," Cameroon shrugged. "Hyperbole is cool. Especially if you're overreaching to make a point. The truth is someone in the elite decides there isn't enough profit margin to pay for their children's education. Or they decide they need to make even more money so they can buy bigger and better Christmas presents. So they shut down the plant, lay off all the workers, and go on a world cruise for a couple of years. And by the time their little darlings are old enough to require tuition, just about that time the state figures out how to come up with 400 million to refurbish the guts of the concentrator and all of the pelletizer. Then the owners concede that, perhaps, maybe, they could reopen the mine. But, of course, as a new corporate entity. And those laid-off workers? They come flooding back from wherever they went to get jobs. They're so eager to go back to work in their home towns that they'll take non-unionized jobs for half the pay they left a couple years earlier."

"Maybe you should cut back on your Falsies meetings, Don. You're going overboard on the conspiracy theories," Jensen said.

"These are not conspiracies my friend. They are just facts. The same thing is happening with Ptarmigan Swing."

"Huh?" Jensen and Fran said simultaneously.

"That big company from Iowa that makes wooden swing sets for yards."

"The one that moved into the industrial park in Ashland?" Jensen asked.

"Yes. Their building burned down when a snowstorm toppled the dry kiln's smoke stack onto the plant's roof."

"What about them?" Fran asked.

"They bussed their employees up here for a while, but then started to make it so hard for them to keep their jobs, all of the original workers ended up quitting."

"And your point is?" Fran asked.

Cameroon inhaled deeply, "Capitalism is bad when greed runs unchecked."

"Now there's a sound bite if ever I heard one. You ever consider running for political office, Don?" Jensen asked.

Fran chuckled.

"I'm too old, and I'm not cut of the right cloth. Besides," Cameroon slurped from his cup, "the trilateral commission would never anoint me. I'm not malleable enough."

"You make it sound as if we're all controlled. Like in *The Matrix*," Jensen said.

"Movies like that don't come out of thin air."

Fran slurped and said, "Oh, so now we're all hooked up to a bio-generating plant and this latte is a dream." She slurped some more. "Ummm. Best dream I've had in ages."

"Not exactly."

"What exactly?" Jensen asked.

"All I'm saying is that THEY make self-interested decisions without regard for society, for the real people who are damaged by their decisions."

Fran eyed Jensen. Neither spoke.

Cameroon drank. Cradling his cup in his hands he said, "Not that long ago someone somewhere decided that half the population 'sitting around home doing nothing' should be put to work. Now, only a relatively few years later, women across the country are working."

"What's so bad about that?" Fran said. Her eyes flashed.

"Don't get your underwear in a bundle, Franny. There are upsides of course. But there's downsides too."

"Like what?"

Cameroon smiled. "Like an entire generation of aimless, unparented children."

"I resent that," Fran said.

"The fact that you do indicates not your dedication to motherhood, but the disproportionate size of your ego."

"Don't you think he's getting a bit senile," Fran asked Jensen.

Cameroon smirked. "Ahhhh attacking the messenger. The last refuge of those in deep denial. Scoff all you like. But you don't laugh when another batch of school children get slaughtered by a socio-path. But, that's not my field. I'm not a psychologist. I really only have just two words for you, remember Reserve Mining."

"That's three," Jensen said.

Hansen laughed.

"That was before our time," Jensen said. He joined Hansen's laughter.

Cameroon scowled. He glared at Jensen. "The two words are... Oh forget it. The same, 'sociological' if you will, scenario took place in Silver Bay," he said. His nostrils flared. "Now it's known as North Shore Steel. But the point is, history is going to repeat itself in Hoyt Lakes."

Fran lounged back, linking her fingers behind her head. "Geeze. It's nice to know there was a point."

"We thought you were just practicing one of your lectures on us," Jensen said. He yawned and continued to absently flip through a six-month-old issue of *Home and Garden*.

Cameroon was undeterred. "You two aren't worth the effort. The real point is, the history of mining will soon repeat itself, but this time with water. With Lake Superior water."

Fran yawned.

Jensen looked up from his magazine. "You're preaching to the choir, Don."

Cameroon shook his head, reached for his coffee. He stared at Simon and Fran. He said, "I hope the choir is ready to sing pretty damn soon."

"Humphf," Hansen said. "When the whole choir is together and singing the same tune, that's when we rock and roll. Not before. But I assure you, when we're all on the same melody, it'll be sweet, sweet music."

"Who's mixing their metaphors now?" Cameroon said.

The trio examined one another.

"If and when the music really starts playing, it won't be sweet to everyone's ears," Jensen said.

"Thank God for that," Cameroon said.

"I thought you were an atheist," Fran said.

"Only in matters of human nature am I that cynical. When it comes to honest-to-goodness nature, God is very much alive and involved. He is there, and he is not silent. In a nature sort of way."

"Your systematic theology has the oddest system, Don," Fran said.

"Must be the company I keep," Cameroon said.

"Ann Rynd said you are who you sleep with," Jensen quipped.

"Thank God I sleep alone," Cameroon answered.

"You sure invoke God's name a lot," Fran said. "Won't your young coed friend be a bit miffed by your blatant double standard?"

Cameroon's eyes blazed. "I highly doubt that Ms. Shyness is incapable of tolerating intrinsic ambiguities in those she highly admires. And besides, soon you'll be glad I'm asking for all His help. We're going to need it."

Hansen looked at Jensen, said, "Ever notice how he starts using all kinds of big words when he gets nervous?"

11

Crazy loves company.

uperior, Wisconsin, if it were located in Maine, would be on the Canadian border. Move Superior to the other side of the globe, it would be north of Stalingrad. Keep it moving east, it would be in Mongolia. A lot of Superior residents think of their town as Mongolia, outer Mongolia. When reporting the temperature, local weathermen often joke, "Temperature in Siberia is..." For all the drawbacks, being located so far north provides one exceptional benefit. Summer days are long. Gloriously long.

Davecki looked at his watch. It was nearly 10 p.m. It was still light. Dusk rose slowly, like a gentle August fog creeping upward from a swamp. Which, in fact, this part of Superior, at one time, was. This was way before humanity had reduced the swamp and pine to asphalt and concrete.

The concrete upon which Davecki stood radiated heat through his boots. The tall, unmown grass in the nearby vacant lot slumped. Full darkness darted furtively around the North End's shabby buildings, waiting for the sun to give up the struggle.

All the darkness wanted to do was grip the rundown buildings in a grim hug that would make them look less dilapidated. For decades the City of Superior relied on the embrace of darkness to cover a multitude of faults. It wasn't such a half-bad planning strategy. Always reliable, darkness never failed to spruce up the notorious old town.

The street light overhead clicked on. The loud buzz from the fluorescent fixture grated Davecki's nerves. He looked up. The light flickered like a blue moth coming awake. He looked down Tower Avenue. In the dim distance, huge concrete grain silos loomed. Once the largest grain elevators in the world, Superior used to publicize their prominence. That was before bigger ones were built in Russia.

Studying the huge concrete monoliths, Davecki thought, *Reminds me of that movie, Dark City. Will things change suddenly and I'll be a new man?* A Honda Accord hummed past as he hung his helmet on the right mirror. The car's horn beeped. People regularly beeped at the man in the red suit. Davecki turned and instinctively scanned the plate. A vanity job, *LUV2DUU.* Two men inside. The driver smiled and waggled his fingers at him. *Girlie wave,* Davecki judged. He grinned and waved back with a masculine salute.

Movement from the picketer caught his eye. Davecki watched as she walked across the street toward the Gentleman's Club. The casino shuttle roared past, honked its horn. She waved her sign at the addiction-mobile. Davecki studied her as her motion turned her away from him toward the north. An inch over five feet tall, longish, straight brown hair. Rubenesque, not statuesque. She was fortyish, round face, features edgy enough to be appealing, yet pleasant. She looked kind.

As she pivoted with the passing of the bus, the back of her denim jacket glowed under the strengthening radiance from the street light overhead. The big bold logo had white lettering silk screened on it: EX-STRIPPERS FOR JESUS. The words formed the top half of a circle. In the center was a boldly rendered gold cross with an ambulance speeding by in the background. The bottom half of the circle read: EX-NUDES AGAINST LEWD DUDES. A flowered print dress of many bright hues hung beneath the jacket to the woman's brown clogs. *Is this for real?* Davecki cleared his throat.

The woman turned. "Hi," she said. Her voice was clear and direct, close to aggressive, but, he noted, far from anger. She held her sign. Davecki held his breath. After five seconds of Mexican-standoff type silence he realized, *She's a coy one, this.*

On the outside, Davecki smiled. On the inside, he careened through the standard profile-building every cop does when facing someone new. He looked closely at the woman's eyes. Brown. Shiny. Her body language said, relaxed. The sign didn't waver. *She's not smiling*, Davecki thought. *I guess I have to break down first.* He grinned slightly.

Then her curvaceous lips also rose slightly at the corners. *Very shapely lips.*

"Breathe, Officer," the woman said.

Like a good little lap dog, Davecki inhaled. "It's that obvious?"

"Like a lighthouse."

Phallic reference. Davecki, you're sick. He felt a far part of his brain at work. The activity in the outlying district of mental topography was like a big German Shepherd chewing loudly on a bone. *Better let sleeping dogs lay. Lie? Damn, I can never remember.* "I'm Dave Davecki," he said extending his hand.

"I'm Clara." She shook the hand.

Firm grip.

"What can I do for you?" Her voice was tranquil.

I have no idea. Then the gruesome seagull-pecked face of Little Willie Horton popped into his head. *Get it together, Alphonse.* "I'm looking for a stripper."

"Step inside officer. The joint is full of the poor souls," Clara said.

That far part of his brain crunched out another bone, *why don't I just go inside? Why did I stop here? What made me think this nut case can help?* "Gee, thanks. You have a firm grasp of the obvious. But I'm hoping you can ID a particular girl."

"Girl?"

Come on Dave. Get it together. "Umm. Woman?"

"That's better," Clara said with a broad smile.

"Seriously, it's official business."

The yummy lips curved up further. "I can try."

Oh great. I don't know diddly about my prime suspect. "Umm. She's brunette."

Clara laughed, a high, silvery laugh that echoed between the buildings. "Hair colors change daily, sometimes hourly, around here."

"Right. Oh, sure. I should have known. Ah. She's got a tattoo."

She snorted again. "Most do."

"It's a Ross Verba tattoo."

"A what?"

"It's a bracelet tattoo that goes around the entire bicep, like those barbed wire ones the behemoth NFL linemen wear."

"Right side or left?"

Gol dang it! You should have asked Rose that. Some cop you are. "I don't know," he admitted.

"Only ones with those tattoos that I know of are Crystal and Angel," Clara said. "Was she tall or short?"

"Short!" Davecki smiled, glad to get one right. "Petite," he corrected hastily, looking at Clara's own smallish stature.

"That's probably Crystal. Crystal Cathedral," Clara said with a wry smile. "But I'm just guessing."

Crystal Cathedral? Geeze. "That's gotta be her stage name. Right?"

"That's all I know her by," Clara said. She shrugged her shoulders.

"Is she working?" Davecki looked at the entrance to the club. *I wonder what this one's stage name was? Clara the Cow? Be nice, Alphonse.*

"She quit."

Dang. "She still around town?"

Clara took the sign off her shoulder. She twirled the placard downward and rested the tip of the handle on the sidewalk, rubbing her shoulder with her other hand. "I don't know. Last I saw her was at a prayer meeting we had at her place up on the North Shore."

Davecki rubbed his chin. He looked around. The darkness was not shy now. The sky was nearly black. Two guys came out of the strip joint's door. "Hey!" bellowed the smaller of the two men. The speaker was a blonde fellow with big muscles bulging from his camouflage tank top. "You the G-strings for Jesus lady?" He guffawed, nudging his buddy.

"God bless you, son," Clara said.

The guy stopped in his tracks. "Hey! Fuck you lady. You look like you got big tits. How about a look-see?"

"Hay is for horses," Clara said.

It sounds like she's singing, Davecki thought.

Steroid Boy frowned, his heavy brow beetling. He took a step toward her.

"Knock it off," Davecki said.

Steroidathon's buddy grabbed the commando wannabe by the arm and tugged him toward the parking lot to the south of the building.

"What's with the suit, buddy?" the body builder shouted. He stepped toward Davecki, dragged his wimpy pal. "You think you're Santa Claus or something?"

"Come on, Joey," the friend urged while tugging on the drunk's arm. "You said we were just going to have fun tonight. I can't afford any more trouble."

"Go on home." Davecki blended his basic training Authority Voice with his Father Figure voice. "Or, if you really, really want to get in a brawl, find the owner," Davecki nodded toward the building, "he takes a beating with good humor."

"Yeah? Up yours, old man!" Joey jerked his improbably large bicep from his friend's grasp and stuck out his lantern jaw toward Davecki.

"Come ON, Joey," The friend insisted.

"Fuck you, Trent!" Joey swaggered toward Davecki. "I got a few things to say to this jerk in his fancy red suit. Who the hell you think you are, giving me orders? A cop or something?"

"As a matter of fact…." Davecki reached inside his Aerostich, pulling his badge from the inside map pocket. "I am."

Joey stopped, mid-swagger.

"Jooooeeeyyy," Trent hissed.

Joey turned on his heel, departing rapidly. "Fucking faggot," he called over his shoulder. He and Trent hustled into the gloom.

Davecki watched them retreat. *Wouldn't it be nice if I could follow them to the alley and fill them full of about fifteen holes thus ridding society of yet another couple of useless bums? Be nice, Dave.*

Clara turned to Davecki. "Well, wasn't that fun?"

"Delightful. Today's youth," he said.

"Well, actually, I wasn't thinking badly of them."

"Who were you thinking badly of? Me?"

"Yes."

"And why? May I ask?"

"Because you stuck your nose into my business."

"How's that?"

"Joey there was speaking to me and you butted right in. I can handle myself. I don't need some knight, or cop, in shining armor to rescue me."

"Well. Excuse me. It just comes naturally to most cops to lead with their nose. It's a part of the job. I apologize."

"Well, isn't that refreshing. I accept. Do you know what I could use right now?"

"I don't."

"A good cup of hot tea."

"That does sound good."

"And...." Clara leaned toward him.

"What?" Davecki looked around.

"A ride on your cycle. We could go to Louis'." Clara's eyes widened.

Davecki looked back. "No way. You got a skirt on," he said.

"It's a dress."

"Irregardless, you can't ride a bike wearing a skirt or a dress."

"Why not? I'll just hike it up. By the way, irregardless isn't a word."

Davecki shook his head. He looked her in the eyes.

She didn't waver.

"If you must," he said, turning toward the VFR.

"Yippee!" Clara said. She raced to the back of an old Ford Fairmont parked on the side street, threw her sign inside, and ran back to Davecki who was unsnapping the rear seat cowl.

"Don't you think it's dangerous to take rides from strangers?" he asked as he stuffed the cowling inside his Aerostich.

"Usually. Not with you, though."

"Why not with me?"

"I trust you."

He looked at her. "That's not saying much. I mean, coming from someone who owns a Fairmont. That fact alone puts your judgment seriously in question."

"I prayed about it," she said simply.

"What? Buying a Fairmont or accepting a ride?"

Clara grinned. "Why both, silly!"

"And you get answers to your prayers that quickly?"

"Of course. Don't you?"

Davecki plucked his helmet from the mirror, unplugged the headset and offered it to Clara. "You should wear this."

"No thanks. You wear it. I want to feel the wind in my face."

Davecki replugged the electronics, bucketed-up and threw a leg over. He grabbed the grips and locked his elbows and planted his feet. He looked back at Clara and nodded. She smiled and hiked her skirt.

Davecki looked away and closed his eyes.

Clara grabbed Davecki's arm and leaped like a gazelle onto the back of the bike.

"Take it easy!" he yelled into the full-face helmet.

"What?" she yelled as she thrashed around getting her feet on the high pegs.

Davecki lowered his head. All the bouncing around behind him was irritating. The contact was embarrassing.

He nudged the start button. The YokoOno pipe sang. She wiggled into a compact snuggle at his back. Davecki thought of lady bugs on the beach at Wisconsin Point. A couple more guys came out of the cabaret. "Nice legs!" one of the cretins cat-called. Clara clamped Davecki between her knees and budged him strongly. "Move it!" she yelled above the rumble of the exhaust.

"Hang on," Davecki yelled back before flipping his face shield down. He revved the V-Four high and launched away from the curb like it was a drag race out on County Highway UU. Once he got the bike jetted away from the wrong side of the tracks, he settled it down for a nice, sedate cruise down Tower Avenue.

"Come on! Go fast!" Clara squeezed him hard around the waist.

His Aerostich, which would protect him from a three hundred foot skid along rough pavement, did nothing to shield him from the invading femininity of her clench.   *This is a mistake.*

Being the distracted personality that he was, Davecki did what comes naturally.

He pulled in the clutch lever.

The V-four built high Rs fast.

He downshifted.

When the tachometer needle reached six grand, he dumped the clutch.

The VFR launched south on Tower like a cat with a lit firecracker tied to its tail.

Clara's clench around his chest competed with Davecki's ability to inhale.

They wheelied through the stop lights at Broadway.

Clara screamed and squeezed harder.

Davecki let inertia end the wheelie softly.

When the front wheel touched down, he shifted to third and let the throttle snap shut. The bike rolled forward while slowing. *This is just about the time one of those testy rookies would try and ticket me.*

The vice grip on his chest continued. "DO IT AGAIN. DO IT AGAIN," Clara yelled.

He considered. But decided to be law abiding for once.

The python squeeze let up. Clara yelled, "You're no fun."

12

Women speak two languages, one of which is verbal.

—Steve Rubenstein

ommercial fishermen of the previous century supported large families netting the vast schools of fishes in Lake Superior. All the old timers referred to the Big Lake as she, her or The Lady. This lady, while not a tramp, cares little about fashion or human comfort. As usual, it was chilling the city of Superior like a fine wine.

"It's so cold," Clara said jumping off the VFR.

Davecki yanked his helmet. He patted the thick fabric of his red suit. "That's why I bought this."

"Yeah," Clara said, "what's up with that? It seems sorta femmy. I've never seen any other biker wearing anything like it." They walked from the bike toward Louis' restaurant.

"Biker's don't wear these."

"You're a biker."

"I'm a motorcyclist."

"What's the difference?"

"Bikers ride Harleys."

"That's it?" Clara asked.

"Pretty much. Bikers are big, bad, and beautiful; bedecked as they pretty much always are, in black leather."

"And what are you? Small, good, and ugly?"

Davecki snorted, reached for the front door handle. "That about covers it."

Clara walked through the opened door. "Thanks," she said over her shoulder.

Davecki, reaching around to open the second door, bumped into her. She tipped to one side. "Careful!"

"Oops. Sorry." He yanked the door open. In the tight confines of the entry, his helmet clunked loudly into the door frame.

"Are you always this clumsy?" Clara asked.

"I guess that about covers it."

"Besides," she said, "that suit's *red* is off a little. It clashes with your bike."

Davecki laughed. "Oh, that was one of my primary concerns. I wanted a candy apple red suit, but Andy only makes off red."

"Andy?"

"Andy Goldfine. He's the guy who came up with the idea." They ascended the ramp toward the no-smoking section of the restaurant.

"What idea?"

"For the suit. What's the matter? You growing potatoes in your ears?"

"What in the world are you talking about?" Clara asked.

"It's something my Ma always used to say when I didn't pay attention to her."

"I'm paying attention. You're just not making sense."

"Anything you say. Anyway, the story goes... he, as in Andy Goldfine—just so I'm making perfect sense—was sitting on the steps of his apartment building one night. He says to his neighbor lady who was sitting on the steps of her apartment building next door, 'Ginny'—that was his neighbor's name, just so I'm being perfectly clear—'Ginny,' he says, 'wouldn't it be cool if you could ride your bike to work wearing a suit and tie and not get dirty or wet?' and the Aerostich was born."

"Oh," Clara said. They stopped at the cash register. "I understand perfectly. You're making perfect sense now. It's a stupid story, but you're being clear at least."

"Okay. Don't get your undies in a bundle. Imagine this. James Bond in a tuxedo. Imagine he's going to a formal party, but he doesn't want to take the Ferrari. He wants to ride his Ducati. But, he doesn't want to mess up his fancy tux. All he has to do is put on his Aerostich and boogie. When he rides up to the chateau, he gets off, takes off his helmet, unzips his suit and presto! He's instantly transformed from a mere motorcyclist to the dashing, well-dressed, and handsome hero."

"I can't quite see all that. But I can see you've rehearsed it quite often in your own mind," Clara said.

"Table for two, Dave?" The speaker was an elegant lady, obviously tired, but with vibrant gray/blue eyes and a warm, genuine smile.

"Hey, June," Davecki said. "How are you? And how is that beautiful granddaughter of yours?"

"Kelly's just fine, and the great-granddaughter is even better."

"Awesome! Great. Glad to hear it."

June's eyes slid to Clara and then back to Davecki. "Your usual booth in the corner?"

"Absolutely. Yes."

"You can just go on up. Sandra will be right with you."

"Thanks."

As they moved up to Davecki's booth, Clara said, "You seem to be pretty familiar around here."

"Been a regular for two and a half decades."

They sat in the back corner of the balcony section, Davecki's back to the wall. He took a moment to tuck his helmet into the corner and allow Clara to get settled, then he cleared his throat. "Now, about this co-worker of yours."

"Co-worker?"

"Crystal."

Clara stared at him.

Davecki stared back. "You know, the brunette with the arm tattoo. We talked about her back at…"

"I know whom you're talking about. I just find it intriguing that you called her my co-worker. Would you mind explaining that?"

"I assumed from your jacket that you were an ex-stripper."

Clara folded her hands on the table and gazed steadily at him. "Just because I lead a stripper support group doesn't mean I was one."

"Well excuse me. I am sorry. Maybe you shouldn't wear that jacket. It gives the wrong impression."

Davecki watched her watching him. Her face was neutral for a few seconds. Then a smile seeped up from the corners of her lips the way light appeared in the east at dawn. "I accept your apology. Actually, I get that all the time."

"Okay. So now that you've pinned my ears back, are you happy? Why don't you tell me your story?"

Clara laughed lightly. "Well, I grew up in, shall we say, less-than-optimum circumstances. I became a Christian when I was eighteen and spent a long time being prepared for this ministry. God loves strippers, too. There aren't any ministries to strippers you know."

"I think there's a priest in New York City who ministers to them."

"Really?"

Davecki was about to reply, but the waitress walked up. Sandra, tall and stately, with dark hair and dramatic features adorning a pleasant, slender face, was carrying a tea set-up and one menu. "Here's your tea, Officer." She handed the menu to Clara. "I'll be right back to take your order, ma'am," she said and turned to leave.

"Hey, Sandra, what gives? You haven't worked a late shift since forever," Davecki asked.

Sandra rolled her eyes. "Tell me about it. Believe you me, I'd rather be home. But Celia got cancer. She needs chemo and I need the extra money for the treatments and working is way better than betting on the Pack." As she spoke, she glanced around the room, scanning the other tables.

"Sorry to hear that," Davecki said.

"Yeah, me too. I'll be right back. I've got an order up." Sandra glided away.

"Clara's going to have some tea too," Davecki called after her.

"Sure thing," Sandra called back without turning. "Be right back."

Clara stared after her. Davecki didn't. "She seems pretty casual about cancer," Clara finally said.

"It's all an act. Sandra's a marshmallow. Especially when it comes to her kitties."

Clara's eyebrows rose.

"Celia's one of her cats," Davecki explained.

"Oh."

"Now," said Davecki, leaning forward. "About this person you're ministering to, Crystal."

Clara tilted her head to one side and smiled.

Whoa! Lips like those are way too scarce in the general population.

"After years of going to church and learning the Scriptures, God just put the call on me one morning during my prayers that I was to start reaching out to these women."

Does she ever answer a question directly? "God said this to you?" Davecki asked.

She sighed. "No, I don't hear voices, Officer. It was that still, small, voice; really more of a knowing. But it's just easier to say, 'God said.'"

"I'll give you that."

"You see, when they leave the life they need to fill the empty spot with something. Protesting against their former exploiters helps take up some of that space. It's in the Bible, you know."

"Really? Where?"

"Well, ummm. Let's see, I think it's in—oh shoot, I can't remember right now. But it says that the vacancy has to be filled or the demons will return sevenfold and make life even more miserable."

"So what's with the sign? Be good doesn't seem to be all that inspiring. "

"Carl Jung said he would rather be whole than good." Clara rested her chin in her hand. "Did you know he was the son of a minister?"

"No, I didn't."

"He was. But anyway, there's no substitute for good behavior. So I remind people what they were probably told when they were little: be good. It's amazing how well it works. Lot's of people talk to me about what my sign means. I always get the chance to tell them that a relationship with Christ can restore them to sanity."

Davecki looked Clara in the eyes, said nothing.

"It means that talk is cheap. Actions speak louder than words."

"Oh. I get it. Bullshit walks. Money talks, is that what you're trying to say?"

Clara harumphed. "NO! That's not what my sign means. It means if you sincerely believe what you're doing is good, then fine, okay. Don't stop."

"You remind me of my daughter Bethany," he said.

"What's that mean?" Clara asked.

"She thinks in strange ways too."

"What's strange about my thinking?"

Davecki started his tea ritual. He said, "Sociopaths think they're doing the right thing. Timothy McVeigh thought he was doing the right thing."

Clara said, "McVeigh's behavior is between him and God. I'm not talking mass murder. I'm talking about examining your own conscience and doing what's right. I'm simply called to stimulate the conscience of those God brings in my path."

"Including motorcyclists?" Davecki smirked. "What I was going to say was, that my daughter, while taking a round about path at times, always seems to come to the right conclusion."

"Humph," Clara said softly.

He nodded.

Sandra came with another tea set-up. "Is this man being mean to you?" Sandra asked. "If he is, we can call the cops and have him thrown out on his ear."

Davecki leaned back and watched the women at their work.

"He's not being mean. But does think he's clever and witty."

Sandra put her hands on her slender hips. "Isn't that the way it always goes? Men are just so predictable. You have my condolences."

Clara's sensuous eyebrows arched steeply. "Condolences?"

"For having to actually spend time with this character here," she said.

"Oh thank you. It's so nice to know someone understands," Clara said. She handed the menu to Sandra. "I'll have an English muffin with peanut butter and honey."

"Great. Be right back," Sandra pivoted smartly and took off.

"What about you? You're not having anything?" Clara asked Davecki.

Sandra said over her shoulder, "Oh he always has Louis' Choice; over easy, whole-wheat, hash browns."

"Don't you know there's no such thing as whole-wheat hash browns, Sandra?" Davecki said.

Over her shoulder, Sandra said, "Oh darn. I forgot. I'll tell the cook to make them out of potatoes."

Davecki fiddled open his tea bag.

"She knows what you have?" Clara asked. She fiddled with her tea bag.

"Like I said, I've been coming here for twenty-five years. So. This Crystal Cathedral. What makes you think she's the one I'm looking for?"

"Not really sure. Both her and Angel have tattoos. But, Angel is still working. Crystal just quit the biz. She's in transition. It would be like her to look for a little medication in a new guy. What do you want with her, anyway?"

Davecki gave her the bare facts. Clara listened, winced at the description of Little Willie. "I think she may have been the last, or one of the last, persons to see him alive," he concluded.

"You think she murdered your friend?"

"I didn't say that. There's no reason to believe there was a murder. No bullet holes in the body. No signs of a struggle."

"Yet you're investigating. Something must be suspicious," Clara said.

"Every death gets looked into. This one isn't a murder by a long shot. We're just looking into it."

"Well, it's not like some little old man died in his La-Z-Boy in front of a boring Packers-Vikings game. You wouldn't look into that would you?"

"No. That would be a simple case of death by NFL boredom. Death by too many commercials. It would be open and shut."

"What's not shut about this?"

Davecki spooned honey from the rectangular honey container into his cup. "Lots of things." *Don't mention the money.* "Well, for one thing. There was a lot of cash involved." *God I hate when I do that.* He stirred his tea, clanking the spoon against the side of the cup.

Clara smiled. "Well, Crystal either has or comes from a lot of that."

"How so?" Davecki asked. He stirred his tea, clanking the spoon against the side of the cup.

"The cabin. She called it a cabin and it's got to be worth a few million dollars at least."

"I heard strippers make a lot of money." He stirred his tea, clanking the spoon against the side of the cup.

"They do. But not that much. How else is this thing unshut?"

"Unshut? That's quite a word." He stirred his tea, continuing to clank the spoon against the side of the cup.

"I'm particularly fond of it. It's a word that covers a lot of ground," Clara said. She sipped her tea.

"Little Willie was floating around out on Lake Superior, and nobody bothered to mention that he was missing. But, it's early. Nothing much makes sense early in an investigation. What I do know is, Little Willie was reported to be with a woman the last night he was seen. She may have been either a stripper or a coffee shop clerk. She has a tattoo on her arm. And, she is my only lead right now. It might not seem like much, but investigations are like romance…" He stirred his tea, clanking the spoon against the side of the cup.

"What?" Clara asked. Her eyebrows arched again.

"Investigations are like romance. One thing leads to another. So, you were at a meeting at her cabin?" He stirred his tea, clanking the spoon against the side of the cup.

Clara folded her hands into a tent and rested her dainty chin on the folds of her knuckles. "Why are you trying to aggravate me?"

"How's that?" Davecki asked.

"The tea stirring thing," she said. She nodded toward the still-clanking cup.

"Oh. That. Sorry," Davecki said. He pulled his spoon out. "It's not a ploy, honest. It's just that most people don't realize how long it takes honey to dissolve. I don't like it all sitting at the bottom. I like it well stirred in." Davecki squeezed a lemon slice. The juice trickled down his fingers and splashed into the cup. This he raised in a salute. "Cheers," Davecki said.

Clara raised her cup and said, "Likewise." She set her cup down and said, "Like I said. She called it a cabin. But it was a mansion to me."

"That's interesting."

"How's that?" Clara asked.

Davecki looked at her. "Are you mocking me to my face?"

"How's that?" Clara said.

Just then, Sandra approached. In her hands were plates. Crawling up her arms were more plates. All were loaded with food. "Is he weirding you out, Miss?"

"Sort of," Clara said.

"Well, don't you worry. He's mostly harmless, if you don't consider being weird, bizarre, and strange a serious set of character flaws."

"I love you too, Sandra," Davecki said.

"See what I mean?" Sandra said directly to Clara. "Takes everything so personally. Thinks the world revolves around him. He's just like my kittens."

"Wow! I never knew you thought so highly of me, Sandra."

"Oh, you're the best, Dave. The best," Sandra said backing away from the table. "If you need anything else, just holler."

"No rush, Sandra. Take your time," Davecki said.

"Don't worry. I will," she said turning toward the main dining room.

"You two act like you're married."

Davecki, already spreading strawberry jam on his whole wheat toast, said, "Then it's probably the most successful marriage in Superior." He stabbed the pointy end of his toast into the soft yolk of his over easy eggs. "So, about this cabin/mansion-prayer-meeting?"

Clara prepped her English muffin with peanut butter and honey. "About a month ago we were supposed to do a weekend retreat. It was a prayer and fasting vigil, but I only stayed the first night."

"You didn't eat all weekend?"

"I wanted to fast all weekend, but the whole thing went terribly wrong. I couldn't discipline myself. I needed food."

Davecki stopped the mouthward progress of his hash browns. He said, "I'd love to hear how a religious retreat can go horribly wrong. But, what I really want to know is, can you tell me how to get to this mansion?"

Clara paused. "This is official? I mean, you're supposed to be talking to her? I mean, as a police officer."

Davecki looked up from his food, flicked a quick glance at her like a snake sticking out its tongue. She was looking directly at him. "I'm investigating a crime. I HAVE to talk with her."

"You said it wasn't a murder."

Davecki sighed. "Okay. You're right. I'm investigating a potential crime."

"I just want to be sure you're not a stalker or anything. These girls get some pretty strange men chasing them," she finished.

"What about weird and bizarre?" Davecki asked.

"That, too," Clara said as she picked up her knife. "I don't think I can tell you how to get there. I might be able to show you. I wasn't the one driving." She squeezed a lemon slice above her cup. "I would remember if we retraced the route."

Silence visited briefly as the two sipped their tea and ate.

"When would you be free to go up there?" Davecki asked.

"I could go tomorrow afternoon."

"Good. That works for me." He spread more jam on another piece of toast.

"When you said your suspect might have worked at a coffee shop, I remembered Crystal saying she worked at one."

Davecki looked at her without raising his head. "That's a pretty important detail to suddenly 'just remember.'"

"She didn't work there long. Only a couple of days I think." Clara spoke around a mouthful of muffin. A drop of honey dripped off the muffin onto her chin.

"You know," he said, "it is always particularly endearing when a woman wears her lunch on her chin." Davecki gestured with his finger.

"Huh? Oh, thanks." Clara wiped the honey with her index finger and licked it.

Talk about aggravating. "That's corroborating information. My sources didn't specify if the woman was a stripper or a coffee shop girl. Now I know she was both and that there's lots of money involved. Where there's lots of money, there's always lots of questions that don't want answers."

Clara bit the corner of her lower lip with her left incisor. "I bet your job isn't much fun most of the time."

"That's why they call it work," Davecki said. "I don't imagine picketing strip joints is a barrel of laughs, either."

"No. Sometimes," she leaned forward. She pushed her plate out of the way of the rest of her. She looked down at the table, then up at Davecki. She spoke in a whisper. "Most of the time I'm not even sure I'm going about it the right way."

"Ya think?" said Davecki.

She leaned back in the booth.

Be nice Alphonse. Davecki leaned away from the table. "What do you do for a living? Besides the anti-stripping thing?"

"I'm retired," she said.

Davecki raised his eyebrows now. "Aren't you a little young to be retired?"

"I'm frugal."

"That's no answer."

"It is to me."

Davecki turned his full attention to his eggs and hash browns.

Clara sipped her tea. There was a silence. "Are you pouting?" she asked.

Davecki chewed, taking his time. "I was going to ask the same of you."

"You remind me of an eighth grader."

"How kind."

Clara laughed her silvery laugh.

"What's so funny?" he demanded.

"You."

"Yeah?" He shoveled in some hash browns.

Clara suddenly leaned forward, chin in hand again. "Maybe it's because you're a cop."

"What's that mean?"

"Well, I'm not sure. I thought you were just a big adolescent. But maybe that's not it. Maybe it's *because* you're a cop, and you've got all this power and people always have to answer your questions. So it's different in a social situation. When someone who isn't intimidated by your position declines to answer one of your questions, you don't like it."

He swallowed hard. It could have been a Tonka truck going down. "I could pick you up at two o'clock tomorrow."

Clara laughed again.

"Now what?" he asked.

"You actually do real police work? I thought all you did was drive around on your motorcycle, go from restaurant to restaurant, and make witty repartee with the regulars."

"You're right again. What are you, clairvoyant?"

"I'm just trying to be witty and charming like you," Clara said.

"Clara the Clairvoyant. I like that," Davecki said. He speared the last bit of toast with his fork and swept the plate. "Shall we go? I should get you back to your picketing. And I've got an early start tomorrow." He leaned toward the edge of the booth.

Clara didn't budge. She smiled, a full-face smile.

Davecki halted his go motions. "What are you so happy about?" he asked.

Clara slid out of the booth. "I would say amused," she said as she stood.

Davecki eyed her from his seat. "Do I have permission to stand now?"

She waved her hand. It was a practiced, imperial gesture. "You may rise."

Davecki got to his feet and gestured toward the exit. "Exactly how am I amusing?"

Without moving, Clara said, "Ooooh. You know, that's actually a pretty good question. I think I should try to answer it."

"Don't overtax yourself."

Clara laughed.

Davecki stole a glance at her as he pulled out his wallet. *Now her lips look like the Joker lips from Batman.*

She said, "You really are quite funny. I think you're probably a humorous person. Deep down."

Davecki dropped some bills on the table and indicated the exit again. "So?"

"So what?"

Sew buttons on your underwear. "So, what's the answer? What's so amusing about me?"

Clara turned, leading her lamb to the slaughter. "I'm thinking."

They walked to the bike in silence. As Davecki pulled on his helmet, Clara said, "I guess amusing isn't the right word after all."

"Oh? What's the right one?"

"I think refreshing is more apt."

You forgot powerful and manly.

"Well... maybe that's not right, either."

Make up your mind lady.

Clara smiled again. She ran her fingers through her hair. "I've got it," she said.

"I can hardly wait," Davecki said.

"Entertaining. That's it. You're very entertaining."

"And that's good?" Davecki asked, facing his tormentor.

"It's good if it's adult. It's bad if it's adolescent."

Davecki looked Clara in the face. She wasn't smiling, wasn't frowning. She was watching with a neutral expression. The one she had worn when he thought she was a stripper. *I'm not going to give you the satisfaction lady.* "You ready?"

Clara's face dropped neutral and shifted into pleasant. "Ready," she said.

They got on the VFR. Davecki drove sedately into the full darkness. He pulled to the curb in front of the Gentlemen's Club and didn't shut the bike down. Clara jumped off and faced him with yet another smile. He flipped his visor and said, "Where should I pick you up tomorrow?"

"I'll meet you," she answered. "Where's good for you?"

Davecki sniffed. "Big Apple Bagel at two o'clock?"

"Looking forward to it," she said.

"Me too," he said. He nodded his head strongly enough to flip his face shield down and zoomed into the darkness thinking, *She sure turned out to be a pain.*

13

If you expect the wise man to be as angry as the baseness of crime requires,
Then he must not only be angry but go insane.

—Seneca, *On Anger*

evada Henderson sat propped up against the headboard of a large bed, in a large room, in a huge log house perched atop one of the most prominent cliffs along the so-called "North Shore" of Lake Superior, between Duluth, and Silver Bay, Minnesota. The room had twenty-foot-high walls built with thirty-inch-thick white pine logs. The vaulted ceiling was paneled with five-inch wide tongue and groove bird's eye maple boards that would have brought tears to the eyes of Nikos. The one-inch, polycoated, white oak flooring glistened in the even light flooding through the vinyl-extruded, French-cathedral windows placed high in the gable ends of the room. Covering the expansive oak floor were four lush Persian rugs. Standing on one of those rugs were bed posts of burnished cherry with strategically placed burls into which the bed's frame was anchored. Intricate hand-carved twines of deeply stained ivy writhed up the bed posts. The canopy over the bed was rich, maroon brocade. On Henderson's bare lap, a thin and humming computer cast a bluish tint from its backlit screen. The light made Henderson's craggy face appear ghoulish. He clicked and clacked the keyboard, staring intensely at the screen. He seemed completely unaware of the nearly naked woman next to him.

The woman was young. Her skin was smooth and alabaster in color and texture. She wore only a pair of black cotton panties. Around her upper right bicep a bracelet tattoo of red hearts, yellow flames and blue ivy danced. It was a new tattoo, the ink was vibrant and, as yet, unfaded. She was tucked into a fetal position. The top of the woman's head touched Henderson at his hip. It appeared as if she were an appendage bulging from his side. Her hands covered her face. Her body shook slightly.

Henderson's long, strong fingers clicked furiously at the keys and then rested.

From behind the woman's hands, a muffled sniffling filtered upwards as if radiating from the quilted down comforter. "I didn't mean any harm,"the woman said through her fingers.

Henderson didn't respond.

The woman squirmed, detached herself from his hip and nudged her head upwards, trying to wedge under his left arm.

Henderson elbowed her away. "Quit bothering me, Dolly."

"What's the bother about snuggling?" She threw herself back on the bed and pouted. Short dark hair against a fair complexion gave her the look of a geisha.

"It wrecks my typing speed," he said. "It makes ICQing with your daddy very frustrating if I can't type fast enough."

The woman's face brightened. "Did Daddy ask about me?"

"I'll be done in a minute, darlin'."

She stuck out her tongue, rolled away from Henderson and buried her face in a large pillow.

"That's a sweet thing," Henderson mumbled. His fingers flew over the keyboard. The message scrolled out across the screen: *The woman from the city knows a guy who knows a guy. She arranged a meeting with a man named Knute who is a Falsie. I'm going to tell him I'm a writer and pump him for info. It shouldn't be too hard to get an invite to their next meeting. Those groups are always suckers for free publicity.* His fingers stopped moving.

In four seconds, another line of message emerged below the sentence Henderson had typed.

Good work. Keep me posted. The Rio Salado is filling up nicely. We're getting more good press. I'm happy. Don't let those fools ruin our fun.

Henderson snorted. He typed: *I wouldn't call them fools. Anyone with the motivation to blow up the pipeline with fertilizer and fuel oil is dangerous. I'd call them gutsy as hell. Plus they have the perfect cover. El Qaeda will take the rap gladly and they'll let it go that way. If the Falsies claimed responsibility, there'd be a big investigation and everyone would find out we're transshipping water instead of oil. We could just claim it was your standard pipeline explosion incident.* Henderson stopped typing.

Words scrolled out in response: *Lighten up, Nevada. If it ever comes to that, I'll spin the media coverage with the help of FEMA laws. You just better not be getting sympathetic with these hayseeds. They're a bunch of numb-nuts who don't know their ass from a hole in the ground.*

You're the boss. Henderson typed.

And don't you forget it. Talia and I are actually going to leave for Hawaii tonight, IF there aren't any more delays. Any developments on the biker thing?

Nothing. Don't worry. Lake Superior doesn't give up her dead.

Now you're quoting Gordon Lightfoot? Christ Nevada are you going soft on me?

Gordon Lightfoot is a great man.

Trust me Nevada. That body is going to show up.

If and when it does show up, there's no way it'll come home to roost on us. There was enough stray money flying around on the wind to make it look like a drug deal gone bad, Henderson typed.

I agree with you there, but, still, be on the lookout. Every time Dolly's involved things go to hell in a handbasket.

Hey, it's already handled. It's a done deal. The Falsie's didn't get any of the money and we can easily assume they're like most terrorists, short on cash and long on talk. If they have any sense of reality, they'll figure out they're playing with the big dogs and won't push their luck. I don't think there's one of them that wants to end up like their biker buddy... very dead.

I hope, for your sake, you're right. I'll log-on in Hawaii. If needed we can ICQ from there. Albertson out.

Henderson closed the Dell and moved it to the antique, birch night stand on his right.

Dolly removed her face from the pillow. "He didn't even mention me, did he?"

"As a matter of fact your name did come up darlin'," he said.

Dolly smiled. "What did he say?"

Henderson sighed. "He said that everything you touch goes to hell in a handbasket."

Dolly's face fell into pain. Then she said, "I HATE YOU!" She swung a fist.

Henderson grabbed her arm in mid-swing.

"Ouch!" she cried. "You're hurting me."

"I feel real sorry for you, Dolly. Truth is, no matter what you do, it will never be enough to get your daddy's attention."

"If I help blow up his precious pipeline, he'll notice."

Henderson put the arm in his hand down. She immediately moved in against his chest. She slipped her arm across his wool shirt. "Why do you have to wear these scratchy shirts?"

"Because they keep me warm in the winter, cool in the summer." Dolly frowned. "How can it do both?"

Henderson smiled. "You're too young to understand the benefits of a good wool shirt, honey. And don't frown like that. You'll wrinkle."

She kneed his leg. "You're *mean*."

Henderson laid his head back against the carved headboard. "Yes I am. Why, at one time I was called the Meanest Man in Texas. Did I ever tell you that?"

She rolled her eyes. "About a MILLION times. So what did Daddy want?"

"Oh, he was just askin' about your boyfriend," said Henderson.

She slapped his chest. "Quit being so awful!"

"I used to think I was awful. But watching you operate baby doll, well, I'm a piker compared to you."

"I've heard enough. I'm leaving." The woman pushed away.

Henderson was silent.

"I mean it, Nevada. I'm going now."

"Have a good one, baby doll."

Dolly stared at Henderson. She leaned back toward him. "You're mad now, aren't you?" Her lower lip stuck out.

"Dolly," he sighed, "I was born mad and raised mad, and I'm paid lots and lots of money to stay mad. I'll die mad, and I'll go to hell mad. Me being mad is a given."

Dolly opened her mouth. Wide, white teeth glared. She growled and advanced toward his arm.

Henderson gazed at her. "Don't you bite me, girl."

She picked up his arm. Placed her teeth on the heel of his leathery hand.

"You do it, I'll knock those beautiful expensive teeth out of your mouth."

Dolly held her pose for a second. Then she threw herself on the pillows once more. She made a fist and whacked him on the chest, hard. "I hate you."

"That's a good girl," said Henderson. "Now tell me what your dirt bag boyfriend said. Did he come right out and ask for the money?"

Dolly raised her chin and looked at the wall.

"Now, don't get all frowny-face on me, sweet thing," Henderson commanded.

"I'm not going to say anything until you promise to stop calling him my boyfriend. You're my boyfriend."

Henderson stared at the high ceiling. He sighed. "I promise."

"Thank you."

Dolly continued to look at the wall.

Henderson continued to look at Dolly. "Come on now, Doll Face." His voice quavered slightly. "Tell me what I want to know."

"Ohhh, men are such jerks. The only time they're nice is when they want something." She sat up, crossing her arms. "You are my boyfriend, aren't you?"

"Dolly. Honey. Can we talk about what the man said? Please?"

"All he asked was if there was any money around!"

"And this was where?"

Dolly covered her face with her hands. "Nevadaaa," she whined. "Why do we have to talk about this?"

Henderson put his hand on her knee. "Because it's important, darlin'."

"Important to who?"

"It's important to me. And to your daddy. And to you, if you care to remember which side your bread is buttered on."

"All Daddy cares about are his projects, that damn pipeline."

"Dolly, if it weren't for your daddy's projects, you'd be living in a cheap hotel in Vegas, hooking for a living."

Dolly jerked her head up, her mouth a sneer. "I hate you!"

"Yes, I know. It's been well established that you hate your boyfriend. Now, what'd the dirt bag say, honey? Tell Nevada the whole story."

Dolly sighed. She moved closer, rested her cheek on Henderson's chest. "We were in here. We were pretty drunk. Pretty high, too. Or I was, anyway."

"Like I said. A piker."

"You want to hear this?"

"Of course I do darlin'. You want me to express myself honestly, isn't that what you said?"

"I'm sorry," she said.

"Keep talking, baby doll."

"I thought it would be fun to show him the money."

"You WHAT?"

"Well, I was thinking about that movie where Cuba Gooding, Jr. keeps saying, 'SHOW ME THE MONEY!' And, besides, he said he was going to need some money for gas. You know, to get home…" Dolly's voice trailed off.

"So you decided to open the safe and show him two million in cash just sitting in a closet in a house on the North Shore in the middle of the Minnesota woods?"

Dolly nodded.

Henderson extended a long forefinger and placed it in the middle of Dolly's forehead. "Dolly Darlin', whenever I think you're just as stupid as stupid can be, you always surprise me by takin' it one step further." He lifted her head, slipped out from under her and dropped his burden down. He got off the bed and asked, "Just where did all that extra money come from anyway?"

Dolly began sobbing. "You hate me, don't you? Don't you?" She clutched up the bedspread and rolled herself into it.

"Dolly honey, there's nothing to hate. You think you know what you're doing, but you don't have a frigging clue."

Dolly wailed, kicked her legs and pounded her fists under the bedspread.

Henderson sighed. "Just what were you planning on doing with all that money, Doll?" He placed a hand on the bed post.

Dolly stopped thrashing the bed and pulled the covering from her face. "I was going to buy Daddy a brand new boat that he and Talia and you and I could drive around on his brand new lake." She looked at Henderson square in the face. "You don't believe me?"

"No honey, I don't."

"What do you believe?"

"I believe you were fixing to give the Falsies the money they needed to destroy all our hard work."

She jumped up fast and slapped him hard.

He rubbed his cheek. Glared at her.

"I would never do that. Not really. I was just leading the guy on."

"No you weren't. You were planning on helping the guy until I came along and broke up your little love-tumble."

"You don't know what you're talking about. I love you, not that dirty old biker."

"You don't love anybody, honey. Not even yourself."

"What's that supposed to mean?"

Henderson shook his head. "It means you think you have a plan. You think you know what you're doing, but you haven't got the foggiest."

"I do have a plan. I know what I'm doing," she said. She scooted across the bed and started to get up.

Henderson grabbed her and pulled her back. "Well then, your plan sucks."

"Let go of me," she yelped.

He set the limb free.

"You don't know anything," she said.

"I know you dance and take your clothes off in front of people for no reason. You screw total strangers for money. You..."

Dolly jumped off the bed and stomped to the door.

Henderson watched her. He didn't move a muscle. He watched her jerk open the door and just before she slammed it shut he said, "Know what else?" He smiled. Waited.

In three seconds the door opened. "What?"

"Thirty seconds before I tossed your boyfriend off of Palisade Head he told me you were in on it."

Dolly stared at him. "You killed him?"

"Yep."

"He's *dead*?"

"Yep. He fell off a two hundred-foot cliff onto a big bunch of hard rocks. He's real, real dead."

Dolly drew in a deep breath. "You're lying." Tears sprang to her eyes. "I'm calling Daddy. I'm going home."

Henderson huffed lightly. "Your daddy and Talia are going to Hawaii. You call him now and ruin his plans to get away, he'll be real, real mad."

"I don't care," she sobbed. "I'm calling him, and I'm going to tell him what you did to Willie. And I'm going to tell him what you did to me, when I was only fourteen. About how you're a sexual predator."

"The predator, honey, is you. It was you who started it back then. I won't have any trouble convincing everyone you're the one who's kept coming back for more."

"You think Daddy will believe that? He's going to believe his— his hired help, over his own daughter?"

"As a matter of fact I do believe that, and you know it's true. He's ignored you for the last twenty-four years. I don't see why he should stop now."

"You heartless bastard," she yelped, turning away.

"That's me. Hey, Dolly?"

She looked at him, her face white.

"Your daddy already knows what I did to your boyfriend."

"You're lying!"

"No I'm not. We discussed it in great detail. See, your friend smashed against the rocks and his eyeballs flew out and his big fat belly exploded and—"

"STOP!" Dolly reached for the door frame to steady herself.

"Yeah, he hit the rocks like a sack of shit. Pretty much exploded."

Dolly sank to the floor. "Shut up! Just shut up!"

Henderson's lips went white. "You know, I think you're right. The time for talking is through." Like a cat closing in on a hapless mouse, he fairly flowed in a stealthy stalk across the room while unhooking his belt. As he pulled it from around his waist he said, "I think it's about time you got the lesson your Daddy should have given you a long time ago."

14

> *It was a puzzling thing.*
> *The truth knocks on your door and you say,*
> *"Go away, I'm looking for the truth,"*
> *and so it goes away. Puzzling.*

—Robert M. Pirsig, *Zen and the Art of*
Motorcycle Maintenance

Davecki knew he needed sleep. He also knew why he had been putting it off. If he waited until he was about to drop from exhaustion, he wouldn't have to think about falling asleep. Not that he had anything against thinking. Despite what B.D. might say in angrier moments, Davecki was actually too thoughtful. But he just didn't want to think about Little Willie floating in the water.

He had even dreaded returning to *Steak Warning*, as if somehow some trace of his friend's body, or indeed, the spirit of Willie, remained. Willie was gone now. *In Hog heaven.* Davecki grinned.

After his frustrating, Jekyll-and-Hyde encounter with Clara, he had driven back home. Fast. As he had roared down Highway 2/53, well over the speed limit, he came up with any number of smart-ass comebacks he could have used on Clara. Key words: COULD HAVE. Instead, what had he done? Sat there like a half-wit eating his hash browns and getting laughed at. *Yah damn fool! Too bad you need her to find Crystal's Palace.*

Aboard *Steak Warning* he stomped around angrily. Took his Glock out of his holster and stuffed both in their hidden compartment. He stomped some more. *This is nuts. Get a grip, Alphonse.* He put both palms on the counters port and starboard and started push-ups. When his shoulder muscles screamed he stopped and sucked air heavily.

But the sound was relentless, the sound of the waves. Their whispers, usually so soothing, were irritating. "If I'd have known how damn noisy living on a boat would be, I'd have kept the minicamper," Davecki said to the refrigerator.

He tucked down onto the floor and started sit-ups. When his gut muscles screeched, he heaved up and sat on the edge of the bunk. After his breathing regulated, he flopped back.

He lay there. *Okay, what's going on, Alphonse?* The closeness of the deck overhead made him close his eyes. *I'm angry with Willie for ending up dead. No. There's more. I'm pissed that he ended up dead and came floating back into my life.*

He rolled to his side.

Yeah, that's it. Willie, you jerk. Why couldn't you still be alive and bugging somebody else?

The waves laughed against the hull.

"Would you shut up?" he whispered to the water. He flopped to his other side. *Frigging Clara. Who does she think she is anyway? The Queen of Sheba? I'm going to tell her off.*

The waves chuckled, but, they refrained from outright guffaws.

Would you please shut up?

The lake rolled under him, murmuring, sloshing.

He sat up and whacked his head.

Damn it! He rolled out of the bunk and staggered to his feet. "Shut up!" He pounded the counter. "Shut UP!"

The lake stilled. Immediately there was a sudden silence. The only sound was his own ragged breathing.

Davecki sat back heavily on his bunk. He realized what an ass he'd been. Here he was, tired, confused, and mourning his friend, and he was screaming at a lake. "Sorry," he said out loud. *No point in trying to sleep now.* He rose and shuffled to the sink and pumped water into the copper kettle to heat water for tea.

Sitting at his small table, head in his hands, he gave up. The image that had plagued him all day played itself out. The money. Little Willie. Floating. The eyes…

Davecki felt a prickling in the back of his own eyes. He took a deep breath and focused intently on his tea. Steep. Half spoon of honey. Half squeeze of lemon. All the while, thinking.

He and Willie hadn't seen much of each other as adults, but whenever they did, they had a great time recalling the fond past life of carefree teenagers.

Willie looked rough—hell, he *was* rough—but he had a heart of gold. He didn't mistreat anyone who didn't deserve mistreatment.

Nice to animals and kids. Polite to the ladies; almost chivalrous.

Davecki smiled. Though once at WalMart Little Willie held a door open for a little old lady from South Superior and she walked to the door furthest from the bruising biker and let herself in.

Davecki sipped his tea, tried to remember when he had last seen his friend. *Must have been two, three months ago. At the Anchor.*

"That a new tatt?" Davecki said taking a stool next to Willie.

Willie looked left and right, then leaned close.

"I can tell you," he half-whispered in his rumbling voice. "I joined a group that's concerned with taking care of the lake."

"Oh, FALSIES?"

Willie looked shocked, then suspicious. "Who told you?"

Davecki laughed. "It's a secret society, remember? That means everybody knows about it. Seriously, I know a couple of eggheads from the UW-S. Actually, I don't really know them all that well, but we've talked. They hang out at that coffee shop on Tower. We've chatted. It's amazing what people will tell a cop. They're kind of kooky, but, hey, aren't we all? So what's the group up to these days?" Davecki asked.

"It's not all that big a deal," Willie said.

They drank their beer. Willie finished his Anchor Burger, downed the rest of his brewski and stood. "The lake's in trouble," he said. And he walked out the door.

Davecki stared into his now-empty teacup. *That was the last time I saw him alive and breathing.* He shoved the cup across the table.

He grabbed a set of keys from the back of the table. *I should take this tub out and give the carburetors a good cleaning out.*

He tossed the keys back on the table. They clattered loudly in the unusually silent cabin. *Nawww. Too expensive. Too much gas.*

Then he snapped his fingers. "Dang!" he cussed. *I forgot to call Sulu! I suppose they know by now. I'll have to call Niilo or go visit Knute. Have a cup of coffee, talk about Willie.*

He stood and leaned left and fell into the bed. *But before that, I got to find this Crystal. And before that, I need some sleep.* He punched up the pillows, curled into a ball and thought, *The waves are talking again. What are you saying my little ones?*

Before they could formulate an answer that would reach his consciousness, he was fast and sound asleep.

15

The hurrier I go, the behinder I get.

—Rodril Heukenlein

In the morning sun, Davecki pointed his cheery red motorcycle south on Tower Avenue. This early in the morning the wide roadway was deserted. Tower Avenue, between Belknap and 18th, gave him space to get up to 80 mph. At the Nottingham Building, he two fingered the front brake lever, did a stoppie, and tipped the bike left across the lane and into a parking spot. He looked up at one of Superior's finest old structures, the Nottingham Building. This centenarian building was home to Northland Coffee, a place reputed to have possibly employed one Crystal Cathedral.

As he started pulling his gloves off, Pammy Oakley emerged from the western wear shop next door. The petite clerk leaned against the doorpost and lit a cigarette, eyeing Davecki. She nodded a greeting.

Davecki raised his gloved index finger and nodded back. He heeled the kick stand down and dismounted. He was about to unplug his electric vest and communications pigtail when the cell phone built into his helmet chirped. He thumbed the PTT button. "Davecki," he growled, his eyes still on Pam. Her slouch against the door frame looked like a cheetah lounging in the sun.

"This is Callahan," the voice in his earpiece vibrated. "St. Louis County called. They're on the scene of a motorcycle accident up at Palisade Head. The plate they ran was that of a Superior resident: one William J. Horton. They want someone up there to ID the wreck. Seems they've got some extenuating circumstances. Sign out a squad car and get going."

"What's the magic word, Chief?"

"I've got two magic words for you Davecki, but I won't say them over the air. Now get moving... please?"

"I love you too, Chief," Davecki said. He thumbed the PTT button twice to hang up.

"You too good to say hi?" Pammy drawled.

Davecki flipped his face shield up and said, "Not too good. Too slow. I gotta run up the Shore. Can't be polite."

"You could at least say 'hi.' "

"Hi."

She took a long deep drag on her cigarette. "You always in such a rush? You look sorta uptight."

"I am. Too many things to do at once. I needed to ask Scotty in there," Davecki nodded toward the coffee shop, "about Crystal Cathedral."

Pammy laughed. "You want to find out about Crystal, you'll have to ask about Dolly."

"What's that supposed to mean?"

Pam blew a stream of smoke up and out. It ruffled the hair that fell over her forehead. "I mean, Scotty hired Dolly, not Crystal."

"In plain English please?"

"My my, aren't we testy this morning." Pam took another drag, then tossed the butt onto the sidewalk, crushing it with the sole of her frilled cowboy boot. She bent down to pick it up. "Don't like to litter, you know," she explained with an innocent smile.

Davecki's gloved fingers drummed the VFR's gas tank. "Hey Pammy. I know what a neat person you are. Anyone can tell that from how cute you are. But, I'm in a bit of a rush here."

"A'right, a'right." She roused from her slouch against the door frame and sauntered over to the bike. "Crystal's real name is Dolly. Kind of a mixed-up kid, but nice. We sort of hit it off. She had a couple of jobs, far as I know. One was here," Pammy jerked her head in the direction of the coffee shop, "the other was at the Gentleman's Club. Crystal Cathedral was her stage name."

"That's a long way from Dolly. You know her last name?"

"Nope. She only worked here a few days. Scotty says one Sunday morning she just never showed. Never even came for her pay."

"How long ago was that?"

"A month, I suppose."

"You know where she lived?"

"Nope."

He sighed. "Okay. Thanks, Pammy. Gotta go."

"No rest for the wicked," Pammy said. She ambled back and assumed her slouch.

Davecki thumbed the start button, flipped his face shield down, and zoomed away. He sang, "Hello Dolly, well hello Dolly. It's so nice to have you back where you belong," while shifting.

16

Sometimes it's better to travel than to arrive.

—Robert M. Pirsig,
Zen and the Art of Motorcycle Maintenance

ooming was one of Davecki's favorite things. It kept his body busy while his intellect was otherwise occupied. He zoomed the VFR down Tower Avenue to the whine of the gear-driven overhead cams and the roar of the YokoOno exhaust pipe. The stoplight on Belknap turned yellow. In response, he downshifted and wrenched the throttle backwards, dropped his left knee and dove around the corner. Coming upright, he twisted the right grip even more. The VFR stood on its back wheel and screamed through its high-tech muffler.

Cool. Okay. Think Alphonse.

Davecki mulled the situation while reflexively dealing with traffic, road surface, angle of incline, apex of corner, tangent of wheelie, coefficient of drag. Is the fun factor high enough? All the usual minutiae of motorcycling.

Okay, I find Little Willie floating. He's last seen with a dancer with two names. Dancer's from the North Shore somewhere. Now his bike turns up wrecked, also on the North Shore. Seems like the North Shore's a good place to avoid.

Meanwhile, Davecki was hauling ass across the Bong Bridge. Shortly after zipping under the center span, the responsible part of his brain notified him that he was, at the moment, a Superior cop speeding in Duluth.

Oops.

Minnesota State Troopers had been known to lurk just below the sight line beyond the big blue arches of the massive bridge, and even a mildly comatose trooper would get a real hot flash at the sight of a bright red sport bike going over 100 mph. Glancing out at the upper St. Louis river shipping channel, he throttled down to 70.

He thumbed the PTT and spoke a chain of numbers into his chin guard microphone.

The sound of one phone ringing in the wilderness echoed in his earpiece. "Police desk," a bored-sounding voice intoned.

"Hey Con. Tell Callahan I decided not to waste time by checking out a squad."

"He's going to be maaaad," Connie trilled.

"Fine, if he wants to chew my ass, he can call my cell number." Davecki double-punched the PTT. Instantly his spirits lifted. It was a great day for a ride, especially to Palisade Head. Didn't the Chief say to get up there ASAP? So wasn't it perfectly reasonable to save the time of signing out a squad? Wasn't it way faster to pound up the North Shore on the most convenient vehicle available? *Yes. Of course. Very sensible.*

One of the kickiest places to speed in Duluth was through the three and a half underground tunnels that bulged on the end of I-35's long trail from Texas to Duluth. Sure it was a thrill to zoom along the Duluth waterfront, past the can of worms, past the Aquarium of Few Fish; but, the best pop came from speeding through the underground passages honking the horn and yelling into the face shield.

However, by far the greatest gas, way better than even the speed, was to pop out of the last tunnel and take the full visual blast of seeing the great big expanse of Lake Superior looming off to the horizon.

Every speeder had a choice in that last tunnel. There was the occasional State Trooper lurking out of sight just beyond the bend in the highway. It was either look carefully down the road for evidence of the Law, or scope out the bold, sapphire-blue Inland Sea stretching to infinity.

Davecki never bothered with the Law. It paled beside the enormity of the lake. Today, the lake's greeting was tense. Like bumping into the Ex in a restaurant. The waves were gray and choppy. He responded to the tense greeting by opening the throttle more.

17

You gotta walk slow, talk low, and don't say too much.

—John Wayne

avecki raced up the contorted roadway leading to Palisade Head. He knew there would be no oncoming traffic; the deputy at the entrance was stopping all vehicles and had told him everyone was up top waiting for the guy from Superior.

The guy from Superior reached up and flipped open the Plexiglas face shield, eager to breathe in the fresh lake air. A cold brace of Gitchee Gummi wind slapped his cheeks. Reprimanded by the icy slap, Davecki slowed the VFR down to plodding speed, his eyes streaming tears.

At a pockmarked, shotgun-scarred One Way sign, he turned right and ascended toward the apogee that was Palisade Head. He crested the top of the knob, tore his vision from the gigantic radio tower looming into the blue, blue sky and looked down into the parking lot. A row of vehicles about twenty-five yards away stood all lined up like ponies in front of a saloon. He drove up and maneuvered the VFR into the row next to a maroon and white Minnesota State Trooper cruiser.

Two other cop cars, an emergency rescue vehicle, a full sized camper van and a red four-wheel-drive tow truck were also in the lot. The tow truck was backed up snug against the retaining wall. A five-eighths inch cable snaked away from the winch at the bottom of the flatbed and ran through a clump of bushes toward the lake beyond.

Davecki plunked his helmet and gloves on his side mirror, followed the cable through the low bushes. He stopped, shading his eyes with his hand and squinting into the brilliant sunlight. Stretching out to infinity and beyond was the big sea shining waters, the Father of Waters, the inland sea. And somewhere across the shining waters of Nakomis was his home on the "north coast" of Wisconsin.

And directly before him—though not quite so scenic—was a group of men, gathered in a semicircle at the end of the tow truck's cable. *They look like a bunch of fishermen standing around a big catch.* It wasn't a lake trout on the line that held everyone's attention. The catch of the day was an utterly demolished Harley Davidson.

Their attention to the wreck was so complete that no one noticed Davecki parting the bushes and approaching across the uneven mound of rock. Not until he was nearly to the group did one of the men look up. Through a gap in the circle Davecki saw what had them so engrossed.

Spilling out of the Hog's mangled saddlebags was money, a lot of money. Little bundles, all splashed out like packing peanuts around a hastily opened box.

At the sight of the money, every instinct in Davecki itched to take command of what was obviously a crime scene. *Don't be stupid, Dave. Let the energy here do its thing.*

The man who noticed Davecki broke off from the group and started toward him. He watched the man approach. The man reached back and hitched up his pants. *This here is the top dog.* Davecki didn't move. The man drew closer, and Davecki saw the tension evident on his face. *Oooh, ouch and owie. It's an irritated top dog to boot.*

"Miller. Splake County Sheriff," the man said as he reached out his hand.

18

Men should be what they seem.

—William Shakespeare, *Othello*

Nevada Henderson smiled. The man seated across the table from him at the Perkins Restaurant on Superior's lakefront stared at the silverware. He smelled powerfully of fish. A brownish Dickies work shirt, decorated with stains and old flecks of dried catsup, was pinned to the man's chest by two wide suspenders. Wool longjohn lapels peeked out from beneath the shirt collar. The slender curve of a hand-carved pipe stem stuck out from the breast pocket like a twig that had been broken off a low hanging branch and gotten stuck under the suspender strap.

"So, anything you can tell me, Knute, would be very helpful for my book on Finnish secret societies."

The old man reached for his coffee cup. The gray hair growing out of Knute's ears bobbed like long grass in a summer wind as he swallowed. He put his cup down. Said nothing.

Not very talkative, Henderson thought. *Crafty son-of-a-bitch.*

"Knute? Anything at all."

The old man's wrinkled face rearranged itself. Creases disappeared and reappeared.

Henderson watched and waited in silence. After a long silence the old man's thin lips moved. They curled upward at the corners in what appeared to be a faint smile. *He seems to be enjoying this. The old coot.*

"Ain't no more secret societies in Oulu, Mr. Hallstrom," Knute said.

"Please, call me Kevin." Henderson gave the old man another smile. Knute said nothing. Henderson cleared his throat and hurried on. "I'm sure there aren't *now*. But according to Lance Dryborough, there used to be several of them."

Knute drained his coffee cup and held it up in the direction of a passing waitress. She flashed Knute a smile as she breezed past. "Be right back."

Henderson watched the old man watch the woman's backside heading toward the kitchen. *Not a chance.* He pressed on. "I'm trying to do as thorough a job as I can. I want to actually put the reader *inside* a secret society. Just like they were there."

Knute glanced briefly at Henderson, then looked away.

"One reason I asked you is, that your name is obviously not Finnish, so, I thought you might have been able to observe the societies from an objective distance," Henderson said. He smiled again. *If you can't dazzle 'em with brilliance, baffle 'em with bullshit.*

"Well you got one ting right. I'm obviously not Finnish. But you got a nudder ting wrong too I bet. I'm not Swedish either. I'm Churman, and I saw some tings in my time. But dem days is over. Besides, puttin' someone inside a fiction... dat's a big yob."

"Not so big. Especially if you can do what Lance said you could."

Knute looked at the table.

"Knute?"

Knute looked out the window.

If I can't get this old guy to talk, we'll be up shit creek. Henderson leaned forward. "Knute," he said in a low voice. "I'll be candid. I don't just want you to tell me about the old days. I don't just want to *hear* about the secret societies. I want to actually go to a meeting or two. I want to be introduced. I want in." He leaned back suddenly as the waitress brought the coffee pot. Smiling, she refilled Knute's cup.

Henderson read the name tag. "Thanks Rose Darlin'," Henderson said.

She smiled. Said nothing.

"Danke," Knute murmured.

She smiled and turned toward Knute. "You're welcome," she said and headed for the kitchen.

I'll be damned.

"Der ain't no more secret societies," Knute repeated.

Henderson said, "Well, that's too bad. No, really, it's more than that. It's a shame."

"Vhy's dat?" Knute asked. The old guy eyed Henderson with

chin lowered. The effect was like looking over eyeglasses. Only Knute wore no eyeglasses. He did, however, seem to be peering through the bushy eyebrows that sprouted like weeds above the deep set eyes.

Henderson said, "Well, those dissenters of old were a source of real social vitality. I wish I could have been a part of that back then. Now that they're gone, all that's left is us. A bunch of sheep. It's just too bad." Henderson sighed. "So I guess Lance was wrong. I'll just have to make it up."

Henderson sighed again. He rubbed his eyes and forehead and picked up his fork. Then he remembered the unwritten law of northern Wisconsin society: *to be accepted, you must talk while chewing.* He loaded his fork with a heap of eggs. He unloaded the huge pile of cholesterol in his mouth. Shifting the cooked chicken embryos around to make clearance for words to pass, he said, "So, okay. Let's just pretend I was going to go to one of those old-time secret meetings. Where would I have gone? How would I get in?"

Knute eyed Henderson.

Henderson's face remained blank. *This old coot is one tough poker player.*

Knute stabbed three layers of pancake, lifted same. Before inserting the cake pieces, he said, "Not as good as panukaku." He took the carbo load into his mouth. After chewing, before swallowing, Knute said, "Way back den you'd go to da Corner Co-op and ask Suzy vhere da brookies vas bitin'."

"This is great," Henderson said. He scrawled notes on a dictation pad flopped out on the table. *Keep it coming old man.* "Really? And what would she say?"

"She might say dey vere catchin' some at da bend in da creek vhere it passes tru da Maki farm's back forty."

"That's some sort of code isn't it?"

Knute sighed. "Not really."

"Oh? Yeah. What a dummy. That would be where the meeting was being held wouldn't it?"

Must have been the food-in-mouth ploy, Henderson figured.

The false journalist took a large bite of omelet. "And what kind of places did the societies meet in?" At the word societies, a chunk of egg flew out of Henderson's mouth and kerplopped right in Knute's coffee. A little splash sloshed onto the table.

Knute didn't flinch. He picked up his cup and drank. Swallowing hard, he said, "Anyvere. Som'times here, som'times der. Alvays out of doors. Lot of times, Maki's back forty, smack-dab in da middle of some old grote pine next to a cedar svamp between Maki's pasture and Laakson's pulpwoods."

Henderson laughed. Another piece of egg flew out of his mouth and landed in the water glass on Knute's side of the table. "This is great," he said as he scrawled notes fast and furiously. Then he stopped writing. "Was Suzy talking in some kind of code?"

Knute shook his head. "No. No code. Dat vas yust a test. Anyvun askin' about fishin' on da Maki place vasn't s'posed to be at no meetin'."

"I don't get it."

Knute shifted his weight around in the seat. "If anyvun in Oulu got asted about da best spot to catch brookies on Crystal Creek, dey ver sposed to say, 'Vhere da creek cuts tru da Maki place.'"

"Okay. I'm with you so far," Henderson said.

"Den if dey ver asted for more directions dey vere be told it vas hard to describe and dat dey should talk to Pastor Rantala."

"And what would the Pastor tell dem, er, them?"

Knute ate more pancake. "Vouldn't tell 'em nuttin'."

"I don't get it," Henderson said.

"Because dere's no such person as Pastor Rantala. Rantala's a farmer."

"So the rube would be asking all around and everyone would know there was some snooping going on. I get it," Henderson said. He forked a load of hash browns in. "But what about a map? Why wouldn't anyone wanting to find a meeting just look at a map and figure out where the creek cut through the Maki place?"

"Dat dey could do. But it vouldn't do 'em no good."

Henderson scratched his head with the eraser on his pencil. "Why's dat?"

"'Cause der ain't no such ting Crystal Creek. Only creek out der in dat part of Oulu is Reefer Creek and it don't go nowhere near da Maki place."

"Whoa! So der, er, there was no way to find out where the meeting was?"

"If you vas smart enough you could. And der vere plenty of smart

Federal Agents who got in. Dat's vhat kilt da meetin's off. Or, you could yust get invited. Dat vas da easiest vay. Gettin' into da piney woods wit'out getting' lost, eaten alive by mosquitos in da summer, or trippin' over a cedar root and breakin' yer leg vas next to impossible back den."

"I suppose they held their meetings at odd times too. To keep the riff-raff out."

"It vas alvays after milkin'. Dairy farmers are ruled by dere cow's udders, Mr. Hallstrom."

"In the vinter too?"

"Tings slowed down in da vinter. But durin' da summer, it vas full bore. And never on Vensday."

A short silence ensued while Henderson scrawled notes. "Why never, never on a Wednesday?" he eventually asked.

"'Cause dat's church night. Everyvon vas in church on Vensdays."

Henderson scribbled. He laid down the pencil. He looked at his watch. "Hey! Today's Wednesday. If there was a meeting tonight, would you take me?"

Knute drained his coffee cup and put it down with a thud. "I tank you for da breakfast. I got to go. Got to get up to Canada and get dem walleyes back down here in time for Friday night fish fry. Sorry I can't help you more."

"The Lord helps doze who help demselves," Henderson said. "If you are serious about helping me more, you could make a call and get me in. After all, there are no more secret societies. Right?"

Knute looked Henderson straight in the eyes, answered with silence and stood up.

Henderson stopped his fork in mid-flight. A clump of hash browns fell back to the plate. "Hey! I was just getting going. There's so much more to ask."

Knute stopped, turned. He pulled his Kromer on and said, "Yeah, and more to tell. But not by me. I got to go but I will make dat call. If you can find da meetin', dey'll let you in." He adjusted the Kromer and left the restaurant, taking with him the bountiful fragrance of fresh fish.

Henderson reforked the hash browns and filled his maw just as Rosey walked past. He hoisted his cup and motioned the way Knute did.

Rosey walked on without acknowledgment.

He put the cup down. *Damn this is a tough room.* He chortled. *No matter. All I've got to do now is get a Bayfield County plat book, some aerial forest survey photos and show up tonight just after milking, whatever the hell time that is. Then, provided I make it through the swamp in tact, by seven thirty Kevin Hallstrom should be attending his first FALSIES meeting.*

19

Lake Superior is down several inches from last year's level.
A typical 1,000-foot laker must reduce its cargo by up to 4,000 tons
in order to avoid scraping bottom.

—From a story by Paul Adams,
Duluth News Tribune June 19, 1999

Cameroon eyed Fran, who lay slouched on the couch at Northwoods Coffee. He leaned across the low table toward her. "You remind me of my grandma's quilt."
She raised an eyebrow. "Dare I ask?"

"You look flung across the cushions, like a tossed aside quilt. Quite alluring I must say."

"Of course you must say." She tipped her cup gingerly toward her lips. Sipping her Double-A Kenyan cappuccino, she added, "What else on earth might you feel compelled to say. You're a dirty old man after all. It's your duty to be insulting and suggestive."

Cameroon snorted. "I'm not a dirty old man. I'm a slightly soiled elderly professor of equal worth and dignity. Not that you care about my self image."

Hansen sat up and set her coffee on the table. "Anyway. There's no stopping it. It's already been decided at the highest bureaucratic levels. The water *will* flow south. And with all this terrorism terror dominating the country's communal consciousness, there won't even be a period of public discomfort. They'll just enact legislation while everyone's hunkering down in their fight against biological warfare. In the meantime, we should act. It's the perfect time. We've got the perfect cover. I wish I was a bank robber. That would be fun. What better time to become a professional criminal. You two could go in and do the heist. I'd be the driver. Fantastic Fran drives the getaway van!"

"Come on, Fran, you can't mean that!"

"Mean what?"

Jensen rubbed his hands together. They looked like fresh-caught trout flipping themselves in the creel. From his end of the couch, he glanced nervously across the counter to the back of the coffee shop kitchen. Two people stood at the sink washing dishes.

"I am serious, Simon." Fran replied. "There's no other real option. Sure we could wait and let things develop. But that's what the U.S. Government did with Osama. I've given this a lot of thought. The time to act is now. All you two need to do is tell me if you're willing to proceed." She looked from Jensen to Cameroon.

"But how can you possibly know for sure?" Jensen asked.

Fran looked down. "I have a source of course," she said.

Cameroon held his gaze on Fran. Jensen looked at the silent professor and then back at Hansen. He laughed. "I'm going to need more than that, Fran."

Hansen's face went tense. "This is no laughing matter, Simon. I have a good friend in high places. She tells me the money flowing up here from Arizona is like an artesian well."

Cameroon broke his silence. "She's right, Simon. The time to act is now. Nobody cares about water diversion with smallpox and anthrax on the rampage and the looting of Social Security. We should go for it."

Hansen added, "The amount of water being taken, the way it's being done—it's all damaging to the ecosystem in the long term."

"If your friend is so highly placed, why doesn't she blow the whistle? Why's it up to us?"

"You're kidding. Right? She'd be dead in a week if she made credible revelations. You know the only way a bureaucrat can truly be a whistleblower is if they don't care about living. The witness protection program is a myth for all intents and purposes."

"So, I'm just supposed to take the word of Frantastic Hansen and risk my life? I should think you'd give me more to go on than 'highly placed,'" Simon said.

Hansen sighed. She sipped her coffee. "You have no idea what those people are like." She glanced at Cameroon. "She dated a guy. This man she was involved with for a short time is some sort of henchman who does all the dirty work. He doesn't have a conscience. My friend believes she would be killed if she tried to back out."

"Back out?" Cameroon said.

"What's that mean?" Jensen asked.

"It means she's involved financially and can't suddenly find morality. And besides, she doesn't know how far up the ladder the corruption goes, but there's a lot of money changing hands. So, either WE do something, or we don't, and these people not only get away with the greatest theft of the century, they put our entire ecosystem at risk." Fran flopped back heavily on the couch, her cheeks flushed.

Cameroon sat in his chair, motionless except for one index finger tapping the rim of his coffee cup.

Jensen leaned forward, his forearms on his knees, staring at the floor.

Still staring down, Jensen said, "I suppose you're right. I mean, if anyone can do the dive, I can. But geeze," he raised his face toward Hansen, "the suction..."

Hansen smiled, sat forward.

"I'm not sure I could even pop the release under those conditions."

"Of course you can do it. You're Simon Jensen," Hansen said.

Jensen nodded, "You've got a point there. The more I think about it, the more I guess it could be done."

"For all five inlets?" Cameroon asked.

Jensen looked at the white-haired professor. "If it can be done at one, it can be done at all of them." He looked at Hansen. "You got enough raw material?"

"Not yet. But soon. I'm working overtime on it," Fran answered.

Jensen looked over his shoulder again. Two people stood at the sink at the back of the room. "I'm not sure it's the wisest move in the world, though."

Fran snorted. "It's a lot wiser than Sulu's plan. At least this way, nobody goes to prison."

"Now that you've got to like," Jensen said. "Are you two going to bring it up at the next meeting?"

"If we three are agreed and committed to action... of course," Cameroon said.

"You think it's okay to spill the beans?" Simon asked.

"We've got to. I don't want to be accused of acting arbitrarily," Cameroon said.

"Besides, if anyone can keep a secret, it's Finns. They hardly talk to each other, much less outsiders!" Fran laughed.

Jensen said, "But the group isn't all Finns anymore. I'm just not so sure about some of the newbies. What's with their obsession with fertilizer and fuel oil?"

"Well, they've kept their mouths shut so far," Cameroon said. "I mean, they're pretty much all in favor of blowing up a large part of Kansas real estate. I'm sure each and every one of them is well aware of the loss of our civil liberties. They probably wouldn't get across Iowa without being arrested. Our plan is a way out for them."

"That's a good point," Fran said.

"Hey guys!" Scotty the coffee shop guy said as he scooted from behind the counter. He was wiping a cup with a white cotton cloth. "What's a good point?" he asked.

The trio looked each other over. Hansen said, "Putting the water issue up before the WTO again," Fran said.

"You three are like dogs worrying a bone. When are you going to give that subject a rest?"

Hansen reached into the inside pocket of her black blazer and extricated a crumpled newspaper clipping. "This is from way back in nineteen ninety nine. It says here, and I quote, *Great Lakes Water Concerns Rebuffed By Administration.*"

"Old news," Scotty said.

"Let me see that!" Jensen said. He lunged across the couch for the paper.

"MINE!" Fran yelped. She flicked the paper up and away from the snatch of Jensen's hand. She held it over her head and out of his reach.

"For Cripe's sake," Jensen crabbed as he palmed the back of the couch to keep himself from falling into Fran's lap.

Fran fluttered the paper. "No. I'll read it aloud."

"Brat," Jensen said.

"Takes one to know one," Fran replied.

"Just read it," Cameroon commanded, rolling his eyes.

Fran brandished the clipping with a flourish. "Remember the WTO riots?"

"Yeah. They called it The Battle in Seattle didn't they?" Jensen asked.

"Exactly. This article is the account of several Great Lakes lawmakers requesting that the issue of wholesale diversion of Great Lakes water be put on the WTO agenda. Clinton quashed it."

"Why wouldn't they put it on the agenda?" Scotty asked.

"The same reason the Bushies refuse to discuss it now. They all made billions on oil. They want to repeat that story line only with water," Fran said. She tossed her head. Her silky black hair shuddered in shimmering waves. "The bottom line is..."

"MONEY," Cameroon said.

"The Bushies are saying the same thing the Clintonions said, that it would be creating an issue where there currently isn't one. He said current law and treaties prohibit any such thing from ever happening."

"Tell that to the Canadians," Cameroon snorted.

"No kidding," Jensen said. "They're the ones who started this whole mess. They were actually going to ship tanker loads of Lake Superior water to Japan."

"Too little, too late," Fran replied. "The U.N. already owns all the water—it says so right in the NAFTA treaty. The new world order already has everything in place that enables them to dismiss the will of the people of the Great Lakes Region and use the water for whatever reason they deem appropriate."

"And to make matters even easier for them, all they need to do is say the magic words..."

"For reasons of national security," Jensen said.

"I don't think people would let that happen to Lake Superior," Scotty said.

"That may be well and good for the loyal citizens of the United States of America who believe we still have rights. But any resistance by people wanting to preserve the integrity of Lake Superior would be squashed by our own military, under martial law," Fran said.

Scotty looked out the windows at the front of the building. "No way they would do that."

"Ever hear of FEMA?" Cameroon asked.

"The disaster relief people?" Scotty asked.

Cameroon sighed. "Federal Emergency Management Authority. They have the power to declare martial law and order military strikes against the American people. Besides, FEMA's no big deal. The U.S. Government stomps on the rights of the people any time someone in authority gets a groin itch. They've done it many, many times already."

"When?" Scotty asked.

"Nineteen seventy-one for instance," Fran answered. "The May Day Peace Demonstrations in Washington D.C. Over eighteen thousand people were arrested in a single day. Helicopters were dropping tear gas bombs. Police were herding people into buses by beating them with their nightsticks. Entire crowds of students were being corralled like cattle and hauled off to RFK Stadium for detention."

"I've never heard of that." Scotty said.

"The media was a government lap dog back then too. They kept quiet."

"How do *you* know about it, then?"

"I was there."

"You got arrested?"

"No, I got lucky. I camouflaged myself by following an ABC camera crew around. The cops figured I wasn't a radical out to overthrow the government. So I got back to campus in time for my ten o'clock Monday morning physics class."

"What was weird was, nobody ever heard anything about the riots and the detentions. It was weird enough back then. Now after WTC, if that kind of thing ever happens again, over water or anything else, the government won't even bother declaring martial law. Any resistance, armed or otherwise, will be squashed like a misguided spider crossing the kitchen table during Christmas dinner."

"Do the Canadians know about this?" Scotty asked.

"Who cares about Canada? When the U.S. sneezes, Canada catches a cold," Cameroon said.

"Simmer down, Don," Fran said.

He glared at her.

"I say the Canadians will be very upset if we start stealing Lake Superior from them," Scotty said.

"Not if the Colorado River is a precedent," Cameroon said.

"What's that mean?" Scotty asked.

"Any Canadian with half a brain knows that Great Lakes water is going to be going south someday. Look what they did to the Colorado River. It's all used up way before Yuma, Arizona. Not a trickle makes it to the Sea of Cortez anymore and Mexico, couldn't, didn't, and hasn't done diddly-squat about it."

"Canada's not Mexico and that was then. This is now," Scotty said.

"Maybe," said Fran, "but a California company is suing the Province of British Columbia because the Provincial government rescinded their permit to pipe Canadian Rocky Mountain water south."

"No kidding?" Scotty exclaimed.

"No kidding," Fran said.

Cameroon slapped his hands on his knees. "Good enough. Let 'em battle it out in the west. That'll take the spotlight off Lake Superior."

"Nothing can take the spotlight off Lake Superior," Fran sighed. "It's just too big to ignore."

20

It is easy to make things difficult.

—Uvegeney Uvstinko

ou must be the famous Dave Davecki." The cop extended his hand. The black nose of a webbed nylon holster poked out from the waistband of his jacket.

"More like Infamous." Davecki shook the hand.

"Dan Miller, Splake County Undersheriff."

"I've always wanted to come up your way and catch some of those legendary splake," Davecki said. "They as good-tasting as they say?"

A smile eased Miller's strained face. "Better. Only you can hardly catch one nowadays. Ever since Babs Wrinkleman put splake fishing on her TV show, they've been overfished to the max."

"Too bad."

"Tell me about it."

"Hey, Danno," one of men called from the cliff's edge. "You want I should winch it up? I gotta get going."

"Hold on, I'll be right there," Miller called back. "You wanna look before Glenn gives himself a shit fit?"

"Nothing to it, but to do it," Davecki said.

The two started toward the cliff's brow. Miller narrated, "Some girl climbers found the bike at the bottom and used their cell phone to call it in. They're waiting in their van."

"What's with all the money?"

"Drug deal probably. There's a Canuck cycle gang operating a regular pipeline pumping meth, deth, ecstacy—anything brewable in a bathtub—south. Coke, hash, marijuana, whatever returns. The stiff must have gotten high on product and tried to take a shortcut back home to Wisconsin."

As they neared the Harley, Davecki said, "That's definitely Willie's bike."

"You know that for sure?" Miller asked.

"I'd know it anywhere. One-of-a-kind FLH. Only shovelhead around with those big leather bags and all those silver conches."

"You sound pretty familiar with the bike."

"I was familiar with the deceased."

Miller was instantly alert. "Deceased?"

"I pulled Little Willie out of the lake myself, two days ago."

They approached the group of men. A State Trooper and a guy in dirty blue jeans and a grubby Vikings windbreaker stood by the mangled Hog. "This is Detective Davecki from Superior," Miller said.

The trooper extended his hand and smiled. "Monty Hall," he said.

Davecki snickered, shook Hall's hand.

"I get that all the time. Ma was a fan of General Montgomery. My old man was in the 125th Field Artillery in North Africa. Actually drove the real Monty around for a few days. I just go with it."

The Vikings fan looked up. He pointed a stubby finger at Davecki, grinning around a sizeable wad of tobacco. "Hey—you're that famous cop who roasted the firebug in St. Paul like a marshmallow."

"That's not quite how it was," Davecki said.

"Knock it off, Glenn," Miller said. "Detective Davecki says the owner of this bike is recently deceased."

Glenn smirked. "So, ya think he was a druggie?"

"Not that I know of," replied Davecki.

"Yeah right."

"Cool it, Glenn," Miller growled.

"Mind if I touch your evidence?" Davecki asked Miller.

"Ain't evidence. Knock yourself out."

Davecki squatted. Bundles of hundreds had spilled from the saddlebags. *Geeze, look at all that money.*

"Guy drove it right off the cliff. He had to have been flying," Trooper Hall said as he shook his head.

Davecki let his eyes rove thoroughly over the remains of the formerly classic motorcycle. It was an unmitigated mess. The forks were utterly destroyed, bent back and looking like limbs with compound fractures. The front wheel was broken in half. The Continental tire was twisted around the axle like a pretzel. The tanks, the seat, the sissy bar, the rear fender were all scuffed, smashed, and generally ravaged. The cone-bottom points-case was shattered. Gear fragments clung to the side case, adhered by thick black oil. The wreck looked just like it should look; wrecked. "Something about this doesn't fit the owner's profile," Davecki said.

"What? He wasn't a big winner at the Black Bear Casino? I've heard that more than once," Miller said.

"How much is there do you think?" Glenn asked.

"Couple hundred thousand at least," Hall said.

Davecki look up at the trooper.

Hall said, "I went to drug interdiction school in Miami. They showed us stacks and stacks of cash. A one-inch stack of new hundreds is twenty thousand. A standard briefcase can hold three quarters of a mill."

Miller added, "There's a lot of it blowing in the wind, thank you Bob Dylan. But, I'd say there's almost that on the bike, with more down below." He gestured toward the cliff's edge.

"Down in the water?"

"In the water. On the rocks. Blowing in the wind. It's everywhere. A lot of it floated in and was wedged between the rocks. Couple of deputies are down there now. Picking hundred dollar bills like they were blueberries."

"Those dike climbers probably scored a bunch," Tow Truck Man said.

"I'm thinking of searching their van," Miller said.

"Are they suspects?" Davecki asked.

"Ain't no crime. Just an accident here," Miller said.

"Then what's your probable cause?" Hall asked.

"Who needs probable cause these days? I'll just tell 'em it's in the interest of national security."

"It took me twelve minutes to get up here after I got the initial call," Hall said. "They couldn't have had all that much time to bring in the sheaves. They were up top here when I drove in."

"Gotta give these new type girls credit," Glenn said. "They've got balls."

Davecki looked back at the bike. *Who cares if they picked up a few grand? What I want to know is what's wrong with the picture here?* He stood and walked to the edge of the cliff. "It flew off over here?"

Miller said, "Glenn, don't you touch anything. Monty, watch him like a hawk."

"You're a real jerk, Barney. No wonder everyone calls you Lite. Miller Lite. I don't know what my sister ever saw in you."

"Cool it, Glenn," Miller commanded. He stepped toward Davecki.

"Why are all cops losers?" Glenn groused.

Miller walked up to Davecki. "Don't go getting all fancy on us, Davecki. This is an accident scene, not a crime scene."

21

There are an infinite number of facts about the motorcycle, and the right ones don't just dance up and introduce themselves. The right ones, the ones we really need, are not only passive, they are damned elusive, and we're not going to just sit back and "observe" them. We're going to have to be in there looking for them or we're going to be here a long time.

—Robert M. Pirsig,
Zen and the Art of Motorcycle Maintenance

avecki got down on all fours and inched to the lip of the precipice. He peered over the edge. *THAT is a long way down.* He backed away, lowered himself to his belly, looked down again. "It flew off here?" he asked again.

"Don't know. This is where we winched it up," Miller said.

Davecki looked out over the water. Crystal blue like a giant soft carpet stretched away to the horizon. He looked down. Two hundred feet below a Lund aluminum boat nuzzled the boulder-strewn shore. A hundred feet away from the boat, two figures in uniforms scuttered over and around the boulders like ants searching for bread crumbs.

Miller lowered himself next to Davecki.

"They picking up money?" Davecki asked.

"Right."

Davecki pushed back from the edge and stood. He walked slowly toward the bike. The lawman followed. Up ahead, Glenn lumbered through the bushes.

"Where's he going?" Miller asked Hall.

"See if he can molest a rock climber or two," Hall said.

"He'll get the short end of that stick in a real hurry," Miller said.

By the wrecked Harley, Davecki squatted again. The exhaust pipes were smashed. One muffler was missing. The saddlebags were mangled but still bolted to the rear fender struts. "It's hard to stop looking at all that money," he said.

"Tell me about it," Hall replied. "The Feds in Miami told some pretty impressive stories about cops finding huge amounts of cash in car trunks. People usually claim they don't know anything at all about it. The temptation is to scoop it up and make it disappear, but they warned us against it. They said most every cop who did something like that eventually got caught, because he couldn't restrain himself from going on a spending spree."

Still staring at the wreck, Davecki said, "Yeah, it would be tough." Then he pointed his index finger to the rear aspect of the Bendix carb. "See that?"

"What?" Hall bent down.

"That." Davecki pointed directly at the carburetor.

"What?" Miller bent down.

"That." Davecki prodded the brass actuating arm on the throttle rod.

"That brass thing?" Miller asked.

"Yeah, the brass thing. That's the throttle arm. It's wide open."

"So?"

Davecki looked up at the mangled handle bars. He pointed at the bottom side of the right twist grip. Although the handlebars were completely twisted around and bent over to where the windshield used to be, the basic structure was still intact.

"See that?" He pointed to the bottom of the twist grip housing where the thumbscrew for locking the throttle protruded.

"That star nut?" asked Miller.

"Right. It's screwed all the way in. The throttle's locked wide open."

"Like I said, so?" Miller asked again.

"Watch this," Davecki said. He loosened the star nut a couple of times. Suddenly the twist grip snapped back to idle position.

Miller stood. "So? What's the deal?"

Davecki stood. He stepped back from the bike and put his fingers to his chin. "On these old bikes, that star nut sets the throttle. It was a kind of crude cruise control."

"And?"

Davecki didn't answer immediately. "And," he said finally, "I don't know for sure. It just seems odd."

"Doesn't seem that odd to me," Miller said. "Guy scores a bunch of cash. Holds back some hash. Comes up here, gets totally wasted. Decides to head home and takes a wrong turn at the end of the parking lot. Takes the commuter flight back to Wisconsin."

"Maybe," Davecki said.

"This is an accident, Davecki," Miller said, and he walked toward the cliff.

Hall said, "What do you think happened?"

Davecki passed a hand over his face. "Hard to say. All I know is that Little Willie, or someone, revved up the bike, locked open the throttle and sent it flying off the cliff."

"He didn't just drive it off?"

"With a locked-open throttle? Highly unlikely."

"So what is likely?"

"If you wanted to ride off this cliff, you wouldn't need to lock the throttle open to do it. I think someone did it for him."

The two looked at the demolished bike.

"Two years ago, some kids stole an S-Ten Blazer and did exactly that," Hall said. "Drove the thing up here, got out, put 'er in gear, and sent it off the cliff at this very spot."

They fell silent again. A rising wind stirred across the cliff. Davecki rubbed the back of his neck and stole a quick glance at the trooper. "All I know is, this is no accident."

"Then what?"

"Murder."

"What's the motive?" Hall asked.

"There's thousands of motives, flying around on the breeze and floating in the water."

"Well, sure. Money's always a motive. But how are you going to prove it was anything but an accident? There were no guns found, no knives, no weapons of any kind. Did your stiff in Superior have any unsightly holes in him? You're going to have a hard time convincing Miller."

"I don't have to convince Miller of anything. This is his scene, his baby. In fact, I'd prefer that it was an accident. But, I do know this, Little Willie would not voluntarily ride his bike off this cliff."

"No one would—that's why it's an accident."

Shaking his head, Davecki walked slowly back toward the cliff. About ten feet from the edge, he stopped. "Well, well."

Miller, who had been gazing out over the inland ocean, turned. "Now what?"

"Look at this."

Hall joined the two of them. They all squatted down. Davecki pointed at the ground, then raised his finger in a trajectory toward the cliff's edge. "Here's the launching pad."

"What makes you think that?" Miller demanded.

Davecki pointed back at the ground. "This is a burn-out mark," he said.

"It sure looks like it," Hall said.

A snaking trail of black inscribed the stone.

"I missed it earlier. But it makes perfect sense. It explains the locked open throttle."

"You can do that?" Hall asked. "Get it in gear while it's over-revving? Wouldn't that just bust the hell out of the transmission?"

"Those old Harley gearboxes are about impossible to blow-up. Sure it's been done. Any tranny will fly apart if subjected to suffi-cient abuse. But, it wouldn't be unheard of to twist open the throttle, lock it wide open, squeeze the clutch and jam it in gear. Then all you'd have to do is step aside and let the clutch go. The whole she-bang shoots off the cliff like a rocket."

Miller shook his head. "I don't know. I still say the most likely explanation is that your friend rode the bike off himself, high, drunk, whatever."

"I know that's the most likely scenario for you. But for me it just doesn't make sense. It's not something Little Willie would do," Davecki said.

"No matter how well you knew him, you can't know that for sure," Miller said.

Tow Truck Glenn approached. "Yo, Danno, look what I found!" He was waving a hundred dollar bill. "Can I keep it?"

Miller rounded on him, eyes flashing. "No, you cannot keep it, Glenn. It's evidence. Hand it over."

"Shit." Glenn scowled. He handed the money to Miller.

Glenn pivoted and retreated toward the parking lot.

Miller gulped air. "Scout around for any signs of a struggle Monty. Maybe there's a shell casing or something. Your dead guy have any holes in him, Davecki?"

"No bullet holes. But the gulls got his eyes," Davecki said.

"If we could only see what he saw last," Miller said.

"Hey, Danno!" Glenn yelled from above and behind the bushes. "This Hawaii five oh crap sucks. I'm wasting all morning here. I'm going to winch that tub-o-shit Harley up and haul it over to Koivistos."

Miller yelled back. "Like hell. This is a crime scene now. Get your ass back down here and hand over any evidence."

"Asshole!" Glenn yelled. "You can frisk me if you want, you homo."

"Get the hell back down here right now, Glenn. And hand over the money in your pockets, or I'll tell your sister about your last visit to St. Paul."

Glenn stomped through the bushes pulling bills from his pockets as he approached. "You're a real prick. You know that, Danno?"

"That's a good boy, Glennie."

"Fuck you, Barney," Glenn said. He bent down, unhooked the cable from the frame of the Harley and stomped toward the lot.

"He's got more on him somewhere," Hall said.

"You want to pat him down?" Miller asked.

"No way."

Davecki said, "Well, my work here is done. I think I'll head back to town and see what kind of trouble I can uncover back there."

"You seem to be good at that," Miller said. "Why don't you make yourself useful and quiz those girls up for me."

22

Power is strength and the ability to see yourself through your own eyes and not through the eyes of another. It is being able to place a circle of power at your feet and not take power from someone else's circle.

—Agnes Whistling Elk

Hall meandered like a mite through the bushy brow of Palisade Head. The sound of a winch being ground into gear preceded the jump of the cable at Miller and Davecki's feet. As the black steel snake slithered into the bushes, Davecki turned to Miller and said, "You know, I just don't think it'd be cool for me to talk to those girls. Jurisdiction and all."

The heavy sound of truck tires squalling against blacktop as they burned rubber announced the departure of Tow Truck Glenn and his four by four from lot. Miller looked up at the sky and sighed. "That guy's a constant pain. And what's with you? You got something against eye candy?"

"No," Davecki answered. "I just don't need some cute young thing who thinks she's properly dressed ruining my day."

"Suit yourself," Miller said. "You're probably right about the jurisdiction thing. Yeah, you can go. I'll call if I need something. We'll need copies of the autopsy. The body back from Anoka yet?"

"Coming back today, probably."

"Okay. Thanks for coming up. I'll call you."

Davecki hesitated. *I wonder if this guy would know anything about this Crystal/Dolly person.* He pulled the stub of an old carrot from the map pocket of his Aerostich.

"What the hell's that?" Miller asked.

"My anti-cholesterol snack."

Miller laughed. "So did you need something, or were you just taking a snack break?"

Davecki crunched his carrot. Did he need something? He decided against it. "Snack break. I'll be going now. Good luck." He headed for the bushes and beyond.

Walking up to the parking lot, he saw two women standing by the VFR, mid-twenties types; fit. One was blonde and willowy, wearing a black t-shirt proclaiming *Shakespeare Rules!* The other was shorter, with an athletic figure and short, unruly hair, precisely the shade of a tangerine.

They both turned at his approach. "You're old!" the blonde exclaimed.

Tangerine Dream glared at her companion. "Kirsten!"

The blonde blushed. "We just thought... I mean, I thought... with the bike and all..."

Davecki smiled. "No problem. I get it all the time."

Tangerine narrowed her eyes, crossed her muscular arms. "We haven't done anything wrong, and we don't have to stay here," she said. "We're leaving. Kirsten?" She spun on her heel and started for the van.

Kirsten hesitated, toeing the dirt next to Davecki's bike with a black strappy sandal. Her toenails were painted pink.

Davecki smiled. "I hope the day's not lost for you. Just go a ways up the shore and you could get in some serious climbing yet. It's a long drive up from the Twin Cities to be turned away at the parking lot."

Her eyes widened. "How did you know we're from the Cities?"

"There aren't any women like you in this neck of the woods." He walked past her and grabbed his helmet. "Actually, though, your friend—what's her name?"

"Alison."

"Your friend Alison's mistaken. You do have to stay here."

"Why?" she asked.

"That bike is evidence in a homicide."

Kirsten's hand flew to her mouth.

"You're not suspects," he said. "They just want to talk to you some more, maybe look around a little..."

Kirsten's eyes flicked toward the van.

He paused. "Is there a problem?"

"No," she said. She shifted weight from foot to foot.

"Okay then." He zipped up his Aerostich. "But if there were a problem, now might be the time to, uh... tidy it up." Davecki glanced toward the van.

Alison was leaning against the van, an ivory Stetson was perched on her head. The orange hair blazed like the Fifth Element from under the brim.

Turning to Kirsten he said, "Geeze, you girls are something else, Minneapple Blossoms, cliff climbers, and now I see you're cowgirls too." He shrugged his head toward the van.

Kirsten stared at him. He stared at her. Her eyes were hazel, flecks of brown against green. "Oh, hah! That Alison, she's got a million interests."

"That's the way it is these days, girl power and all," Davecki said.

Kirsten laughed. "Hah! That's us; Go Girl!" she said as she pumped a fist into the air.

"What?" Alison called.

"Well, I'd better get back to Alison and the van. It is kind of a mess. I'm more the tidy one," she said. Kirsten took off jogging across the parking lot.

Davecki, against everything he'd learned about himself over the past decade, could not resist watching. At the van, Kirsten threw open the side door and plunged inside. He shook his head. Upon that head he pulled his helmet. Into that helmet he plugged the intercom jack for his cell phone. He plugged in the electric connection for the heated vest. He fiddled on his gloves, stretching the hook and loop latch tight across his wrist. He thumbed the starter. In the rear view mirror he saw one of his greatest fears. The form of a young woman standing in a parking lot vibrating at a frequency that was at least a million light years off-cycle from him. Davecki let out the clutch, crested the exit of the parking lot and cranked on the throttle. His direction pointed his mind toward the next woman he needed to see, a woman who knew about a woman in a Crystal palace somewhere in the woods of the North Shore.

23

The heart is deceitful above all things, and desperately wicked: who can know it?

—Jeremiah 17:9 KJV

Davecki was speeding back to Superior at 130 mph, racing the skies. Purple clouds swirled above, getting darker by the minute. He twisted the throttle even more, streaking past cars and SUVs. As he passed through Duluth's Lake Street viaduct, the YokoOno tuned exhaust note bounced off the giant concrete pillars. "WHUMP! WHUMP! WHUMP!" bounced off Davecki like a boom car's sub woofers.

"I feel good! Da, da, da, da, da, da, Dah!" Davecki sang into his helmet. The bike spit out from under the bridge. Immediately, raindrops falling from the purple clouds pelted him. "Ouch! I feel bad! Da, da, da, da, da, da, Dah!" Davecki yelped into the helmet. He hit the brakes and slowed down to double nickels. *I'll bet that's what it feels like to be shot in the Kevlar by a nine-m-m. Mustang, here I come.*

* * * * *

As the rain began to fall in earnest, he drove the Mustang into the Big Apple parking lot. He walked in and looked around. No Clara. Two cute women stood behind the counter. *I wonder why no men work here?* The black haired woman smiled and waved. *But then again, who cares?* He set his helmet on a chair by the window closest to the Douglas County Courthouse and went to the tea boxes displayed atop the muffin case. He pulled a Lemon Zest tea bag from the dispenser. He turned toward the order counter. Bobo and Brenda waved from the kitchen. At the counter Davecki announced, "You know, the most beautiful women in Superior work here. I'll have a cheese twist and tea."

"Quit flirting with the help," Sally said.

"Not flirting. Just facts," Davecki answered.

You're so lame, Dave," Susan said. Her smile was broad and genuine.

"Thank you, Susan. I appreciate being appreciated. Especially by the S&S twins."

Both babes furrowed their beautiful brows momentarily, looked at each other, and said simultaneously, "Sally and Susan."

"I'll get your honey," Susan said.

"I'll take your money," Sally said.

He paid. He paid dearly when Susan returned with a soufflé cup of amber honey and said to Sally, "You think we should call the cops on this guy?"

"On what grounds?" he asked.

"Harassment," Sally said.

"Harassment my... You know, I could arrest myself. That would be different," Davecki said. He smiled, picked up his tray loaded with bagel, honey, tea bag and cup of hot water and retreated. Slouching into his corner with his vittles, Davecki looked out the window. He ripped his bagel in half. The day had turned dark, and it was raining full bore. He thought of *Steak Warning*. The big old houseboat was considerably less delightful in the cold, let alone a driving rain. *You should have never bought that boat, Alphonse. What were you thinking? Winter's coming. What a duffus. When are you going to live like a normal person?* A gusting wind blew a blanket of raindrops against the panes; rain sheeted across the parking lot. *When is summer going to come?* He looked at his watch. *And when is Clara going to get here?*

He sipped tea, slipped into the comfort of reflection induced by being on the right side of a rain-soaked and wind-battered window. *B.D. is going to want some answers. And all I have is, Willie's dead. His girlfriend has two names. His bike's smashed. Inordinate amounts of cash are floating and flying all up and down the North Shore.* He sighed and picked up a newspaper sitting on the next table.

He didn't see her enter. He was minding his own business, munching his own bagel, mired in a story about Minnesota's Governor Boa.

"Detective."

Davecki dropped the paper and raised his eyes. He studied the woman who stood at his table. The woman had bright orange hair, like the Fifth Element.

"You don't know me?"

"Clara?"

"None other."

"I thought it might be a good object lesson on the changeability of hair colors." She looked at him, her brown eyes wide and serious.

Okay. I'm supposed to say something. Get a clue, Alphonse. "It looks good."

Clara rolled her eyes.

Davecki sighed, said, "What? It does!"

Clara tilted her head, studied him for three seconds, "It doesn't look good. It looks ridiculous." Clara pulled out the black chair and sat.

"Can I get you something?" Davecki asked.

"I've heard you're always here. Why is that?"

Davecki glanced toward the back. "Because the most beautiful woman in Superior works here. I can introduce you to them if you want."

Clara looked toward the kitchen. "Which one is she?"

"Huh?"

"Which one is the most beautiful woman in Superior?"

Davecki glanced at the kitchen, he looked back at the new red-haired Clara. "They're all beautiful."

"Then you had a Freudian slip."

"What are you talking about?"

Clara steepled her fingers. "You said woman, singular. You thought you said women. That must mean you're in love with someone here."

Davecki stared. "What on earth are you talking about? I love women. Everyone knows that."

"You don't love women. You hate them," Clara said.

Davecki tore another hunk of cheese bagel free and tucked it into the corner of his cheek. Chewed. "Okaaaay. If you say so. We can get going anytime. Are you sure you can't just tell me where Crystal's Cathedral is?"

"You don't believe me?"

"Why should I?" Davecki sipped tea.

"I guess you shouldn't. I guess you wouldn't."

"I'm ready to go if you are." Davecki stood.

"You know," Clara said looking toward the bagels in the back, "I do think I'll have a bagel. Now that I think of it."

Davecki sat.

Clara looked at him for a second. She got up and went to the counter. She returned, sat.

They looked at each other, out the window, at the table.

Brenda the Bagel Babe brought a green looking bagel and cream cheese.

Clara spread cream cheese. Concentrating on her work she said, "So, here's what I think. You just think you love women." She rolled her eyes up, looked at Davecki without raising her head. "You can't really love women or a woman if you're constantly objectifying them."

Davecki popped a bagel chunk into his maw and chewed. "Mmmph," he said.

Clara chewed.

Davecki chewed.

Just then a twenty-something woman walked in. She wore a tight, flowered miniskirt, a form-fitting blue lycra top, and black platform shoes. Her long legs were encased in pearlescent panty hose. Ample cleavage was on display. *Thank you, God*, Davecki thought.

"You know. I'm usually a 'peace at any price' person, but, I can't help but feel like you should look over your left shoulder and give me that lingo again about me objectifying women."

Clara looked. The young woman strutted her stuff to the order counter.

Davecki said, "As you can plainly see, the object is objectifying herself. She comes sauntering in here looking like that, what am I supposed to do? Pretend it isn't there? Hell, the only thing missing from that package is the one-nine-hundred number on her back."

Clara looked back to Davecki. "She's a victim."

"What?"

"She's a victim of her culture. She's being told what is hot and what is not. If you didn't ogle her all the way to the counter, she wouldn't dress like that."

Davecki chugged his last bit of tea. "You sound certifiable. You know that? You didn't come off as a femi-nazi last night. If I didn't need you to find Crystal, I'd walk out right now."

Clara swallowed bagel. "You see?"

"What now?"

"I'm just an object to you. I'm a means to an end, a utilitarian object."

Davecki laughed. "You got that right. I'm not looking for intimacy here, lady. I just need to talk to Crystal Cathedral."

Clara laughed. "Why are you afraid?"

"You ever see the movie *Braveheart*?"

"Yes." Clara put the last of her bagel in her mouth.

"I'm afraid of ending up like Mel Gibson on the chopping block getting cut open, having his guts drawn out slowly and then being quartered after which his head was chopped off and stuck on a stake for all of London to see."

"Interesting."

"I'm sure it is. As fascinating as all get out."

"Such a Gestalt image. I understand now."

Davecki shook his head. "Can we please go now?"

Clara said, "Sure. It all makes sense. I apologize."

Davecki looked up. "For what?"

"For saying you hated women."

"I'm ever so grateful."

Clara stood up. They walked toward the doors. "I realize now you're just terribly afraid of women."

Davecki stopped. He looked at the door. He looked at Clara. He reached forward and opened the glass door.

"Thank you, Officer," Clara said. She smiled widely.

Davecki grunted. Outside, he asked, "You think you can find Crystal's cabin again?"

Standing in the entry, looking out at the rain, Clara didn't answer for a moment. "I don't know for sure. All I know is, we drove Highway 61 for about an hour. When we got to some big pine trees, we turned left and went another ten or fifteen minutes down a long, long driveway, climbed up a steep and twisty road along a hillside, and there it was: the biggest log cabin on the tallest hill for miles. The view of the lake was extraordinary."

"For someone who wasn't paying attention, you remember an

awful lot. Do you have the GPS coordinates, by any chance?"

She smiled, fiddled with her raincoat. "I kept waking up last night. All I could think about was Willie; how he died. I mean, you know, err, I know I should be happy for him—"

"Happy for him?"

"Well, of course," she said. "He's left this world and gone to be with Jesus. What better place to be? It's what we all want, even you."

"Now you know what I want?"

"In an overarching way, yes."

Davecki rubbed his chin. "So, Jim Jones was right."

"Of course not. Mass suicide is stupid and wrong. Christ commands us to follow Him, not someone who lords it over the flock. God alone decides when we are to leave this earth. He's got work for each of us down here, personal and otherwise, and we shouldn't leave until it's completed."

The rain fell steadily, straight down, individual rain drops made individual splashes on the blacktop. Davecki asked, "And how do we know what that work is?"

"Jesus said the work of God is to believe in Him whom He sent. So first and foremost, we are to believe."

"Okay. But beyond believing, how do we know we've got a job to do?"

"If you're still here, your work's not done."

"That's easy." Davecki sighed. "So you're happy for Willie?"

"Yes and no. He's at peace now. All the questions he ever had, now he knows the answers. I envy him that. But… whoever killed him committed a grievous sin. I can't help but want to find out what happened so we can bring the evil-doers to justice."

"What makes you think he was killed?"

"If you were more of a spirit detective you wouldn't ask me that."

"Well, I'm not a spirit detective. I'm just a plain old detective. So, I ask again, what makes you think he was murdered?"

"Intuition. And, your investigation."

Davecki smirked. "That's an easy out, but I'll grant this, from what I saw up on Palisade Head this morning, it does look like he was killed."

"You've been up the North Shore once already today?"

"Hey, when you're a cop, you do all kinds of running around

looking like a chicken with its head cut off. It's a part of the job."

"You've actually seen a chicken with its head cut off?"

"Yes. And you? Do you ever take anything at face value? Do you always ask obvious questions?"

"The sure way to ruin an obvious question is to not ask it."

They stood watching the rain.

"I like that sound," Davecki said.

"The sound of traffic going by?"

"That too. But, even more, I like the sound of the soft patter of splashes on the blacktop. Just listen for a second."

There were no cars passing.

They listened.

"Oh, now that you point it out, I can hear it. Very cool," Clara said.

Then a large, maroon pulp truck rumbled past on Belknap Street. Sheets of water splashed up from the many wheels. The name painted on the door was Timber Tim's Trucking.

"Let's stand here a little longer. Maybe it'll let up. I gotta call HQ anyway."

"HQ?"

He grinned, pulling out his cell phone from the inside pocket of his bomber jacket. "Yeah, I know, it sounds like the worst cop show, but we actually do talk like that." He poked a speed dial number. "Connie? Dave," he said in a raspy voice. "I've got a bad cold coming on." He coughed loudly and winked at Clara. "If I stay home and rest, I think I can stave it off." He frowned. "Well, yes, I do happen to be at the bagel shop. But hey, a man's gotta eat, especially one so sick as I." He coughed again. "Oh come on, Con, you can handle B.D. for me. I know you can."

Clara stared.

"Gotta go, Con... love ya. Bye!" He stabbed "end," and stuck the phone back in its pocket.

Clara crossed her arms and looked at him. "You don't seem sick to me."

"Oh, that?" He grinned. "That's just a little game I play with B.D."

"Who's B.D.?"

"My boss. He's a control freak."

"Takes one to know one."

"Man, why are you so grouchy?"

"I'm not grouchy. I'm just wondering how you can call lying to your boss a 'little game?'"

He looked at her. "Huh?"

"You lied on the phone," she said.

"That wasn't a lie. It was just for fun."

"For what?"

"You know, FUN," he said. "Also known as enjoyment. Humor. It's something people do quite often."

"Oh, really? I've also heard it called lying. Not telling the truth. Also known as breaking the Eighth Commandment."

They watched the rain.

"It's letting up," he said, even though it wasn't. "I'll get the door for you." He dashed to the Mustang and yanked open the passenger door. Clara followed him and flung herself in. Davecki slammed her door, ran around the rear of his favorite horsey, and jumped in, dripping. *This should be an interesting ride.*

"Why did you park so far from the door?" she complained, swiping a hand through her hair.

"I wanted to give other people a shorter walk to the door in the rain."

"Oh, I see. An enabler."

Davecki stared out the windshield. *Just shut your yap, Alphonse.* "Oh, and I thought I was being considerate. Are you always so judgmental?"

"First Corinthians says the spiritual man judges all things," she sniffed.

"Matthew Seven says 'judge not, lest ye be judged.'"

Clara scowled. "It says both. I didn't know you were a Bible scholar."

"I'm not. I just remember the important stuff. He rolled his eyes. He started the engine, drove around the building to Cumming, and pulled onto Belknap.

"I think you like lying," Clara said.

She's determined to pick a fight. "Yeah, it's my favorite hobby," he answered.

"It's unbecoming and deceitful."

"*All* cops are deceitful. It's our job."

"Only because you like deceit better than honesty."

"Only because I like my job, I like doing my job, and, because people, especially criminal types, make entire careers out of lying, I occasionally meet them on their own level, tell the rare lie to get them to tell the truth."

"You've rehearsed that answer a lot."

"Only because people like you seem to need reassurance that cops are the good guys."

"Well, just you wait. This terrorist thing is going to expose some very bad apples in the enforcement bushel."

"Enforcement bushel?"

Clara sighed. "Hey, this is all right."

"What's all right?"

"This car. For such an old thing, it's pretty nice. I thought it would be more junky."

"So why do *you* lie?" he asked.

"I don't."

"Never?"

"Accusing me of lying is transferring."

"Transferring?" Davecki accelerated the Mustang toward the Highbridge. A brown UPS truck approached from the east.

Clara pointed. "Look out for that truck!"

"I see it," Davecki said. "Bill would never hit me." He stepped on the gas. The Mustang zoomed up the approach to the bridge. "So... define 'transferring.'"

"You know all the UPS drivers by name?"

"Most of them."

"Transferring is the psychological principle whereby an individual—such as yourself—projects his dysfunction onto the person he's with and in so doing escapes from the responsibility he doesn't want to face."

"Sorry I asked. You've really changed from last night."

"Oh?" Clara said.

Silence.

"Aren't you going to answer me?" Clara demanded.

"I didn't hear a question."

Davecki looked across the bay, across Park Point, at Lake Superior. *The Lady is gray today,* he thought. The windshield wipers thumped.

"I said 'oh' and raised my inflection at the end," she explained. "Which makes it a question."

Davecki said, "I'd be delighted to answer the damn question if you'd be so kind as to tell me what it is."

"There's no need for obscenities." She jerked her head in his direction, held the look for a few seconds. "You're so angry. Is that why you're trying to pick a fight?"

He took his eyes off the road to gape at her. "I'm trying to pick a fight?"

"Oh, trust me. You're one of the angriest men I've ever met."

Davecki giggled. "I'd say it takes one to know one but I'd be accused of transferring."

Clara looked back out the windshield. She sighed. "Touché."

They glanced at one another. Clara looked out the window to the east. Davecki looked at the road. The windshield wipers moved and wiped away all the tears.

They zipped across Rice's Point Flats. "You know, Detective, I was serious about the spirit detective thing. You'd be a lot better off if you trusted your intuition more than your intellect."

"Lord help me," he said.

"He will," Clara said. She smiled.

"Spirit detective?"

"See? You just did it. You raised your inflection at the end. You didn't say, 'What is a spirit detective?' and you expected me to know it was a question. You see? Everyone does it."

"Okay. You got me." Davecki sighed.

Clara clapped her hands and bounced in the seat. She said, "A spirit detective is like Charles Finney."

"Who is that? No inflection intended."

"None taken," Clara said.

"It's a long story."

"How about the short version?"

Clara smiled and waved her hand. "He was a great man of God who figured out all kinds of mysteries from the Word of God and turned into a great evangelist."

"And I should follow in his footsteps?"

"Why of course. You could be a great detective if you acted like Charles Finney."

Davecki snorted. "I thought I already was a great detective. What, should I dig out a Ouija board?"

"No. You should believe in God and trust in your hunches and premonitions and dreams."

Silence elongated. The sounds of the car traveling north on Interstate 35 amplified. Davecki drove. Finally he said, "Look, I'm not exactly sure what you meant about that Charles Finney stuff, but intuition is a big part of being a detective. One or two real clues is all anyone ever gets. The rest is just patience, persistence, plodding, and faith."

"Sounds spiritual to me."

Davecki looked at her. She appeared to be serious.

"It is, and it isn't," he said. "You do have to follow your hunches without always having a rational explanation. And there's a certain amount of letting go. Trying to force outcomes and control events like investigations, confessions, evidence sorting—that gets real frustrating, fast."

"Can you give me an example?"

"Yeah. I can. If you know somebody killed someone and you can't prove it, you've got to let it go. It's either that or frame him, and that's a whole different conversation."

The car rumbled through the tunnels. Davecki drew a deep breath and went on. "It's my experience that murders… they want to be solved. But rationality gets in the way most of the time." The car exited the last tunnel. On the left, the Big Lake. It was unsettled. Fidgety waves danced about under a low hanging, gray mist.

Clara looked out the rain-streaked side window. "The paper said it was an accident, not a murder."

"It was in the paper already?"

"This morning. Don't you read the paper?"

"I was going to read it at the bagel shop, but I was interrupted by a harassing individual."

"Well, excuse me for showing up on time!"

You weren't on time. Wisdom prevailed. They rode in silence.

Still looking out her window, Clara said, "I always get a little feisty when I'm nervous."

Feisty? How about obnoxious? As he turned to suggest a different word choice, she turned to face him. Her eyes were wide and serious. Her beautiful mouth turned down just a little at the corners. A tendril of her hair, still wet from the rain, clung to her cheek.

"I didn't mean to make you angry. I'm sorry."

He cleared his throat. "That's okay. I probably was transgressing, anyway."

"Trans*ferring*. And no, you weren't, really."

On the outside, Davecki smiled. On the inside: *Carefuulllll!*

24

Time has a way of demonstrating the most stubborn are the most intelligent.

—Yevgeny Yevtushenko

O ulu, Wisconsin: one of the country's least known yet enduring enclaves of independent thinkers and political radicals. Deep in the heart of Oulu's piney woods, forty insurgents were gathered, out of doors as always, and united against the exploitation of their most valued natural jewel, Lake Superior.

Oulu was the logical spot for a band of freedom fighters to organize. It was way better than Afghanistan, if nothing more than for the entire lack of thousand-pound bombs. Plus there was the unequalled in the known world Moiaka.

Be that as it may, until very recently, the rural township had been the most densely populated Finnish-American community in North America. For decades, Oulu had been home to true nonconformists who, first and foremost, followed the dictates of their conscience. The U.S. Government kept an eye on this unlikely cauldron of dissent, sometimes agreeing with the political fires burning in the woods, sometimes choosing to overlook their activities, and sometimes, feeling threatened, hunting them down as traitors.

But, the hunting down part hadn't happened in decades. Though in recent years there had been sufficient electronic eavesdropping by the AWACS overhead. For the most part, the hearty band of pioneer thinkers had been left alone.

Way back when, all the old-timers had been through tough times and were themselves tougher than venison jerky. Many had once been blacklisted by Wisconsin demagogue, Joe McCarthy. All worshipped the acceptable Wisconsin demigod, Vince Lombardi.

Most had, as children, fallen on hard times when family members lost their jobs because of political views. More than half had experienced the tragedy of loved ones emigrating to Karelia for political freedom and finding, instead, worse oppression or death. All the old-timers were intimately familiar with the strict requirements for a secret society.

But there was new blood in the group; their half-Finn children and nieces and nephews who brought their friends, youngsters who had never been threatened, or lost their jobs, or been beaten, or had loved ones killed by anti-union thugs. Many of the newcomers saw the old Finns as hopelessly outdated; too slow to act. The old Finns saw the newcomers as upstarts lacking judgment and experience. As a result, there were holes in the group's ideologic fabric, big holes. Large enough to drive a Kenworth logging truck through.

Tonight the cauldron of dissent was bubbling over, and though there might be minor discordancies among them, they were determined to uncover the corruption of their own government and end a great social and ecological injustice.

"This meeting of Finns Against Lake Superior Import Export Schemes will now come to order!" Professor Don Cameroon pounded the butt of his Ruger Blackhawk .44 magnum revolver on the sheet of plywood that served as a table, trying to make himself heard. The pounding was loud. The manifold conversations of the people gathered around the rustic table were louder.

Cameroon pounded the podium again. "ORDER!" At the sound of his barked command, a red squirrel chattered a loud reply from a nearby pine tree.

The group gradually quieted. "Our first order of business is to officially recognize the passing of our dear departed brother, Little Willie Horton."

A large man, six foot six and weighing at least two hundred and eighty pounds, raised his hand.

Cameroon pointed the butt of his Blackhawk at the giant. "Chair recognizes Mr. Box Elder."

Box stood. "I make a motion to recognize Little Willie for the contributions he made to our group," he said in a low voice. He sat. Someone sniffed loudly. A woman in green battle fatigues wiped her eyes.

Cameroon said, "Thank you, Box. Motion has been made. Is there a second?"

A bearded man in the back of the room seconded. Cameroon acknowledged it. "Discussion?"

A woman near the back stood, her eyes red-rimmed. "I knew it was too dangerous!" she shouted. "Why did you make him do it?"

"Nancy, you know Willie volunteered for the job," Cameroon said. "Nobody held a gun to his head."

"A couple of us would have liked to!" a voice chanted.

The group laughed.

"Enough!" Cameroon reprimanded. "We're discussing the dead here. As I was saying. Going undercover as he did was risky."

For the briefest of moments, the face of one man registered surprise, his eyes widening and his mouth going slack. Then, just as quickly, his face hardened, became inscrutable as ever.

"I want whoever did this to him punished!" cried Nancy.

"I must remind you that there is no evidence this was anything other than an accident."

Snorts of disbelief could be heard.

Cameroon raised his hands. "Let it pass, for now. If this turns out not to be as it seems…" his face became grim, "we will take care of it." He drew in a breath. "I call for the vote."

It was, of course, unanimous.

"Our next order of business is to welcome a new member."

Everyone turned to stare at the newcomer, a tall man with angular features. Cameroon said, "The Secret Order of FALSIES does officially welcome Mr. Kevin Hallstrom." Cameroon began reading from a paper. "He is the nephew of the late Gus Hall, former beloved president of the Communist Party of America. His mother, Rose Black Bear, was a healer in the Navajo nation. Mr. Black Bear is an elder of NDNZ, the militant arm of the United Southwestern Tribes. He comes to us tonight with a recommendation from Knute the Fishman." Cameroon tossed the paper down. "Would you please stand, Mr. Black Bear."

Nevada Henderson removed his ivory Stetson and stood. Smiling, he turned to and fro, nodding his greeting at one and all. There were murmurs all around.

"Is there any discussion?"

"If he's good enough for Knute, I guess he's good enough for me," called an old man, his hands resting on the butt of a 30.06.

"Thank you, Cronke. I'll take that as a motion. Second?"

Box Elder raised his hand. "I second."

"Thank you, Box." Cameroon scanned the group. Black Bear remained standing, erect and still, his hands folded before him solemnly. "Any other discussion? There being none, Chair calls for the question. All in favor say aye."

"Aye."

Cameroon glanced all around. A row of old Finns, seated all in a line near the front, had not voted. "Seven abstentions?" Cameroon asked.

Seven nods.

"Motion passes; Mr. Black Bear is accepted into membership."

Henderson/Black Bear inclined his head humbly. "I'm happy and proud to be here. Thank you." He sat down to a spatter of applause. The old Finns moved not a muscle. They stared at a point just over Black Bear's shoulder.

"A man of few words," Cameroon said. "Good. You'll fit in well around here. We could use more people who talk less."

A muscular looking woman in a t-shirt and fatigue pants raised her hand. Cameroon sighed. "Kristina?"

She stood. Her fatigue pants were bloused at the top of her combat boots. An olive t-shirt stretched over her rippling torso. Aside from her hair, which was half blonde and half bright purple, she looked like Linda Hamilton in *Terminator II*. "I think we should start legislation to ban cars. Cars and trucks. Way more people are killed every day by cars than by gunfire." She jabbed her finger in a southeasterly direction. "When those nine kids selling magazine subscriptions were killed in that van down by Madison, CNN never even raised an eyebrow. That was just as tragic as Littleton." The amazon sat, patting the Glock 40 napping in the leather half-holster on her right hip. Her smile was triumphant.

"All righty then," Cameroon said slowly. "Thank you, Kristina. Second?"

"I second that," said a bulky man in the outer rim of the circle.

"Motion seconded by Evad Larson. Discussion?"

A neatly dressed, brown-haired man raised his hand. In the sea of flannel and camouflage, his khakis and button-down Oxford stood out. "I'm just wondering, Kristina, how did you get here tonight?"

"In my truck," she answered. "Why?"

"Never mind."

"Point taken, Brooksie," said Cameroon, suppressing a smile. "Any further discussion?"

"Call for the question," called a willowy woman with white-blonde hair and high cheekbones.

"Question has been called for. All in favor say 'aye.'"

A chorus of "ayes" resounded.

"Opposed, same," Cameroon intoned, already checking his agenda for the next item of business.

A man in a yellow chamois shirt stood. He was steroid bulky. His head was shaved. "I'm opposed," he said in a squeaky voice. "We're wasting valuable time on this ban-the-cars-and-trucks bullshit. We can't do anything about traffic."

Kristina also rose. "Point of order," she hissed, glaring at the chamois shirt wearer. Her back stiffened; her chest heaved.

Cameroon opened his mouth to attempt regaining control. Before he could speak, Chamois Man shouted, "Just 'cause you got big tits don't mean you're the boss of the group, Kristina."

Kristina's hand flicked to her Glock. Alarmed, Cameroon whanged on the plywood bench of justice with the butt of his .44. "You're out of order, Frank!"

"No, YOU'RE out of order, Cameroon," Chamois Man shouted.

"You're BOTH out of order," Kristina yelled.

A sixtyish man with black hair threw up his hands in exasperation. "Frank, why don't you just bone her and do us all a favor?"

"WHAT?" Kristina screamed.

"Oh, for God's sake!" Cameroon shouted. "That was uncalled for, Joe."

Joe stood and said, "Anybody here NOT know about the love spat these two have been carrying on for the last six months?"

Silence.

"Anybody give a shit about it?"

Nobody gave a shit.

"I rest my case." He sat.

Frank shrugged. He walked over to Kristina. He threw his large arm across her shoulders. The long plank bench sagged as they sat down together.

A strange moment of suspended animation hung in the air.

Cameroon took advantage of the confusion. "All righty then," he said. "I suggest we move on to the business at hand. For that, I call upon our esteemed research biologist, Fran Hansen."

Fran stood and moved to the plywood podium. Cameroon sidled to the right. The two of them were framed by the American and State of Wisconsin flags hanging from their poles which were stabbed firmly into the soil.

"You are all familiar with the suction dredging that's been going on around the harbor?"

Many people nodded. "I hear it's to keep the channel at twenty-six feet, so ore boats can have enough draft now that the water level is so low," Bill Peltonen said.

"And didn't the paper say they were filling the deep hole off Park Point?" asked Kristina. "The one that was dredged out years and years ago?"

Cameroon said, "We have it on good authority that both these projects are a front. That what is really happening, is an attempt to increase the number of gallons flowing to Arizona per day, far above what the lake can support. That they have, in fact, already begun this."

"Why would they do that?" asked Bill's wife, Nancy.

"Money," Fran answered. "Obviously someone at the IJC is cashing in."

"Obviously?" Joe asked. "Just how obvious is it and why, Miss Frantastic?"

"Alright, Joe. Settle down. You can pick on Kristina but not Fran," Cameroon jumped in.

"I can defend myself, Don," Fran said. "You just like to pick fights, Joe. You don't really care. It's as plain as your big purple nose that there are highly placed government officials at all levels involved."

Nancy shook her head. "I don't see how they could get away with that in this day and age."

Joe said, "That's because they aren't getting away with anything, Nancy. You can't see it, because it isn't there and all Fran's faith in conspiracies can't make it be there."

"Oh for Christ's sake, Joe. We're the original conspiracy theorists. Isn't that why you're here?" Cameroon asked. "They are getting away with it. They did it twenty years ago and they are continuing to do it, especially with the demand rising exponentially. Listen to this." Cameroon pulled a piece of newsprint from a folder. "I have here a news clipping from the Nebraska *Daily Observer*." He unfolded the creased, yellowed paper.

He raised his voice and read. "The Missouri aquifer is thirty feet below normal levels, scientists said today in a press conference at Lincoln College. Predictions are that wells will be running dry in two years." He looked up. "The date on this article is 1972. Has anyone here heard of any major drought or well failures in Nebraska since that time? Nebraska didn't have unusually high precipitation between 1972 and 1974, yet somehow the Missouri aquifer topped itself off. How? Where did they get the water?"

Silence. "I have another." He shuffled the papers in his hand. "This is a news story from the *Toronto Globe and Mail* dated July 3, 1999, and I quote, 'Commercial bottlers have been given the right to drain, free of charge, more than 18 billion litres a year from Ontario's supply of high quality water, fueling fears that nature will be unable to replace the loss. Figures obtained by the Globe and Mail show that bottlers are now permitted to process five litres a day for every person in the Province. That's thirty times the amount allocated to a company planning to export Lake Superior water to Asia before a public outcry prompted the Province to rescind its permission.' The article goes on to say that billions more liters worth of permits are being issued. So now what do you think?"

"Nuke Canada!" Frank shouted.

Fran spoke up. "Canada is not responsible for the current situation, Frank. This problem is homegrown. As you can imagine, this pipeline moving our water to Arizona will never be 'discovered.' Either there's a ton of graft and payoff money flowing along with the water, or there's been enough clandestine legislation pushed through by now to make it legal though not public knowledge. Or both."

A raw-boned old man with bushy white hair and eyebrows, wearing a black cassock stood. He said, "It's just like Roswell. They're here, and the government knows it and is helping 'em. All they're waiting for is how to go public with the information without causing a riot."

Fran smiled. "Interesting theory, Jaako. I didn't know priests believed in aliens." A few chuckles came from the group.

Jaako crossed his thin arms over his pectoral cross. "You watch. Won't be long and those skinny gray fellers with the big eyes and no ears are running the country."

"THEY ALREADY ARE!" a voice cat-called from the back.

Everyone laughed and Fran continued. "What we figure is, all the connecting and construction was done when they put in the sewer lines on Wisconsin Point and when they installed the new water supply lines under Minnesota Point. We knew there must be a tertiary line somewhere feeding the pipeline, so we introduced dye in an attempt to find the right inlet."

Frank struck his knees with his fists. "This is all taking too much *time*! Their pipeline is up and running, and while we're here dickin' around with dye and sewer lines, the lake is losing twenty million gallons every twenty-four hours." He glared around the circle. "I say we send a fertilizer truck to Kansas and blow their damned pipe all to hell!"

Cameroon spoke. "Thank you for your input, Frank. But if you recall, we've discussed it before and agreed to refrain from blowing things all to hell. Unless, FRANK, you want to end up on the list of domestic terrorists and incarcerated like a Muslim money launderer."

Jaako jumped to his feet. "But the lake is being drained dry! And the government's blaming it all on global warming!"

"Sit down please, Jaako," said Cameroon firmly.

Jaako stared at him defiantly.

Cameroon sighed. "Jaako, if you don't restrain yourself, I'll have to ask Mr. Rossem to remove you. Again."

Every eye was on the old priest who stared jut-jawed at Cameroon. Jaako then turned his gaze to Rossem, the barrel-chested sergeant-at-arms, a steroid-packed man even bulkier than Kristina's Frank.

Rossem smiled, said, "It would be fun to have a little Jaako-removal action. I haven't had much practice bludgeoning the clergy since Bosnia."

Jaako glared at Cameroon. "I'll sit down. But just so's I can have my say." He jabbed a bony finger at Rossem. "Otherwise, if I didn't have more to say, I could kick his ass if I felt like it."

"Father Jaako!" Kristina said. "Watch your language!"

"Since when are you so religious, Kristina?" mocked Joe.

"Since God told me to boot your skinny butt all the way across the back forty and into tomorrow," Kristina said.

"You're welcome to try," Joe said.

"All right, all RIGHT!" said Cameroon. "Jaako, we all appreciate your self-control. Joe, Kristina, behave yourselves. Now, can we proceed? Fran?"

Fran said, "Frank, you know we can't blow up their pipeline, and you know why. It looks like an oil pipeline and it quacks like an oil pipeline, therefore, to everyone but us, it is an oil pipeline. If we blow the thing, we're terrorists. They'll hunt us down, and when they catch us—and they *will* catch us, make no mistake—we'll be sent away for life."

"Or we'll get death, depending on what state we're in," added Box Elder. "I seen a show on A&E about the electric chair. I don't want to get the chair, no thank you."

"They don't do the chair anymore," Joe told him. "They do lethal injection. I hear it's not that bad."

"Really?" Box looked interested.

Bill Peltonen cut in. "But while we're figuring out what to do, the IJC keeps asking for more time to study diversion. Seems to me all's they're really doing is stalling for time, while they're trying to figure out ways to make it palatable to the public."

"The IJC has held a dozen meetings in the last year or so," said Fran. "So far their opinion is that no *large-scale* water movements should be allowed, as they would constitute a threat to the ecosystem."

"I'd say twenty million gallons a day is pretty large-scale!" Peltonen said.

"Not really," Fran argued. "According to the Milwaukee *Journal/Sentinel*, 960 billion gallons a day are withdrawn from the Great Lakes. All but 2.5 billion gallons are returned. When you consider the mass and amount of water there actually is in Lake Superior alone, to say nothing of the other four Great Lakes, 20 million gallons is not terribly significant."

"Didn't the IJC suggest that diversion would be appropriate in the event of a catastrophic drought or something like that?" asked a Nordic-looking woman with white-blonde hair.

"I haven't heard that, Helmi, but then I'm not all that up on all the information out there."

Helmi shrugged. "I don't see the problem. Twenty million gallons. Duluth alone uses two million a day. So what's the big deal? It's a drop in the bucket. Plus it's good for the economy, national *and* local. That graft money has probably already paid for the free sidewalk improvement program in Superior and the longer runways at the airport, plus helped finance the new prison and gave both the County *and* the City new administrative buildings."

"How do you know all this, Helmi?" asked Fran.

"I don't. But the money's got to be coming from someone and going to someone."

Cameroon interjected, "This issue isn't germane. I'm going to ask the floor to please defer their comments until the question and answer session after Fran has given her full report."

There was grumbling, but the general assembly quieted.

"Thanks, Don. The lake is down eight or nine inches. And *not* from global warming, no matter how hard local 'scientists' try to tell you it is. This scheme is nothing more than a global-sized, money-making rip-off of one of our most precious local natural resources."

"Yeah!" Frank shouted.

Kristina added, "Plus it's Mr. Big-Wig's way of getting back at the shipping families. He's still pissed about that Reform Party presidential bid."

"What in hell are you talking about Kristina?" Cameroon asked.

"Aw, she's love starved. Out of her head with passion," Joe called.

Cameroon pounded his .44.

Box Elder raised his hand. "I'm just curious, Fran. You told Frank that 20 million gallons isn't significant. If that's so, why should we care? Do you agree with Helmi, that it's good for Superior financially?"

"No," Fran answered. "It most definitely is not good for Superior. And we should care, because it's been done under the table, when it should have been publicly discussed and debated and put to a vote in a referendum. We should care because twenty million gallons is only the start. What's to stop them from taking fifty million gallons a day? Or a hundred? Or five hundred? As I said, we—Don and I and my colleague Simon Jensen—have done some investigating and research, and have drawn some conclusions. However, before I present them, I think it would be good to open this up for some debate."

Jaako stood immediately. "It's obvious you people are thinking too small," he announced. "This type of project, this scheme—there's gotta be more to this. What with the bureaucratic hoops, the paperwork, the construction—it's just too big to be engineered by one man like Kristina suggests."

There was a collective sigh.

Jaako rubbed his hands together, he smiled, "Aliens," he said. "It's aliens who need the water. They fly over the lake at night while we're all sleeping or they subject us to mass hypnosis like in the movie Dark City. And, while we're all hypnotized or whatever, they suck the water up with big vacuum hoses. Hell, it's no mystery that hydrogen powers space ships."

"So, we could be like, the new OPEC. We could all be rich! All we have to do is cut a deal with the aliens and we'd all be richer than Saudi princes," Evad called out.

"This is serious business Evad," Jaako said. "Quit your joking around."

25

Having lived for several years beside "the shining big sea water," I've decided that Lake Superior is God.

—Barton Sutter,
in his book *Cold Comfort*

 To date, time is God's most closely guarded secret. String theorists know more about time than anyone but babies. Some day they'll figure out what babies already know. After all, newborns just arrived from before-time. Because Alphonse Dave Davecki was basically a big baby, he consistently displayed unique ways of looking at the world. A lot of people called him quirky. Some said he was weird. Others, bizarre. Suffice it to say, he could always be counted on to strange a situation out.

Davecki looked at Lake Superior passing on the right. He jigged his head at the lake. "See that?"

"The lake?" Clara asked.

"Yes. It's that big blue thing over there on the right."

"Of course I see it."

"What's it look like?"

"Water."

"Besides that," Davecki said.

"I have no idea what you're talking about. Where are you going with this?" Clara asked.

"It looks like a huge, sleeping amoeba."

Clara stared at the huge sleeping amoeba, said nothing.

"No, seriously," he said. "If you look out across it, without focusing, just look way far away and just above the surface, try to see through all of the space above it all at the same time, it seems like there's some sort of life bulging up from the surface that rises up like a bubble. Whenever I get it right and see all of it at once, it's very clear to me that the lake is trying to change everything."

"Did you do LSD when you were in college?" Clara asked.

"Of course. Didn't everyone?" He sighed. He drummed the steering wheel.

"What, are you nervous?"

"No, just frustrated."

"Why?" She eyed him. "And what kind of frustrated?"

"Because I can't communicate."

"Oh, boo hoo," Clara said.

He winced. *Just stop talking, Alphonse.* His eyes shifted once more from the highway to the lake. "It's like a woman giving birth."

Clara sighed. "I thought it was an amoeba. Quit mixing your metaphors."

"Well, it's both."

"You are so strange."

Davecki sighed. *I told you so,* said the snide voice in his head. *Yeah? Shut up,* he answered. He looked quickly at Clara. *Did I say that out loud?* She was combing her hair back with her fingers. *Whew.*

He looked past her. There, stabbing through the openings in the balsam and poplar trees were flickering glitters of white light.

She said, "Tell me what you meant."

"I have no idea. I look at the lake all the time when I drive, and, you know, living on a boat and all, and one time I just flashed on an image of an amoeba. Like in science class, when you look through a microscope the first time and low and behold there it is, a tiny invisible life floating before your eyes."

She said, "So, you're saying that big huge thing out there," she pointed at the lake, "is really a tiny one-celled organism?"

Davecki drove his Mustang straight forward, "At one level of perception, that's exactly what it is."

"And what level of perception are you talking about?"

"Actually there's two levels, now that I think of it. There's the cosmic slash amoeba level and then there's the geopolitical level."

"Geopolitical? You're starting to sound like a professor I once had in college."

"Really? I'm not that smart."

"How do you mean geopolitical."

"I mean that, at a national and international level, excluding Canada of course, the largest fresh water lake in the world is insignificant."

"So what else is new? The lake is just water. It sits there. It makes bad weather. It's a source of water. It's just a lake."

"All that amoeba thing is... sometimes, I just get this huge feeling that it's way more than an inanimate object."

"And the birth image?"

"Well, other times, it seems to bulge. Like something's under the water, something ancient but at the same time new and completely different from anything we've seen or known, and this incredibly new thing is about to burst up. Burst out."

Clara made a noise as if to speak, but when Davecki looked over, she shook her head no and said, "Go on."

"This is hard to put into words. I usually don't try. I'm not sure why I'm even trying now."

"Because I'm such a soothing presence," Clara said.

"Yeah, as soothing as sandpaper. All I'm trying to say is, sometimes when I look at the lake, I feel as if it's some sort of eternal, alive thing. Something truly alive, that already *is* but at the same time is waiting to be born. Like there's something in the water that's outside of time wanting to come in."

"Like the Incarnation."

"What?"

"You've heard of the Incarnation, haven't you?"

"Remind me," Davecki said.

"Well, God is, was, and will be. You know..."

"Eternal," he said.

"You're such a good student. Now, follow me on this. At the same time that God is out there being eternal, He was born in Jesus Christ. Something outside of time that came in."

The car drove them along in silence for a bit, then Davecki said, "You are so weird, bizarre and strange." And he laughed.

"No more than you. It's just that, when you were talking about perceiving the lake differently, well it made me flash on a vision of Jesus alive and walking around on the ground here. If you make your 'eternal thing' Jesus instead of a lake... well." She stopped herself and looked out the window quickly.

Nice and light now, Davecki, a virtually obscure part of his brain advised, "Your lips are cute."

She laughed.

The rain ended as the forest marched southward. The road curved around the shoreline and climbed up the rocky inclines before plunging into the steep ravines, cut deep by centuries of rushing water on its course from the northern hills to the great lake. The clouds appeared to descend, almost meeting the water. The tires hummed an agreeable tune on the still-wet pavement.

Davecki yawned.

Clara yawned.

As they rounded a turn, a silver Thunderbird car careened at them from the opposite direction.

Davecki reefed the steering wheel hard to the right. The silver car missed them by inches. He exhaled and gently moved the Mustang back onto the highway.

"I'm not sleepy now," Clara said.

"Women drivers," he said.

"God help me," she said.

"He will," he said.

She huffed, and, after a moment, asked, "Is there no chance that Willie's death could be a tragic accident?"

Davecki stared straight ahead. The song of the tires reclaimed center stage. He remained motionless except for the occasional flick of the wrist that kept the car in control. "I've asked myself that about a hundred times. But what it comes down to is human nature."

"Pardon?"

"Everything I know about Willie tells me—no, screams at me—that he wouldn't have done it himself. He wasn't suicidal. Homicidal on occasion, but he wasn't the self-loathing type." Davecki's voice heated up. "And you know what else? Little Willie loved that bike. If he had wanted to off himself, he wouldn't have mangled up his Hog to do it. That would have been like a murder to him. Weird as that might sound, anyone who owns a bike would understand. And then there's the cash. I think Willie got in the way of something big, and that kind of money makes people expendable."

Suddenly she pointed. "Hey, I think this is the turn. I remember those big pine trees."

"Those are white pines," he said.

"You can't tell what kind of pine they are from this distance!"

"Sure I can. Can't everyone?"

"We'll see," she muttered.

Davecki slowed the Mustang and turned in the direction Clara had pointed. He could see her squinting at the pines as they drove past. He slowed down to give her a good look. "As you can see from the unmistakable bundles of five armed bluish-green needles, these are indeed white pines."

"All right, all right," Clara grouched.

Davecki came to a full stop and rolled down his window. He stuck his head out and looked up. "Left undisturbed in rich soil, the majestic white pine can reach a height of 150 feet. The cones of this noble tree take two years to mature. The seed-bearing—"

Clara socked him in the shoulder. "I said all *right*, Mr. Nature."

"Ow!" He held his shoulder. "Boy, you Christians hit hard."

"The Lord disciplines those He loves."

"The Lord is in favor of assault and battery? Haven't you heard that domestic violence is against the law?"

"This isn't domestic," she said and whacked him again. "It's to get you to shut up. I can't stand it. You sound just like one of those awful junior high filmstrips. I thought any minute you were going to start in on the Journey of the Spawning Salmon, or something."

"My personal favorite was 'The Wily Sea Cucumber: Animal or Vegetable?'"

She wiped at her eyes. "Please tell me you're making that up."

He shook his head no. Chuckling he added, "Sad but true. Actually, the best one was the praying mantis. That sucker just chopped up and devoured..."

"STOP! It was disgusting back then, and it's disgusting now."

By way of an answer, Davecki shifted into gear and punched the accelerator. He jerked the wheel and the Mustang fishtailed on the gravel road. Clara reached for the dash, shrieking. The car rolled onto a section of stiff washboard and started skittering around like a scared beetle on top of a hot tackle box. "EEEEE HAWWWW!" Davecki hollered. He counter-steered the pony just enough to control the whipsaw fishtailing, but not enough to cancel it. He looked over at Clara.

"AIEEEE," she shrieked in delight, her arms braced against the dashboard.

He eased up on the gas. The car settled down.

"I liked that."

"It is kinda fun, isn't it?"

"Have you ever played Best Worst?"

Davecki took his eyes from the road. "Can't say that I have."

"It's fun too. You say the best and I say the worst. Then you say the worst and I say the best."

He looked back at his driving. "Okay. That does sound fun. Best burger: Anchor."

"Worst: White Castle. Now you have to say worst something. But it has to be about a castle."

Davecki didn't say anything for a few seconds. "That's a hard one."

"Worst soap, Castille," Clara said.

"Oh that's no fair. I was thinking about castles and fortresses and things."

"Worst attribute: Complaining," Clara said.

"Best thing about complaining: Complaining."

"Worst smelling bathroom..."

Davecki snorted. "What's that got to do with anything?"

"I've got to tinkle."

"Best bathroom: In the piney woods," Davecki said as he put on the brakes.

"Worst moment on a first date: Laughing so hard you pee your pants."

"Worst moment is saying: This isn't a date."

"Best moment: Tricking a clever cop," Clara said as she opened the door.

"Best moment: Ditching a bossy babe in the boonies."

Clara put her foot out and started exiting. "Worst moment: Being ditched. Best moment: Still being a babe at this age."

Silence. "Just go pee will ya? We've got a crystal cathedral to find."

26

*Important things are rarely urgent. Eagle feathers don't fall from the sky,
they grow very slowly from the butt of a large winged scavenger.*

—John Eagle-Feather Bishop

The road through the pine grove was dim but not dreary. The sky's light was occluded by the tall crowns of the looming pines. Just beyond the ditch, gathered around the huge trunks like acolytes, spindly red-armed dogwood bushes and the dark mahogany of alder reached upward in continual praise of their majesties, the white pines. "So what do you remember about the place?" Davecki asked.

"Big. Expensive. Secluded."

"How secluded?"

"Crystal played the music so loud it hurt. When I suggested the neighbors might complain, she said there were no neighbors, and the moose didn't care."

"That's not how I picture a prayer vigil."

Clara pulled a face. "Me neither. I'm still not sure what the deal was; whether I misunderstood, or if Dolly just lied to get me there. In any case, it wasn't really my scene, which is why I spent the better part of the night outside with the lake."

"Anyone else at this meeting?"

"Some tall, mean-looking guy was already there when Crystal, err Dolly, and I got there. He seemed crabby."

"Did Crabby have a name?"

"I'm sure he did, but he didn't share it with me."

"Hmmmm." The dark road climbed up, up, up, carving a series of sharp turns around the steep elevation of the hillside. "I feel like I'm on the road to a haunted house," he remarked.

"It's up on top of a bluff. You can see the whole sweep of the lake. The sunrise is beautiful from up there."

He raised his eyebrows. "You were there until dawn? Must have been some party."

"Well, you'll recall I wasn't there for a party. That's what it turned into though. You may also recall that I wasn't inside with the revelers," she said. "I was outside alone, which I'm sure was the better view. The light sort of spilled over the edge of the lake and spread as I sat and watched. Like I was watching it—"

"Wake up?" he said.

"Now that you mention it, that's what it looked like."

"I can see it now," Davecki said.

A cozy silence filled the Mustang. After a moment, Clara leaned forward. "I think we're close now." The car crested a little knob, the road curved down and ended at a large concrete apron that spread out like a bridal train. Set back from the apron was a colossal log home.

Davecki stopped the Mustang a hundred feet up the driveway. "That's it?"

"That's it."

"Wow."

Just beyond the concrete pad, a five-car garage rested. A breezeway led from the garage to the house. A wrap-around porch guarded by a banister made of thick, hand-peeled cedar, supported a covered walkway to the two-story gabled entrance. Around the saddle-notched corner logs, Davecki could just see the front of the house nearly hanging over the edge of the bluff, protruding like the prow of a ship.

"Quite a spread," Davecki said.

"You should see the inside."

"Good idea," Davecki said. He let the car roll down to the concrete pad, parked, and got out. They walked to the door. He knocked, stood back, locked his fingers together behind his back in parade rest. Thirty seconds later, he knocked again. After knocking a third time, he jumped down off the porch and looked up at the towering peak of logs. A three-foot overhang shadowed the walls. He jumped back to the pine plank porch and walked around to the nearest window. He cupped his hands around his face and peered in. He walked back to the door, opened the screen, and tried the brass handle. It turned.

"You can't just walk in! Don't you need a search warrant or something?" Clara said.

"I'm interested in the architecture," he said. "I would simply like to see if the inside is as beautiful as the outside, if the entire design has the structural integrity of the outside."

"Structural integrity, pashaw! You just want to snoop!"

Davecki turned to face her. The door was half open. "Pashaw?" he asked.

Clara put on a wounded look. "It's a great word. My grandmother used it all the time. And didn't I read somewhere that a police officer can't commit a crime to stop a crime?"

"There's nothing more dangerous than a half-informed person. You really shouldn't believe everything you read," he said.

She glared at him.

"Okay, what you read is true. That's the law. But the reality is, every cop I know lives by the real law."

"Which is?"

"Which is, we rule. And it's even more true since nine-one-one. Any cop worth his salt never let a little thing like the rules stand in the way of solving a murder." He pushed the door open all the way.

"Worth his salt?"

"My grandfather used to say that all the time," Davecki said as he walked in.

Clara stayed on the porch.

Davecki stopped just inside. "You coming?"

"I'm no trespasser."

"Suit yourself. But, it's a known fact, studies have shown that the vast majority of domestic killings occur outside the home. Just outside the front door, in fact."

"You're making that up!"

Laughing, Davecki walked in. Noting that the screen door didn't slam behind him, he whispered over his shoulder, "Ah, an accomplice to breaking, entering, and burglary!"

"I'm not your accomplice! I just want to see the place again. Why in the world would they leave their door unlocked?"

"You gotta remember these people are rich. One of the reasons they spend millions to move north and build mansions in the sticks is to create the illusion that they belong. It's a point of pride that they leave their doors unlocked. It says that they belong to the local community, that they trust and are trusted."

"What are you? Some sort of expert on the rich and famous?"

"Who said anything about famous? You sure do assume a lot."

"And you're opinionated."

The narrow hall ended at a great room with log beams crisscrossing the vaulted ceiling high above their heads.

Davecki stopped abruptly.

Clara, gaping up at the ceiling, bumped into him.

"What's that?" Davecki asked.

"What's what?" Clara whispered.

They cocked their heads in tandem. Above them and to the right a thump-thump-thump oozed through the thick log walls.

Clara's body was still pressed against Davecki. "I'm shaking," she whispered.

"I can tell," Davecki said. "From within or without?"

"Without," Clara said. "The floor's vibrating."

He quick-stepped away toward an elegant half-log staircase, which ascended to the right of the open great room to a second floor. Taking the steps two at a time, he followed the sound down another long hallway. The sound changed from a thump-thump-thump to a whir. He sprinted to a set of French doors at the end of the wood-paneled hall and peered through the glass in time to see a Bell Jet Ranger III swooping away over the treetops toward the southeast. He felt Clara's hand on his shoulder.

"What's going on?" she asked.

Davecki turned away from the window. "A chopper. He must have already been in it when we drove up, otherwise he'd have heard us." They turned and started back down the long hallway. "Plus he's headed in the opposite direction. That's why he didn't see the Mustang."

"He? I thought we were looking for Crystal up here."

Davecki considered. "Hmmmm. We were. We are. I'm just assuming a guy would be piloting a helicopter. Probably some ex-warrant officer from 'Nam."

"You sure do assume a lot." She planted a hand on her hip and cocked her head. "Females can pilot helicopters, too."

"Oh? Can you?"

She hesitated.

"Remember, you *never* lie."

She scowled. "Can we just get out of here?"

Davecki chuckled wickedly. "Well, as long as we're here, we might as well take a look around…." He reached for a brass door-knob on his left and pushed the door open.

The room was dominated by an immense, custom-made, cherry wood canopy bed, which sat atop a sumptuous Persian carpet. Pale light seeped in from high cathedral windows. The bed was unmade; the air was warm. Davecki turned. He bumped directly into Clara, who was again hovering right behind him.

"Are you trying to do that?" she asked.

Huh? He looked down at her face.

"You keep bumping into me on purpose don't you?"

"No. You keep hovering. I think you want me to bump into you."

"Well, you've got another think coming buster. I'm as steeped in denial as you."

"Methinks thou dost protest too much," he offered. He backed up. He cleared his throat. "Well, will you look at this room? See those windows up there?" he pointed. "Those are Andco windows made in South Superior."

"You can tell that from here?" Clara asked.

"Of course. Can't everybody?"

"Don't give me the old white pine lecture. What's your point?"

"My point is, the money it takes to not only buy Andco windows, but to build and outfit a place like this has got ruthless written all over it. There's an old saying, 'Behind every great fortune is a great crime.' I get suspicious around lots and lots of money. Bell helicopters aren't cheap. This house built on top of a big rock, with no neighbors for miles and with the most fantastic view of Lake Superior," he swept his arm across the bank of windows facing the lake, "cost more than my department's yearly budget. My guess, there's some wrongdoing behind all this."

"That's your *intuition?*"

"Yes, Miss Smarty. I'm a spirit detective, I get a sense for these things."

She brushed by him. "Let me see."

He didn't jump back from the fleeting contact.

She walked into the middle of the room, paused, and sniffed the air. "Wait, what do you smell?"

Davecki walked close to her and sniffed.

"Vanilla," they said together. They laughed.

Clara walked over to the night stand. "It's this. An aroma-therapy candle." She handed it to Davecki.

"The wax is still melted." He jiggled the candle slightly and held it out. "See?"

Clara bent to look. Her left breast touched Davecki's right elbow. She sniffed the candle. "That thing was burning not more than a few minutes ago."

She's not moving. He looked at the big bed. It was unmade. "It's warm," he said.

"The candle?"

Get a grip Alphonse, say yes. "Ahh, yes."

Clara stepped back, looked up, smiled. "For a cop you're not very good at prevarication."

"Um." *Say something, you fool.* "Good cops don't lie well." He inhaled. *I feel dizzy.*

"That's funny. Just today you told me all cops are deceitful."

"Oh? I guess I was lying." He turned toward the door. "I wonder what's in the other rooms?" Behind him he heard laughter. "What's so funny?"

"You're amusing me again. Oh, sorry, you're *refreshing* me."

"Hey look, if you want to go flinging your—your bosom around, that's your business. I'm just trying to be a gentleman here."

She smiled. "Proverbs five warns against becoming infatuated with a loose woman and embracing the bosom of an adventuress."

"I wasn't *embracing* anything. You're the one who came up and..."

She giggled. "All right, I'm sorry. It really was an accident, but you looked so flustered that my wickedness took hold of me." She cast her eyes down.

"Wicked is right," he muttered, walking into the hall. "So are we going to look at the rest of the house? Or are you going to put the moves on me again?"

"I didn't 'put the moves' on you! I was just—"

"I wonder what's in here?" Davecki reached for the next door-knob down the hall. He pushed the door open.

A huge desk with inlaid leather sat on luxurious gray carpeting in the far corner of the room. An occupant, seated in the matching leather chair, would be afforded a panoramic view of Lake Superior through full-length windows. Built-in bookcases and file cabinets lined the wall behind the desk. A fax machine and computer sat on a separate workstation in the opposite corner.

"Pretty lavish hey?" Clara said as she moved past, without making contact, toward the nearest window.

Davecki walked over to the desk and rifled through the few papers on its leather surface.

"Hey Clara," he said. "Listen to this: 'Isak: FALSIES meeting tonight. Dolly arrives 9:55 p.m. Flight 348, Sky Harbor.'"

"Is it signed?"

"We should be so lucky."

She said, "Wait, they're flying into Park Point? Why would they be leaving now? It shouldn't take them more than a half hour or so in that helicopter."

"No, look at the letterhead." He handed her the sheet.

"Albertson Enterprises, 1 Superstition Mountain Parkway, Scottsdale, Arizona," she read.

Davecki looked through the other papers. "There's an airport in Phoenix called Sky Harbor. This operation is probably based there."

"So they're flying all the way to Phoenix?"

"Dolly is, anyway."

"What's that say?" Clara indicated the other paper.

"It doesn't say anything. It's a photocopy of a plat map."

"What's a plat map?"

"It shows the boundaries of land parcels."

"Oh! The kind of information on a tax assessment?"

"Exactly."

"How did Crystal get a copy?"

"Anyone can have a copy. You just walk in the County Clerk's office and ask for one. This," he indicated the map in his hand, "this is a plat of the south half of the southwest quarter of section nine in the Town of Oulu."

"That's east of Superior isn't it?" She stepped closer and took the corner of the map.

He leaned into her.

"You putting the moves on me?" she asked.

"Nope. I'm just showing you the lay of the land. See this?" he pointed. "That line is the county line between Douglas and Bayfield County." Davecki shifted the sheet slightly. "See that?" He pointed again.

"That pencil dot?"

"Looks like someone has plans to visit scenic Oulu, Wisconsin." He rubbed his chin. "Well, I can't follow Dolly to Arizona, so I had better go to Oulu. Wanna go?"

"Why not? Just run me by my place so I can pick up my other jacket?"

"Sure." He looked at her feet, clad in canvas sneakers. "Better get some heavier shoes, too. We might be in for a tromp through the swamp. Hey, hand me that letterhead."

She picked it off the desk and handed it over.

Davecki went to the fax machine, positioned the letterhead and the memo in the receiver, and pressed a green button. The machine whirred. He pocketed his copies and carefully placed the originals back on the desk. He looked at Clara. "Ready?"

She nodded. As they reached the hallway, he turned. "You know anything about FALSIES?"

"Well, in junior high..."

Davecki held up his hands. "I don't want to know!"

"All right, I haven't a clue."

"Well, I know a little."

"A little knowledge is a dangerous thing," Clara said.

"True. And, if whoever lives here knows even half of what I know, my guess is they're headed for Oulu too."

27

Men of few words are the best men.

—William Shakespeare, *Henry V*

he pine trees creaked. In the distance to the west, a dog barked.

"*Älä nÿt,*" muttered Bill Peltonen. The other old Finns all in a row, wagged their heads. "What next?" someone muttered.

"Sit down, you old crackpot," shouted Frank.

"Order!" Cameroon called.

Jaako pointed at Frank. "That's *Father* Crackpot to you, *poika.*"

"Order!" Cameroon pounded the plywood with his pistol butt.

"Hey, Jaako! I got abducted last night too and I saw you with one of them alien women," someone guffawed. "I thought you was celibate!"

Cameroon raised his arm and fired his Ruger through the pine boughs. Like a bunch of prairie dogs, everyone ducked and covered. Everyone, that is, except the old Finns. One was trimming his fingernails with his pocketknife. The others sat, arms folded, staring at Cameroon.

"You should'a warned us!" Frank said as he regained his seat. He rubbed his ears. "I won't be hearing right for a week."

As the assembly reconfigured itself, one of the old Finns rose. He stood in silence, arms still folded across his chest. On his head, a magnificent shock of snow-white hair. About his body, an aura of power. He impassively scanned the 30 or so people regrouping themselves. He then turned his gaze to Cameroon.

"Chair recognizes Niilo Rantala." Cameroon said.

Rantala nodded. "It don't matter who's getting da water." His heavy accent drew out the vowels long and easy, his words waltzing. "What matters is dat da lake is being raped, and we got to stop it."

The old Finn who had been trimming his nails snicked his knife shut, pocketed it and gathered himself to his feet.

Rantala looked at him.

Allowing a few more seconds of silence to tick, Rantala began to sit and said, "I yield to Sulu Mikkola."

Sulu Mikkola, a slight man with deep-set eyes, dark hair and dark skin, surveyed the group with a grave stare. "Most of you know I was passing out da *Työmies* with my grampa when I was a boy."

There were nods of agreement all around the room.

Fran looked at Cameroon. She raised her shoulders and eyebrows.

Cameroon raised his palm toward her and motioned for her to sit.

As Fran lowered herself to her seat, Cameroon whispered, "A leftist Finnish newspaper once published in Superior. *Työmies-Etenpäin, The Worker-Forward,*" he whispered.

Sulu glanced at Cameroon and spoke a little louder, "Grampa worked for da pipe-liners when dey first put in dat tube. It's been sucking the lake dry for twelve years now. Ain't no mystery how dey did it. Government by-and-for-da-people don't exist no more. It's government by-and-for-greedy-politicians and greedy rich folks. If you got enough money you can get anything done in this country."

Mikkola paused. He looked around the room some more. "What is a mystery to me is why we ain't doing nothing about it. All we do is talk and talk and talk, and do research." He shot a withering glance at Cameroon and Fran. "I say, blow da damn thing up!"

Cheers and applause exploded from about half the crowd, while others shook their heads or stared at the floor. Mikkola nodded his head in a dignified acceptance and sat down heavily on his plank.

Jaako stood.

"Chair recognizes Father Luoma," Cameroon sighed.

"We all know the Mikkolas, a courageous family whose ancestors, the Black Finns, journeyed across Siberia centuries ago." He bowed slightly toward Sulu.

Mikkola nodded slightly at Jaako.

Jakko continued, "No disrespect intended, Sulu, but if we blow up the pipeline, there's no telling what evil them aliens will blast us with."

Groans erupted.

"I seen that on the *X-Files*!" someone yelled.

"*Mars Attacks* the Twin Ports!" another voice called.

Fran looked at Cameroon.

The professor glanced at her, but said and did nothing.

Rantala rose. The group fell silent. He cleared his throat. "My old Pa used to say, 'Da hurrier I go, da behinder I get.' We rush into blowing up da pipeline," he looked at Sulu, "It'll be a big mistake. What we got to do is expose 'em to da media so da public finds out, gets mad, and shuts it down. My son knows a girl who works at dat Minnesota Pubic Radio. He thinks she'll do a story on dis."

A buzz rippled through the group.

Nancy stood.

Niilo nodded and sat.

"I agree with Niilo. Though I think it would be better to go to PUBLIC radio," she said.

Many many voices laughed.

"Seriously," Nancy continued. We should do some protesting. That's the American way. Freedom of Speech. I made up some signs that we could carry on a picket line in front of the Douglas County Courthouse." She held up a handful of handsome placards.

"I can't read it from here," a voice yelled from the back.

"Show the entire group," Cameroon said.

Nancy raised her hands over her head and spun around. The sign read, HELL NO! WATER WON'T GO! "This one is a takeoff from the Vietnam War protests."

She shuffled the placards and raised the next one high. WATER 'BOUT IT! the sign read. "This is designed to prick the conscience of anyone who reads it."

"Speaking of pricks..." Frank started.

"DON'T. JUST DON'T FRANK," Cameroon yelled.

"Thank you, Doctor," Nancy said. She shuffled her cards again. This sign had bright blue waves bordering the entire surface area. Big bold letters in red read, KNOW YOUR H_2O.

Smatterings of applause rippled around the group.

"Thank you very much," Nancy said. She flipped cards like Vanna White. Turning around, Nancy read aloud, "H_2O NO GO! If we march around and keep chanting "H_2O NO GO H_2O NO GO! It's bound to attract the television cameras."

"Dat and da men in white jackets from da looney bin," Sulu said.

Nancy lowered her cards. She huffed in Sulu's direction, "Well! I think it's a lot better idea than blowing things up."

Fran quietly rose.

Cameroon waved her on. "Chair recognizes Fran Hansen."

Fran scanned the crowd like a wary whitetail doe. "I believe what Sulu says, that most of you support him and his desire for immediate and violent action." Cheers from the assembly echoed softly off pine trunks.

"I also noticed that at least half of you seemed to approve of Mr. Rantala's idea."

More cheers.

"And many of you think Nancy's idea is best."

The same smattering of applause.

"It seems to me that everyone here is of at least two or three minds on this issue. Four minds, if you count Jaako's...theory."

Jaako beamed at her.

"I myself have doubts, often, but as I said before, I came here tonight to offer you another option. Though this has its own risks." She paused, running her hand through her black hair. "I'm reminded of what Job said in the Bible: 'The thing that I fear comes upon me, and what I dread befalls me.' What I'm talking about is—the zebra mussel."

Silence.

Then Waako spoke up. "Come again?"

"Zebra mussel," Fran said again.

"Ain't that some kind of striped clam?" Box Elder asked. "I seen a show about them once."

"Box, don't you do nothing besides sit and watch cable TV?" Waako said.

Box looked injured. "I most certainly do not. I'll have you know this was on PBS."

"You're close, Box," said Fran. "A zebra mussel is a variety of bivalve mollusk."

"Oh, that clears things up real nicely," Waako said.

Frank jumped into the dialogue. "Fantastic Fran has a plan," he mocked. "A mollusk! That will really get 'em! And here I was advocating the use of high explosives."

"A zebra mussel will do just as much damage Frank. In fact,

that's the risk I spoke of. As a biologist, I have long feared the zebra mussel's destructive power. I still do. It has the potential to radically change the ecology of the lake as much as any biological threat. But the wholesale diversion of massive amounts of water for commercial purposes is what I fear most."

"You wanna tell me how some clams is going to save the lake?" Sinto asked.

"Good question, Sinto. I've come to expect cogent questions from our resident publisher."

"I think I'll go with Jaako's aliens," Mikko cat-called.

"Don't you be flippant about them aliens," Jaako warned.

Rantala stood. "*Ole hiljaa*!"

"What's that mean?" Kristina asked.

"Shut up!" Bill Peltonen said.

Kristina flushed. "Well, you don't have to get snippy about it. I was just asking a question."

Frank glared at Bill.

Helmi leaned forward. "No. That's what Niilo said. Ole hiljaa means, be quiet or shut up."

"Oh," Kristina said.

Frank subsided in his seat.

Niilo Rantala stared slowly around the gathering. All quieted. "We're all here for the same reason, right?"

"That's right, Niilo," Waako said as heads nodded all around the group.

"We all got ideas. Some of 'em"—he looked hard at Jaako—"don't sound like much at first. But it don't hurt none to listen. Now, before we go and blow up dis pipeline, maybe blow ourselves up in da process, I want to hear what Miss Hansen's idea is." Rantala nodded toward Henderson. "I just wish everyone here would be as polite as Mr. Big Bear here and listen quietly. Anyone got any problems with dat?"

Henderson smiled and nodded.

Rantala looked at Mikkola.

Mikkola nodded, said, "No problem."

"Miss Hansen?" Rantala sat.

Fran smiled. "Thank you, gentlemen. It's so unusual to be treated like a lady." She flipped a quick look at Cameroon. She scanned the group and continued. "As I said, the zebra mussel can do as much damage as explosives. If you'll bear with me for a moment, I brought some things to show you." She reached under the plywood table and brought out several pieces of poster board. She held one up for them to see. "This is a zebra mussel, magnified to 30 times its actual size."

"Eww!" squealed Nancy.

"What, are we going to ugly them to death?" asked Waako.

Mikkola made a solemn turn and glared at both Nancy and Waako.

"Oops. Sorry," Nancy giggled.

"Yeah, sorry," Waako said.

Fran lowered the illustration and produced a quart jar from below the table. It was filled with mussels. "The average zebra mussel colonizes very quickly. But, my friends here in this jar," and she looked directly at Sulu, "thanks to some fortuitous gene splicing, colonize twice as fast, at double the rate, which means they reproduce in densities of 600,000 to two million mussels per square meter. These little gems will destroy the pipeline just as quickly as any Osama action.

"They form thick layers over the top of each other. This has created serious difficulties for water users." She looked around the room for signs of opposition. "No sarcastic comments? Well, then. I'll continue. They plug up intake screens, pipes, anything they come in contact with. And there goes the water supply."

"Well then, we don't want them in our lake!" exclaimed Helmi.

"They're already here. They've been in the Great Lakes since the late 1980s, probably arriving in the ballast water of a European freighter," Fran said.

She glanced at Cameroon. "Professor Cameroon and I were out all weekend helping diver Simon Jensen locate all their inlets. What we propose to do is place a small supply of these hybrid zebra mussels at each location. They will be sucked down the pipe and eventually, somewhere down the line, they will colonize and begin to rapidly reproduce. In their juvenile stage, they are capable of free-swimming activity, so..."

"HEY! They're like tiny terrorists in a jar," Evad yelled.

Fran smiled. "Good thinking, Evad." Fran lifted the jar again. "Think of these little babies as tiny radicals infiltrating the system to destroy it." She paused, put the jar on the table.

"Now, another feature of the zebra mussel is, the warmer the water the longer the breeding season. So in Arizona, the females could potentially lay millions, even billions of eggs during the reproductive season. This would, I believe, completely clog up their water supply."

"Won't they do the same up here?" Helmi asked.

"Not with this," Hansen said, pulling another jar from below the table. The jar was half full of dead mussels. "Thanks to the wonders of research," quick glance at Sulu, "and thanks to gene splicing, I have been able to develop a gene-specific toxin that is harmless in all respects, except, that is, to these particular genetically altered mussels. Because the toxin is genetically tailored to cause mortality in only the mussels we release, no collateral damage will occur anywhere in Lake Superior. Any questions?"

Henderson raised his hand.

"Chair recognizes J. J. Big Bear."

"Uh, it's Black Bear. And thanks for letting me have the opportunity to speak. I think it is absolutely brilliant. When do we start?"

Bill Peltonen said, "Wait a minute! We got to vote on this. And, what do you mean we?" he asked glaring at Henderson.

Henderson smiled. "Well, actually, I'd be willing to help, but, really, I'm not all that familiar yet. I guess I was just trying to show my support."

Fran said. "I appreciate your enthusiasm, Mr. Black Bear. But we don't need more than myself, Dr. Cameroon and Simon on this operation. But we do need consensus from the group. I'm not prepared to move forward with this plan unless I have the support of the group."

"I'm still not convinced," Box Elder said.

Henderson took up the dialogue. "An explosion is too dramatic. Too loud. Plus, thanks to Ashcroft, we would all be hunted down and put to death for sedition. This is the perfect plan. It's invisible, silent and slow. The people responsible for this travesty against nature won't notice the gradual clogging of their pipe. By the time they do, it'll be too late. If the Great Lakes were still free from the zebra mussel, it would be dumb. But they're not. Anyone looking to pin responsibility will only have Mother Nature to blame. We'd be home free! It's absolutely brilliant!"

The group was silent.

"When were you thinking of planting the mussels?" Henderson asked.

"With the group's approval, as soon as possible. We could start tomorrow."

Sulu rose. All eyes locked on the old man's hoary head. "Dees times are terrible with terrorism and war and death and destruction. Dis is serious business. We could all get da death penalty. But, messing with Mudder Nature, dat's bad too. We got to stop dis thing from happening. I move we go ahead with Miss Hansen's plan." The other old Finns nodded their heads, once.

Jaako said, "I second."

Cameroon and Fran looked at each other. Then Cameroon recovered enough to say, "Discussion?" He looked around the room. "Seeing none..."

The vote was unanimous.

28

Everybody helps everybody. As smart as we like to think we are, as independent as we like to think we are, we're all linked up... hooked up and incredibly in touch with each other's needs and desires. Trouble is, all this activity takes place behind the scenes, without us knowing just how supported and cared for we are.

—Rodriel Heukenlein
Famous Finnish Philosopher

ell me about your daughter."

Davecki looked at Clara, startled out of his thoughts.

"You said I remind you of her, back at the cafe. So what is she like?"

He stared ahead at the highway. "I'm still finding out myself."

"Oh," Clara said.

After a substantial pause, he said, "I didn't even know I had a daughter until she called me up one day and told me. I had no idea. I suppose you disapprove."

"Do you disapprove?" she asked.

"Some things could have been different way back when. But they weren't. I was doing the best I could. I'm not sorry she was born."

Clara shook her head. "Of course not. That's not what I was asking you. Do I disapprove? *Everyone* will fall short of doing what's right sometimes. You're not the only one with something like that in his past." She grinned. "I may even have a few skeletons of my own."

"Oh yeah? What?"

She laughed. "That's why they're called skeletons."

He looked across at her. "Come on. Tell Uncle Alphonse."

"I thought your name was Dave."

Oops. "It is. Sort of."

She narrowed her eyes. "Hmm. Well, whatever. I'm not telling you anyway, Mr. Nosy. The thing is, in my view, when you make a mistake—or in the case of your daughter, you do something good in less-than-perfect circumstances—it's not the end of the world. You just have to repent, make things right. I assume you're in contact with her now?"

He smiled. "Oh yes."

"Well then, all's well that ends well." Clara folded her hands in her lap.

He peeked at her. "I'm surprised."

"You thought I would slap a scarlet A on you?"

Davecki said nothing.

"You know, The Scarlet Letter."

Davecki shrugged.

"Nathaniel Hawthorne?" she said desperately. "Hester Prynne? Arthur Dimmsdale?"

"Nope," Davecki said. "No idea."

"Never mind," she sighed.

He laughed. "Hey, I was just yanking your chain! I may not be the best-read guy in the city of Superior, but I have heard of *The Scarlet Letter*. Who knows? I may have even read it back in high school."

"Oh yeah?" Clara said. "What was the name of Hester's daughter?"

It shot miraculously from his memory. "Pearl," he said smugly.

"Lucky guess," she grumbled.

He crowed. "I'll have to save the victory dance for later, when we're out of the car." He wiggled from side to side.

"I'll victory dance my foot right into your behind."

He pointed at her suddenly. "That is what reminds me of Bethany!"

"What? What!"

"See, Bethie, she's got a heart of gold. But she can kick butt."

"Hey!"

"Chew..."

"All right already!"

"But smart? Is she smart! Takes after her old man, I figure."

Clara made a gagging motion.

"Funny as hell. And brave? She even interviewed Jesse Ventura before he was sent up. Then, after he got transferred to the hospital, she even did one of those compassionate follow-up stories. She is something else." He glanced at Clara.

She was gazing steadily at him with those wide brown eyes. His heart suddenly pounded in his chest. "And… you just reminded me of her."

She smiled shyly. "Thanks." She looked down. She re-clasped her hands.

Davecki looked ahead. He drummed the steering wheel with his fingers.

"So," he said abruptly. "What is the mysterious profession that you retired from?"

Big laugh. "I'll tell you when you tell me what the deal is with your name."

"What deal? What are you talking about?"

"I'm talking about the obvious deception centered around your real name. Is it Dave or is is Alphonse?"she said.

He squirmed and hesitated. "Alphonse is my given name. I pre-fer Dave."

"See? That wasn't so bad was it?"

"Easy for you to say, Miss Not-willing-to-share."

"Okay, okay, lighten up. I'm working up the courage." She grit-ted her teeth. "I'm retired from buying lucky lottery tickets," she said.

"What? You won Powerball?" Davecki asked.

"Well, not Powerball, but, it was enough to keep me off the streets."

Davecki snorted. "I found you on the street."

"Off the streets in the unemployment sense. Are you dense or something?"

"You are so warm and fuzzy."

They looked at each other.

In the Mustang, a comfortable silence settled. Clara leaned her head back and hummed softly. Davecki tapped the steering wheel, listening, thinking.

As they pulled onto her street, Davecki spotted movement in the dusk. "You expecting company?"

She sat up. "No. Why?"

He pointed. "There's someone there. There, on the far end of your porch." He pulled the Mustang to the curb. The figure in the shadows ducked. Clara clicked off her seat belt and went to open her door. Davecki put his hand on her shoulder, peering into the shadows. "Let me check it out."

"*No*, thank you. It's *my* house, *I'll* check it out." She gently removed his hand and opened her door.

"You ever seen anyone get shot?" he asked.

She ignored him jumped out of the car, started up the walk.

He scurried after her. "You know this is how all the slasher movies always start, with some girl deciding to play it tough and look into the shadows."

"I'm not a girl."

Clara reached the porch and climbed the three steps. At the top she paused, turning her head back toward Davecki.

He was just reaching the steps when the shadow behind the pillar exploded.

"Clara!" he shouted.

Clara turned toward the danger just as the shadow became a person, and the person crashed into Clara who flew through the air and hit the floor with a terrible crash.

29

The more of doubt, the stronger the faith, I say.

—Robert Browning,
Men and Women (1855)

n Professor Don Cameroon's battered old Plymouth van, on the way down Snyder road, following the FALSIES meeting, Fran Hansen sighed. "I talked to Simon. He said he's willing to try whenever I'm ready."

Cameroon looked at her. "You sound tired."

She shifted in her seat. "I'm restless. I haven't been sleeping. I just lie there, thinking what if the mussels aren't ready? What if we're fighting a losing battle?"

"Don't be so negative," Cameroon said. "Have you never heard of the self-fulfilling prophecy?"

Hansen sighed again, louder. "Don't be so pompous. Of course I've heard of the self-fulfilling prophecy. I have also heard of being realistic."

"You know what Ernest Shackelton said..."

She interrupted, "'Optimism is true moral courage.' Any other questions?"

"You've got to lighten up, Franny. You sounded more confident back at the meeting."

"Don't call me Franny." She laughed a mirthless laugh. "I wish I believed in my plan as strongly as they seem too. I can't believe how easy it was to sell them on the idea."

"I don't think anyone really wants to get into the blowing up business since September eleventh. They have to talk tough though, keep suggesting it lest anyone think they're cowards."

"They're not the only ones doubting their courage."

They rode in silence for a few moments. Cameroon frowned. "I'm curious about why Simon is willing to go forward with this. He didn't seem so eager the other day. What exactly did he say?"

"That he's been searching for the Benjamin Noble for twenty years and that maybe it's time to do something different with his spare time..."

"The Benjamin Noble?"

"You must have heard him mention that old packet steamer that sank a hundred or so years ago. Simon figures it's somewhere off Park Point."

"What's his big interest in it?"

Fran grinned. "Gold. It was carrying payroll for the steamship line's Duluth operation. There were several thousand dollars worth of gold coins aboard."

"How many times has he been down?"

"Hundreds. Plus he's been out there with side scanning sonar and has been dragging magnetometers up and down both coasts and across the state line for days at a time."

"I can't believe I've never heard him talking about it."

"It's not surprising to me. You only hear what you want to hear, Don."

Cameroon braked for the upcoming stop sign at the junction of Highway Two and the Oulu Rock. Fran looked through the darkness at the huge white boulder illuminated by a pair of headlights coming from the east. "Who keeps painting over the OULU sign?" she asked. "And what does that say now? It looks like HUGS."

A huge maroon pulp truck loaded with wood roared past. Cameroon steered the van toward Brule and gunned it. The little vehicle shook with the strain of acceleration. "Someone has been painting HUGHES over the OULU."

"Why on earth?" Fran asked.

"Well, because the Oulu Rock is, technically, in the Town of Hughes. I guess there's a turf war going on."

"There'll be war within the FALSIES if the mussels don't stop the water flow."

"Don't be silly." Cameroon adjusted his rearview mirror. "You're the best genetic engineer in the world today. All you have to do is trust your instinct and everything will be fine. What could go wrong?"

"Don't say that! Read any mystery novel. Any time some fool says 'what could go wrong,' the worst possible thing happens!" Fran waggled her finger at him.

"You shouldn't pollute your mind with such lowbrow material," Cameroon said.

She crossed her arms. "Oh man! Now you've jinxed us. We'll be hijacked. Or sink. Or the mussels will turn on us and attack. Or we'll be devoured by a giant sturgeon. Or—"

"All right! " Cameroon cut in. "The truth is, Fran, that you *will* be ready. You *are* ready. You're Frantastic Fran."

She opened her mouth.

He raised a hand in protest. "DON'T argue. For once, let me finish."

She rolled her eyes, said nothing.

"I happen to know that you expect more from yourself than any reasonable person should." He smiled. "You only feel comfortable when you're doubting yourself while the rest of the world stands by in awe watching you perform virtual miracles. You're ready. I know."

"How do you know?"

"Because I know you, Fran. And you do only one thing better than science."

"And what, may I ask, is that?"

"Worry."

"Shut up, you old goat."

"That's my girl!" He reached between the seats and picked up a cell phone handset and said, "Now, call Simon and tell him to meet us at the dock. If he isn't too crabby, encourage him to have 'er ready to get under way as soon as we get there."

Hansen eyed Cameroon. "God you're getting bossy in your old age."

"Old age and treachery wins over beauty and brains every time, my dear," he said. As she took the phone, he patted her hand.

"Don't pat my hand."

"Why?"

Hansen laughed. "Because it's patronizing."

"You are something else," he said.

30

To dispose a soul to action, we must upset its equilibrium.

—Eric Hoffer

C lara vanished without so much as a whisper of complaint. Adrenaline has strange effects on people. In Davecki's case he usually opted for fight above flight. He was a cop after all. But, some of Chief Callahan's memos had been "encouraging" the force to consider flight as an option, in the interest of public relations, the memos said. A third option Davecki often experienced, despite official inter-department memos, was PANIC!

Davecki, in this state, was not a typical panicker. For him, time slowed. The brain ramps up, augmenting all senses. It was pretty much a god-like experience, and, as such, was something Davecki rather liked. He heard all, saw all, noticed all. And while the brain performs all manner of utterly complicated tasks, the body goes on autopilot.

Omniscience, you gotta love it, Davecki realized.

There were fifteen feet between Davecki and the top of the porch. It looked like fifteen miles. As his body moved, his brain considered what he had seen: it had been a person, obviously. Too dark for description, but whoever it was had jumped directly at Clara, taking her around the neck and dragging her down. No flash of a weapon, but it was too dark to be sure if a weapon was present. No gunshot—yet. He cursed the bare spot at the small of his back where his own piece should have been resting; it was now resting on *Steak Warning*. Choked moans came from the darkness of the porch. Definitely Clara's voice. *I wonder if she makes little sounds like that when... KNOCK it OFF, Alphonse!*

In one and a half seconds he had reached the end of the sidewalk and took all three steps in one bound. His eyes scanned the porch and instantly found what he was seeking. Clara, kneeling. The other figure, standing, right arm outstretched. *Dear God, she's going to be executed.* Without stopping, in one smooth motion, he had his forearm across this person's neck.

"Drop it," he growled.

"Ouch!" A woman's voice.

The object in the woman assailant's hand fell, clattered on the porch boards. The now weaponless female assailant's knees buckled. Davecki maintained his iron grip.

"Arrrgh!" the fallen said.

"Detective!" Clara said. "Let go!"

He tightened his grip.

A labored groan rose from the perp.

"*Alphonse!*"

He let go. The perp collapsed. Sobs rose. His hypervigilance started to recede. He stepped back. His heart hammered in his rib cage. Quiet voices below him.

"Are you all right?"

"Fine. What's up?"

"It's Crystal, err... Dolly."

"What in hell was she doing?"

"Waiting for me. She's upset." The woman was curled into a ball, head on Clara's lap. "When she saw me, she ran to me. I didn't see her coming and she knocked me over."

"That part I saw. What about the weapon?"

Clara said, "It's not a weapon." She lifted her hand. "It's a flashlight."

It's a weapon on every police force in the country. Davecki rubbed his hand over his face. "Is she all right?"

"Yes. And no. You didn't hurt her, but... Crystal, honey, stand up. We've got to get up and get you inside, girl."

Anguished cries of deep intensity rose. It was a keening of such distress that Davecki's skin prickled.

Clara said again, "Crystal honey. It's all right. Stand up." Clara looked upward at Davecki and shrugged.

"It's all right," he said. He squatted. "Dolly?" he said softly. The crying subsided. The woman raised her face to him. Even in the darkness, he could see the tremendous damage that was spread across the woman's features. Her left eye was swollen shut. Her right was open a slit. A large gash in her left cheekbone oozed blood. Her lower lip, also swollen, was cut and crusted over with dark dried blood. Her right jaw was abraded and bruised. Her wrists were rubbed raw. *Rope burns*, Davecki realized.

Looking directly into her wide, frantic eyes, he said, "It's going to be okay."

She stared at him, uncomprehending.

Clara said, "She's going to need stitches."

He leaned toward Dolly and put out his hand to examine the laceration on her cheek.

Dolly whimpered, turned away and tried to burrow even further into Clara's lap.

Davecki rocked back onto his heels and spoke softly, "She's afraid of me. You get her in the house. I'll call for an ambulance. She needs the emergency room."

Clara nodded. "Dolly, honey. Can I call you Dolly now?"

Dolly nodded.

"Okay. Dolly it is. You have some cuts and bruises. In a minute I'm going to need to look at them. Is that all right with you?"

Dolly nodded again.

Clara looked at Davecki.

He nodded, mouthed the word *Good.*

Clara, voice like a lullaby, continued, "I know you're scared and hurt. I'm glad you came to me. You were here once to pick me up. In the spring. Remember?"

Nod.

"I remember because my daffodils were just coming up."

Davecki stood motionless, listening.

Clara stroked Dolly's arm and shoulder. "And you knew I would be able to help you, isn't that right?"

Something was glimmering in the back of Davecki's brain. He closed his eyes, willing it to come forward. Ribbons of thought...

"Now I have a hard question for you, Dolly. Are you ready?"

Dolly's body tensed, but she did nod in the affirmative.

"I need you to get up and go into the house with me and Detective Davecki. Can you do that?"

Dolly started sucking in quick shallow breaths. She threw quick glances around.

"You're safe now, Dolly. Can we go in the house, please?" Clara said.

"Okaaaay," Dolly answered.

Davecki opened and held the door. Clara clutched Dolly and guided her inside and through the living room to the kitchen table.

"Can you tell us what happened and who hurt you?" Clara asked as she guided Dolly to a chair.

Davecki, at the sink, ran water over a crumple of paper toweling he had ripped from the roll suspended under the oak cabinets. He handed the moist towels to Clara and said, "I'm going to call for an ambulance. Where's your phone?"

"In there, at the end of the couch," Clara pointed with her chin.

"NO!" Dolly said.

Davecki looked at Clara.

"We can clean her up a little first. Can't we?"

Davecki didn't move. Nodded his head slightly.

"Okay, honey," Clara said. "We'll wait on the ambulance." Clara ripped the wad of wet paper toweling apart and put a patch over Dolly's eye. "Hold that there, honey. It'll feel better."

Dolly complied.

Clara placed her left hand on Dolly's shoulder and started daubing at bits of crusty blood on Dolly's cheek. "Honey, you've got to tell us what happened."

Dolly sobbed. She inclined her head toward Davecki.

Clara continued to clean up Dolly's face. "If it's too scary to say out loud, you can whisper it in my ear. Does that sound all right?" She began lightly stroking Dolly's arm.

Dolly nodded at Davecki again.

"Honey, that man is a friend of mine. He's a police detective. His name is Dave. Dave, can you say hi to Dolly?"

"Hi, Dolly. Nice to meet you," he said quietly.

"He's here to listen and to help. You can tell me what happened, and I'll tell him. And then we can help. All right?"

"I have to use the bathroom. I'll be back in a few minutes," Davecki said.

"NO!" Dolly yelped.

"It's okay, honey. He's one of the good guys. He doesn't have to leave just yet," Clara said.

Through the open window, a breeze entered. Davecki inhaled. *I smell Lake Superior*. He turned his face into the wisp of wind.

Dolly turned her face toward Clara's ear and whispered something.

Davecki thought, *Little Willie in the lake... Dolly is Crystal...Crystal was Little Willie's girlfriend...Little Willie was a FALSIE...*

"Dolly, who hurt you?" Clara asked.

Long silence. Davecki held his breath.

Dolly's shoulder's started shaking, "Nevada," she said. Her voice was just above a whisper.

Davecki kept looking away, but he strained to hear.

"Who's Nevada?" Clara asked.

No answer.

Davecki closed his eyes. *Plat map of Oulu...FALSIES are in Oulu... meeting tonight...*

Clara and Dolly's voices floated on the evening air. Understanding was just beyond comprehension.

The ribbons in Davecki's head began to weave themselves together. *Finns Against Lake Superior Import Export Schemes... Water... Little Willie... import-export... Arizona... water... export...* "Now I get it," Davecki muttered.

Clara left Dolly's side and ushered Davecki back through the living room and back onto the porch.

"Nevada Henderson," she explained, "is an employee of her father's. Also an off-and-on boyfriend, from the sound of it. They argued about another man..."

"That would be Little Willie," Davecki said.

"He beat her up. She took off in his car." Clara nodded toward the Thunderbird at the curb.

"I think that's the car we almost hit on the way into her place," Davecki said. "Why did she come here and not try to get to her father? Or the police?"

"Henderson told her he'd kill her if she ran to Daddy." She sighed. "As for the police, I'm not sure. Sometimes the SPD isn't all that sympathetic when it comes to domestic violence."

Just as Davecki asked, "I wonder what caused the fight?" Dolly walked out of the house.

"He killed someone I cared about." Her voice was husky but composed.

"Would that someone be Little Willie?" Davecki asked.

Her eyes widened. "Yes."

"Why?" Clara asked.

"Willie knew something that my father and Nevada didn't want him to know. Something to do with water. And they killed him." Her eyes filled with tears but remained steady.

Davecki spoke slowly. "I need to know what this Henderson looks like."

"Tall. Thin. Mean."

"How old is he?"

"I don't know. Old," Dolly said. "In his fifties or sixties I suppose."

"What about his hair? What color?"

"Brown, but you'll never see it."

"Why is that?" Davecki asked.

Dolly said, "Because he's always wearing that silly cowboy hat."

As in ivory Stetson? Davecki thought. "As in an ivory Stetson?" he asked Dolly.

"Yeah. Exactly. How'd you know?"

"I saw one at an accident site up on Palisade Head. I think it belonged to your boyfriend."

"He is NOT my boyfriend," Dolly said.

"Of course. Sorry. Really sorry. Do you know where this Henderson is now?"

"No I don't. He must have taken the helicopter to the Park Point airport to pick up the Blazer. I took his car when I ran away."

"That explains the helicopter," Clara said.

"What color was the Blazer?" Davecki asked.

"Red," Dolly answered.

"Do you know where he was headed?"

"To hell I hope," Dolly said.

"Oh, he'll probably end up there eventually. But for now, I have a pretty good idea it isn't quite hell he's bound for." Davecki looked at his watch. He looked at Clara.

"We'll be fine," Clara said.

"I've got to call this in. It's the law," Davecki said.

"No ambulances," Dolly said.

"They'll send a squad over to take a statement," he said. He jumped down the steps and loped toward the Mustang.

"Where are you going?" Clara asked.

"I'm going to get my gun, my bike and see an old friend who should be able to help."

"Be careful," Clara called out.

He waved without looking back.

The, "Come back soon," that caught up with his rapid exit made him bust a big grin.

31

Let the tail go with the hide.

—Elsie Greener

arkness rose from the clay earth on either side of Bayfield County Highway FF like a wraith exiled from Middle Earth. The red motorcycle sped along the Finlander Freeway at triple digit speed.

I'll never make the FALSIES meeting, Davecki realized.

Ahead, in the glare of the VFR's headlight, stood a deer, straddling the center line. Davecki dynamited the front brake. Coming to a complete stop on the front wheel, the rear wheel smacked down on the blacktop. The sharp noise scared the deer and it scrambled for traction on the hard blacktop. When the frightened whitetail finished skating like a dog on linoleum to the edge of the road, it got purchase and boinged high across the deep ditch and rebounded high across the barbed wire fence coming to a safe landing in the Wicklund's hayfield. Once safe in the field, the doe stopped and stared at the motorcyclist. It snorted and glared at Davecki.

Sorry to have inconvenienced you, darling, Davecki nodded.

The doe blinked, stamped it's right foot and turned to walk away. As it departed toward the tastiest clover at the edge of the field, it twitched its ears forth and back like they were on hinges.

Davecki revved the engine.

The doe jumped and managed to find the energy to sustain a moderate trot into the gloom.

Got to slow down. He let the clutch out and squawked the Dunlop leaving the scene. As the bike hummed along, Davecki reasoned, *How had Henderson managed to get into the meeting? If indeed he did get in. It says volumes about the group, about how things have changed from the old days when strangers brought betrayal and sometimes death. He wouldn't have tricked those old timers. Knute will know.*

When he drove down the driveway to Knute's old farmhouse, the headlight illuminated the wizened old man sitting on his porch, his Valmet shotgun across his knees. Davecki pulled up and dismounted.

"It's me, Knute," he called as he took off his helmet.

"Who da hell else could it be? Yer da only one I know who would be fool enough to announce his coming so loud. I heard dat damn cycle of yours five miles avay." Knute coughed. "Come on up."

Davecki went on up and pulled an old cane-backed chair close. Knute's face was illuminated by the light of a kerosene lamp that sat on the other side of a double hung window and cast its yellow glow feebly through dirty looking lace curtains and onto the porch. The fishy odor that ordinarily surrounded Knute was replaced by the crisp scent of sauna soap.

Davecki eyed the gun. "You waiting for someone?"

"You."

"Planning on shooting me?"

"Depends." A glint of mirth flashed from Knute's eyes, but his face remained stoic.

"You'd get a kick out of blasting someone with that old blunderbus wouldn't you?"

A full scale smile flitted across the weathered face. "I t'ought you'd be comin', but der's someone else I t'ought might come too." His voice grew harsh. "*Dat* guy I *vould* shoot."

Davecki looked at his shoes. "What's going on, Knute?"

"Yer the real smart deeetecktive."

"I learned a long time ago from some old fish monger that the smartest thing is not being too proud to come right out and ask. You gonna tell me?"

Knute snorted. He shifted in his chair. "I can tell you some. A guy comes to me sayin' he's writin' a story 'bout da old days. Secret societies and all dat. I tell him I don't know nuttin'. Den he says he vants to yoin one. So like a yackass, I tell him vhere ve meet." The old wizened head shook.

"And?"

"And he goes to da meetin' tonight, callin' himself an Indian. Tells everyvun *I* sent him. And like yackasses dey let him in, no qvestions asked. Some secret society."

"Don't be so hard on yourself, my friend. Everything I've heard about this guy spells con artist extraordinaire." Davecki looked out over Knute's darkened yard at the looming shadow of the barn. His eyes traveled further. Trails of smoke wisped from the sauna's stone chimney. The silence was telling. "So, what else you got for me?"

Knute stared at the rough planks below their feet. "Ain't naw-ting more dat I got to say about dat guy except to say, he's mixed up in da south end of dis vater business somehow, ain't he?"

"Looks that way."

"And vit Little Villie?"

Davecki nodded. He told Knute everything he knew, from find-ing Willie's body to Dolly's story less than an hour before.

"From what Dolly said, this Henderson is ready for action. If he was at that FALSIES meeting, my gut feeling is that he's going to use whatever he heard there to sabotage the plan. I need to know what was discussed."

Knute stroked the stock of his Valmet. "I vasn't at da meeting. Niilo and Sulu came to see me after. You yoost missed 'em." He looked over at Davecki. "Dat's how I knew dere vas trouble. Dose two don't usually see eye to eye." He continued. "Dose scientists, Cameroon and Hansen, dey got plans to mess up da vater pipeline vit mussel."

"Muscle. They planning on hiring some Chicago muscle to straighten out this Henderson? Or were they planning on asking me to straighten the guy out?" Davecki struck a pose like Arnold Swartzenegger.

Knute snorted. "Vouldn't get much done vit *dose* muscles."

"Look who's talking, ya old coot."

Knute snorted. "I could bust you up real good any time I vanted. Anyvay, it's mussels as in little sucking critters in da vater."

Davecki raised his eyebrows.

Knute coughed. "I don't tink much of da plan eider. But Niilo and Sulu, dey vere convinced. And dey're not easy to convince. Fer shur you can always tell an old Finn, but you shur can't tell 'em much." He shook his gray head, "Fer shur dey're not as smart as us Chermans."

Davecki laughed. "So tell me about this plan of Don and Fran's."

Knute looked at him. "You know dem two?"

"I've seen them at the coffee shop and we've talked some—local politics, job talk. Nothing like this. I should have guessed they were FALSIES."

"Dey're not, really. Some of da Oulu kids had dem as teachers at da University and said dey vere vorried about da lake, too. Vhen ve started hearing stuff about dis vater pipeline business, ve got in touch vit dem." Knute pulled a chamois cloth from the box next to his chair and began rubbing the stock of his gun. "So dey come to da meetins. I guess Fran's got some high powered friend in da government who knows vat's going on, so dat's been helping. Ve don't hear much odervise."

Knute paused, thinking. "Dey're good folks," he said. "I tink dat Fran's a Cherman, but she don't act like vun most of da time. She probly a Norskie or sometin silly like dat."

Davecki asked, "So what's the plan with these mussels?"

"Don't know for real sure. I vasn't there to hear it first hand," Knute said. "But, Sulu said it vas happening soon off Visconsin Point. Problee going to ruint all da fishing."

"You get all your fish from Canada."

Knute hacked up some phlegm and spitooied it off the porch into the night. "Yah. Dat's tru too. You're one sharp fella, Deetecktive."

"Not as sharp as you, Knute."

"You got dat right, Sonny Boy."

"Well, I gotta go, ya old geezer," Davecki said. He stood. "How's the investing going?" He pulled his cycle gloves from the open Aerostich and zipped up.

"Harumph!" Knute harumphed. "Dat Nine-One-One crap da Osamer pulled really shot a hole in it for a vile." The old man grinned and looked quickly up at Davecki.

"And?"

"And vat?"

"And... what should I invest in nowadays?"

Knute snorted. "You take da cake you know dat?" The old guy deployed the Valmet from his lap and leaned it against the porch railing. With a sustained groan, he heaved himself up from the rocker and said, "I'll valk you past da gander. He's a bit cranky."

Davecki looked off the porch. A huge gray gander had appeared at the foot of the steps. It weaved its long neck in circles like a rising cobra. The great orange and hideously humped beak seemed to float dangerously in the dim, dank dark. The feeble yellow light glinted off the creature's perilous looking piebald eyes. "Geeze, that thing looks crazy," Davecki said.

"It ain't no crazier den you or I. He just don't like strangers."

"He should be used to strangers. There's none stranger than you, Knute."

"Takes vun to know vun."

Davecki laughed as the old guy lead the way off the porch. "Shush up, you big ugly varmint," Knute said as he swung his arms at the goose.

The animal weaved its long neck like a wary cobra, squawked loudly once and waddled swiftly into the darkness.

Davecki stayed close to the old man and said, "Seriously, Knute. Ever since you told me to buy Cisco when it was at six, I've been waiting for another great tip. If it weren't for you I couldn't have bought my boat."

"I got a tip for you. Da tip of my boot on your behind."

"You're something else. You know that? You can't give the old dog a little scrap from the master's table?"

The two got to the VFR. Davecki grabbed his helmet.

Knute said, "You are kind of a sorry old dog. I guess I could give you some advice."

"Gee thanks." Davecki pulled his helmet on.

"If I vas you, I'd look into a vay to legally sell dat vater."

"What!?!"

"You heard me."

"But I can't believe my ears." Davecki batted the side of his helmet hard a couple of times with the heel of his hand.

"Quit yer play acting. You look like a damn idjit. 'Cording to da international agreement every citizen living 'round da Great Lakes is entitled to a daily allotment of vater. If you vas smart as you tink you are, you'd figger out a vay to gather up everyone's excess allotment amount and sell it to Mexico or Texas. Dats vhat dey did in Canada."

Davecki stared. His mouth hung open. "I can hardly believe my ears!"

"Dat's *yer* problem. You got so much dirt in dem ears you could grow potatoes in dere. Listen up. See reality for vat it is."

Davecki threw a leg over the bike. "And dat, er, that, reality is?"

Knute snorted. He looked up at the stars. "Dat reality is dat vater is going to be sold and da smart vuns, da vuns who vant to get rich vill figger out how to sell it legal like."

"You are a piece of work, Knute."

"Tank you. Tank you," he looked at Davecki. "If I vas you, I'd run for Mayor and make da City of Superior rich selling the vater dat's rightfully deres."

Davecki, pulling his gloves on, laughed. "There's no way on God's green earth a cop would ever get elected Mayor of Superior. It's so weird hearing you talk like this. Vat, er, what happened to your devotion to FALSIES?"

Knute snorted. He turned and kicked at the gander as it snuck out of the night towards the talking duo. "Get off da VAY! You useless bag-o-feathers!" The bird squawked and retreated. Knute turned back to Davecki. "It's about time Superior made some money. Dere's nawting stopping dem 'cept demselves."

"If Superior got wealthy it would ruin everything," Davecki said.

Knute opened his mouth to say something, but Davecki punched the starter button and the YokoOno muffler rapped out a loud note of satisfaction.

Knute clamped his mouth shut and waved Davecki off with the standard Oulu dismissal.

32

People could survive their natural trouble all right if it weren't for the trouble they make for themselves.

—Ogden Nash

Mr. Nevada Kevin Black Bear Hallstrom Henderson, or whatever his name was supposed to be, plunked the optional remote cell phone antenna on the roof of the S-10. Behind him in the dim light of the parking lot, illuminated by the green glow of mercury vapor lights, a large sign atop an old building said: ROD'S RENTALS.

Henderson opened the cream-colored Vios laptop on the hood of the car. The door ajar chime chimed. A light flicked on inside the rental shop. The light of the computer screen burst out of the computer's lid. Henderson clicked a few keys, wedged his thumb around the mousepad. Inside the rental shop loud talking echoed. From behind the computer, the familiar sound of a modem dialing echoed. Nevada Henderson adjusted the ivory Stetson on his head and twined his arms across his chest. And he smiled.

And waited.

The computer screen flickered and flackered and jumped here and there. Henderson remained motionless. The commotion inside the rental shop subsided. When the computer screen stopped its gyrations, Henderson unfolded his arms and wiggled his fingers like a pianist about to perform Mendelsson's Scherzo in E minor.

I figured you'd be getting up just about now. It's ten hours ahead there, right? Good thing you were on-line, he typed and hit return.

A few seconds later, words scrolled across the next line. *Actually, we're just getting in. Went to a hell of a party at the Governor's mansion last night. Got to talking with Harrison Ford, and it got late.*

Henderson chuckled. *Just like you to be hobnobbing with the rich and famous while I'm up here hustling the hayseeds.*

That's your job. Mine is to keep raising the dough it takes to keep this operation going. What have you got for me?

I conned my way into a meeting and found out these hayseeds aren't so stupid after all. A couple of professors are planning to plug the pipe with genetically-altered zebra mussels.

There was a longer pause, then, if it was possible, Henderson felt the sub-ether tremble just seconds before a huge ***WHAT!!!*** appeared on the screen.

The cowboy laughed again. *Not to worry, Isak. I've got it covered. Right this moment I'm at a boat rental shop and am going out there to stop the insanity.*

Just how do you intend to do that? And why didn't you take the Bertram out from the McQuade Marina? I gave a hell of a lot of money to that PAC to get that put in and now I'm paying a hell of a lot of money to keep that tub moored there, to say nothing of keeping it stocked with munitions.

"Harumph!" Henderson said. He typed, *No time. They left the meeting and I followed them directly to their dock. They were farting around waiting for someone I think, so I hustled over to that rental shop by Nemadji Bay. Woke the guy up, but he came around when I gave him five hundred bucks. Said he had a nice twenty-six foot SeaRay available. I don't have a lot of time. They're probably getting underway as we speak, so to speak, so I've got to get a hustle on.*

In the darkness beyond the old Great Northern ore dock, out on the black waters of Superior Bay, a mighty roaring sound rushed off the water and up the landing slip.

Henderson looked out to sea. "That sounds like a helluva boat," he muttered.

Henderson jumped, startled by a voice behind him. "You got that right," Rental Rod said.

"Whoa. You scared me," Henderson said.

"Oh. Sorry," The six-foot-four, sandy haired man said. "Didn't mean to sneak up on you like that."

"No problem," Henderson said. "You know the sound of that boat?"

"None other like it on the western end of the lake. Guy named Nikos built it by hand from the keel up. Twin supercharged four-fifty-fours in it."

"Holy mackerel," Henderson said. "Why so much horsepower?"

"Oh, it's a huge old tub. Needs every pony it has. But, considering, it's pretty fast for its size and weight."

"I'll bet," Henderson said. "So, what's up? You got a boat for me?"

"Yeah. Friend of mine, Don Garner, said I could rent you his rig for the day. Three hundred bucks. That too steep?"

"Nope." Henderson reached into his front pocket and retrieved a roll of bills. He peeled off three Franklins and handed them to the tall man.

"I'll get the keys."

Henderson returned to his ICQing. A question was laid out behind the blinking cursor, *So what's your plan, Nevada?*

No real plan other than to put a stop to their plan the best way I know how, he typed.

The next line scrolled out, *Do what you gotta do, just try and avoid another loose end like the biker bum.*

I'll do my best boss, Henderson typed.

No doubt. I've got to get some sleep. I'll be home tomorrow night. Albertson out.

Henderson nudged the mouse around with his finger and clicked with his thumb just as the door to the office behind him slammed.

Henderson folded the computer away, jerked the stubby antenna off the roof with a yank on the black cord and threw the entire mess into the back seat. He slammed the door shut.

"Thank god. That chime was driving me nuts," Rod said as he walked over to a Harley sitting beside the steps of the office.

Henderson walked over to the machine. The sparkling gray paint gleamed under the street light's glare. "Nice bike. That's the new V-Rod isn't it?"

"Yeah, it is. I'm sorta fond of my toys. It's Rod's V-Rod," Rod said laughing. "Here's the boat keys. It's a yellow SeaRay. She's moored in slip twenty-one. Garner wasn't all that happy about being woke up at this hour. But the three hundred seems to have calmed him down considerably. It's the last slip on the dock." Rod threw a leg over his bike. "Long as I'm up, I'm going to wash my bike down by the fish cleaning gazebo. You want a ride to the end of the dock? It's a ways down there."

"Sure. Why not?"

Rod fired up the brand spanking new Harley. The throaty bellow of the engine echoed all around the parking lot and surrounding alder bushes along the shore beyond.

"Great sound," Henderson said as he straddled the rear fender.

"Not much of a seat for two," Rod yelled.

"No problem," Henderson yelled back as he settled on to the stingy seat.

Rod drove the bike toward the looming black dock in the distance. As they crested the little rise in the parking lot, Rod cut the engine. "We can coast all the way down this hill and out to the end of the pier. There might be someone sleeping overnight on their boat. No sense in pissing them off too bad. It'll be loud enough as I leave," he explained.

At the end of the pier, Henderson said, "Great Rod. I really appreciate this a lot. My wife will never suspect me now."

The taller man was busy pushing his bike back away from the edge of the dock. With raised eyebrows he said, "You sound like Larry Race all of sudden, Mr. Dosen. You sure you're not up to no good? I don't want any of my consignment boats involved in any shenanigans," the tall man said.

"Who the hell is Larry Race? As if I care. All I'm trying to do is sneak up on my wife while she's on her boyfriend's boat for the night. She thinks I'm in Hawaii on business and will be most upset when I climb aboard and catch them humping away like hamsters in their hutch."

Rental Rod eyeballed Henderson for a few more seconds. "I don't know. Maybe you should just give me back the keys. I don't have any tolerance for domestic disturbances."

Henderson took off his Stetson. He scratched his head and shuffled his feet. The hard leather of his heels thunked on the green treated planks of the dock. The echo reverberated across the dark water. "How's about another couple of hundred?" Henderson said. He pulled out his roll and peeled off two more Franklins.

"Just don't get me in any trouble, Mr. Dosen," Rod said as he took the money.

"Hey, a word to the wise. If I get into any trouble at all, you got my S-10 up there as collateral. The keys are in it. The computer's in it," Henderson said as he bent down to untie the bow line from the cleat on the dock. "And, if you're smart, if I don't come back by dawn, you'll take a peek in the duffel bag in the trunk before the landing starts getting busy."

Rod glanced up toward the landing. "Well, in that case, maybe you should just get yourself in as much trouble as you want, Mr. Dosen," he said.

Henderson scuttled toward the aft mooring line. "I'll do my best," he said.

Rod ignited his V-Rod and idled it back down the dock toward the fish cleaning gazebo.

Henderson fired up the SeaRay and headed out to the inland sea towards his intended victims.

33

Delays have dangerous ends.

—William Shakespear, *Henry VI, Part I*

f course, what he should have done was call B.D. It was standard operating procedure to keep in touch with the boss and report the facts, or the lack thereof, about the case du jour.

Or, in the case of Alphonse "Dave" Davecki, **NOT**.

B.D. always wanted to cut in on the action. For some odd reason the Chief of Police felt that his employees should do as they were told. Davecki was always trying to re-educate Callahan, but, it was tough teaching the old dog new tricks.

Or, Davecki could do what seemed right to his sleep-deprived, overstressed brain: he could head for *Steak Warning*, motor out to sea in search of additional facts to gather before contacting the boss.

You never know when a little thing like luck is going to break a case wide open, Davecki rationalized. His weary right brain added, *Plus, I wouldn't be adverse to a little up close and personal confrontation with the lake-stealing, Little Willie-murdering, Dolly-beating bastard who seems to be causing all this trouble.*

Speeding west at what could only be characterized as a fool-hardy rate, considering the blackness of the night, Davecki stared as far down U.S. Highway Two as was humanly possible considering the candlepower of the VFR's headlight. Suddenly, a flash of red erupted from the dashboard. He looked down. There on the dash the red call light indicator for his cell phone flashed. *Damn! Forgot to plug in the phone jack. Screw it. It's probably B.D. looking to poke his nose into my business.* The light flashed again. *Or, it could be Clara.*

The Blueberry Store flashed past on the left. *Screw it. I'm not stopping. I'm going straight to the dock. I'll check my messages then.*

The light flashed all the way to Maple. Then it stopped until

Poplar. The flashing went on all the way to Rapids Riverside and went out. *Someone's got a lot of patience to keep calling and letting it ring that much.*

Parking the VFR next to the tennis courts on Barker's Island, Davecki hustled down the dock into a fresh and warm southerly breeze to *Steak Warning*. *Should have stopped at Holiday and got some coffee or Vivarin.* He cast off and was out in Superior Bay just in time to open the throttles on the mighty twin V-eights so their roar could drown out the chirping of the cell phone in the cabin below.

Davecki sped past the ore docks, through the Superior Entry and out into the lake. It was pitch black. Vision was limited to seeing the bewitching lights of the Duluth hillside and about a one hundred foot, at best, radius around *Steak Warning*. Heedless of any collision, Davecki zoomed across the water at over forty miles an hour. Then he felt uneasy about his speed. He pulled back on the throttles. *Steak Warning* hauled itself down into the water and settled into a steady throbbing as it plowed H_2O. Looking around, seeing nothing, Davecki said, "This is useless." He cut the engines entirely and the boat collapsed into the murky water. He whetted his finger and held it above his head. *About five knots from the southwest. No need for a sea anchor. Last time I used that, Little Willie came a-calling.*

Davecki went below, fetched his cell phone and returned to the foredeck to set watch. *For what, I have no real idea*, he thought as he raised the phone to dial. Before his finger could touch the three, the Nokia in his hand chirped like a chickadee.

34

Hell is having no boundaries.

—Norm Stramenski
Lutheran cleric and author

t some unholy hour of the night Clara slipped out of the room where Dolly lay, finally asleep. Clara tugged the blanket draped across her shoulders tighter and picked up the cordless as she walked out to the porch.

Dolly had given a report to Officer Jimmy Hix, refused medical treatment, cried, talked, slept, woke screaming, cried some more, talked some more and refused to accept Jesus into her heart.

Clara had washed the wounded soul's wounds, listened, iced her bruises, listened some more, watched her sleep, gave her the plan of salvation three times, held her hand, listened more and accepted that the poor soul was so doubled over from the pain of her privileged life that no amount of salve—spiritual or physical—would be anything more than a temporary bandaid at this time.

Clara backed onto the wooden porch swing and pulled the blanket tight. She shivered in the cool air. She twisted the cordless phone out from under the blanket and dialed a number.

"Hi. My name is Clara Christmann and, I was wondering, um, I've been helping Detective Davecki..."

She smiled.

"Yes, I'm the one. Yes." She chuckled. "Well you tell Officer Hix thank you, but that I couldn't possibly."

Clara listened.

"Yes. Yes. Of course. No, that's not the case. I just wanted, was wondering if I could get his cell phone number to give him a report about Dolly."

Listening.

"No. Not a problem. I was just, hmmm. For some reason I sort of expected to hear from him by now. I'm not sure why I thought he'd check in..."

Listening.

"Oh. *You're* Connie. Yes. Yes he is, I agree."

Clara switched the phone to her other hand and sat silently.

"Okay. Okay. Yes I have it. Thanks."

Listening.

"Yes, I'll tell him. I feel exactly the same way Chief Callahan does. Thanks again."

Clara sighed, punched in seven numbers and waited. And waited. After a long minute or two she looked at the phone and punched the end button. She stared off into the darkness. Her lips moved. Her eyes closed. Her head nodded. Then she jerked awake, pushed the talk button and hit redial. And she waited. "I wonder if he's just being abstinent?" she said as she broke the connection again. She dozed again. She dreamed of birds singing in the lilac bushes beside the porch. She woke. "Ummm," she said, stretching. She dialed again. And... "Hi. Hope I'm not interrupting anything."

Listening.

"It was a lot like washing plastic bags."

Listening.

"That's because you've never had to be frugal in your life."

Listening.

"Washing plastic bags is frustrating and time consuming, but productive because you know you're saving money so you do it despite the frustration."

Listening.

"No, she didn't say much of anything useful about her boyfriend. The useful I had in mind is more of a spiritual nature."

Listening.

"Yes, I am aware that you are trying to be a spirit detective now."

Listening.

"No, I don't think that's funny."

Listening. Clara turned her head to the east. The sky showed a very slight decrease in the amount of darkness over Allouez.

"Yes, I realize the time. I'm too keyed up to sleep. I wanted to fill you in about Dolly."

Listening.

"Okay. Okay. No. She refused medical attention. I cleaned her up and gave her four Ibuprofen and then listened a lot. No. No, she didn't say anything about him. She did ask me to pray for her. I asked her if she wanted to give her life to Jesus, and she said no. She did manage to surprise me though."

Listening.

"She **asked** me to pray for her..." Clara unwrapped herself from the blanket slightly. "...and you, of all people."

Listening.

"No. I did. Wouldn't you like to know."

Clara chuckled.

"Maybe I'll do that sometime. God knows you could use it."

Clara turned her head left. Down the avenue, a slight mist was rising like a ghost from the blacktop under the street light.

"I'm not going to tell you. I will tell you that I asked God to heal Dolly's cuts and bruises and grant her peaceful sleep. I thanked Him that Dolly had come to me and asked that she might see His love for her. It was nice to hear her say 'Amen' when I finished."

Listening.

"No. She fell right into a deep sleep. That wasn't too long ago."

Listening.

Clara coughed out a laugh. "No, I don't think that spirit detectives have guardian angels who get them to their cell phones at just the right time. I think that spirit detectives, the good ones, are conscientious and considerate. They sleep in beds and keep in touch with their loved ones and superiors."

Long silence.

"Yes, I'm here."

Silence.

"No, I'm not speechless. I'm just trying to think of the right answer."

Listening.

"Okay. Okay. I get your point. There is no wrong answer in this case. I'm very, very tired. It was a Freudian slip. I am concerned about you is all. I can't help it if I express myself poorly in an unguarded moment. 'Fatigue makes cowards of us all,' Vince Lombardi said."

Listening.

Silence.

Clara smiled.

"You've got that right, Detective. I wouldn't say it that way, but yes, I'm quite certain your posterior would be in that condition if love did run up and do that."

Clara laughed loudly. A squirrel chattered from the giant hard maple tree across the street.

35

To do a great right, do a little wrong.

—William Shakespeare, *The Merchant of Venice*

In the small hours of the night, one pale light lit up the deck of the *L.L. Bean*. The lake, calm for once, quietly rocked the three people and five barrels of zebra mussels standing on the aft deck. Well wrapped against the chill of predawn, Professors Cameroon and Hansen watched anxiously as Jensen prepared for his dive. The mussels napped.

"Don't forget, Simon—open up the barrels as close to the intakes as you can."

Simon Jensen looked up from spitting on his mask. "I know what I'm doing. And you've told me that at least four times in the last ten minutes."

"Fran. Relax. Let Simon do his work."

Jensen harumphed and swung his tank onto his back.

Cameroon cleared his throat. "Simon…are you going to be warm enough?"

Jensen froze. "Unbelievable," was all he said and he turned away. He back-flapped to the port gunnel and sat. Jensen nodded at the professors. "Okay," he said. "As long as you both have been harassing me, I'll take my turn. When I finish with the first one, I'll surface. Don, you make sure you have the next barrel clamped and winched over the gunnel. Right?"

"Right," Cameroon said.

"Fran, when Don gives you the okay, steer for the next waypoint on the GPS. I'll hang on to the barrel for a tow. It won't exactly be water-skiing, but we'll get to all five inlets fast. We want to be outta here before daylight." He looked over his shoulder. "I'm glad there's no chop, you can keep the barrel closer to the water, Don. I'll be able to hang on better. But don't get it too low while we're under way.

They're heavy as hell and if they start dragging in the water that skimpy deck crane will probably come right off its moorings."

He glanced at the wind vane atop the instrument cluster above the pilot house. "Looks like only a few knots of wind from the southwest, so you won't have too hold to much correction on the wheel, Fran."

"Right," Hansen said.

Jensen reached up to his face mask. "Don, when she cuts the motor, don't start lowering immediately. Let 'er get reversed and stopped before you play out any cable."

"Right," Cameroon said.

Without an instant's hesitation, Jensen seated his mask and mouthpiece and vanished overboard making a loud splash.

Cameroon grabbed the winch's hand control. He toggled the switch. The electric winch whirred. The small gantry crane creaked under the weight, but the heavy barrel moved upward slowly. Cameroon and Hansen pushed the package over the gunnel. The winch whirred as the barrel lowered away. "Not quite as fast and dirty as throwing them overboard wholesale like what Honeywell and the Defense Department did," Cameroon said.

"And, not nearly as mysterious," Hansen added. "At least we know exactly what's in these barrels."

"And we have the antidote," Cameroon said as the winch whirred.

Simon, treading water, reached up and touched the fifty-five gallon drum as it neared the surface. As man and barrel sank from sight, the last thing to be seen above the surface of the black water was Jensen's neoprene hand and arm waving good-bye.

36

One of the great disadvantages of hurry is that it takes such a long time.

—G.K. Chesterton

The lake didn't want to get nervous and make waves that would upset the barrel operation taking place 500 yards offshore. But, on the other hand, the inattentive police officer was once again sound asleep on the job.

Mustering its energy, the mighty lake did everything in its power to initiate a sublime action. Being so huge, the grand stroke, the mighty storm, the huge frightening fog, your basic monster wave or three (the better to sink large ships with) was easier for the Big Lake to pull off. The subtle stuff required a tremendous concentration, a sharp focus of the elemental energy that was the essence of the monster body of water.

But, subtle is as subtle does, and the lake coughed up a sluice of water that soaked Davecki from the waist down.

"Damn!" he yelled as he jumped up from his repose on the foredeck.

"What the?"

He looked around.

Nothing.

"Criminey! What's going on?"

He spun around in search of answers and saw only blackness. But, there was the sound.

The sound of an inboard/outboard motoring across the water not too far in the distance. Davecki scuttered across the deck and jumped into the afterdeck. He reached into the salon and pulled out a pair of compact Nikon binoculars from behind the sink. Sweeping the binocs around in the dark he muttered, "I'd make one sorry bat." Sweeping, sweeping, sweeping the binoculars while trying to triangulate the sound, Davecki shuffled across the deck panning madly for the sight of running lights in the direction the sound seemed to be coming from.

"Gotcha!" he yelped. The light gathering optics enabled him to see a yellow hulled SeaRay humming out from the Superior Entry at full speed. The phosphorescent spray of the bow wave glowed like an old man's white moustache. "There's one boat that absolutely, positively needs to be followed," Davecki said.

He put the binocular strap over his head and rushed to the teakwood dashboard. *Steak Warning* fired up instantly under his command and surged forward at a quarter throttle. Davecki raised the glasses. "Damn!" he cussed. He put the glasses down and steered toward the rapidly diminishing sound of the departing SeaRay's engine noise. After a few moments, Davecki eased his own twin throttle handles forward. *Why'd Nikos make this thing so loud?* Davecki thought.

Once *Steak Warning* was up on plane, Davecki looked through the binocs again. He panned forth and back a few times. "Damn!" He put the binocs down and turned the wheel to the port a few degrees. After a few seconds, *Steak Warning* heaved up. *That's his starboard wake.* Davecki held the port heading less strongly. Seconds later *Steak Warning* started to heave up again. *That's his port wake.* Davecki corrected his heading to the starboard. *I can't see like a bat, but I can drive a boat by the braille method. Good thing the lake is as flat as glass.*

In a few seconds *Steak Warning* rose on the SeaRay's starboard wake and Davecki corrected to the port again. Again he raised the field glasses and scanned across the bow for a few degrees to port and starboard.

There!

Davecki eased back on his power. *Steak Warning* slowed. He brought up the glasses again and checked his quarry. *Lead on, McDuff. I'll just hang back here and see what you're up to*, Davecki thought easing back on the throttle a little more.

After a few minutes of running, and after several port to starboard corrections, Davecki had the hang of braille navigation. He looked to his right. Far, far off in the east, he could actually see a horizon. *Sun-up in an hour or so.* He returned his gaze to zero degrees off the bridge and instantly grabbed the throttle.

The running lights he'd been pursuing were dead in the water ahead only one hundred yards!

Davecki slammed the throttles backwards and rammed the gearbox levers into neutral. *Steak Warning* sank off plane into the water. Davecki looked beyond the SeaRay where a large boat sat. It seemed to be at anchor.

"No!" he said to the steering wheel. "That thing is moving."

At that instant, Davecki saw a flash. An instant later the sound of a small handgun's report boomed in across the water.

"Cripes!" he yelped. He jammed the gearboxes in and rammed the throttles forward.

Steak Warning, for all its monstrous power below decks, was a heavy tub. Its propellers churned for all they were worth, and the boat surged mightily forward, but the effect was rather like a large flat stirring paddle moving slowly, slowly through molasses in January.

Davecki pushed on the steering wheel. Up ahead, he saw and heard more gunfire coming from the SeaRay. He pushed hard on the steering wheel, as if he could make the boat go faster.

As *Steak Warning* surged forward, Davecki yanked hard on the black ash wheel lock handle. Rudder secured, he dove down into the salon and ransacked his Aerostich for his Glock. He hauled ass back topside in time to see the SeaRay start racing away from the scene.

Davecki held his course. The SeaRay swung away to port. In the growing light, Davecki saw, as he closed on the bigger boat, the name *L.L. Bean* painted in white on the black bow.

He pulled back on the throttles and disengaged the gearing.

A man rushed to the gunnel of the big boat. He was holding his right arm with his left hand. Blood flowed from between the fingers that clutched the wound.

"Superior Police!" Davecki yelled. "What's going on?"

"That guy came alongside and started to board us without permission. Then he heard you coming up from behind and all of a sudden started shooting," the white haired gentleman aboard the *Bean* yelled.

"Are you okay?" Davecki asked.

"Just a flesh wound," the man answered.

A woman poked her head out from behind the glass door of the pilot house. Right in the middle of the glass, a wide, circular spider web of broken glass highlighted a bullet hole. "I can take care of him," she yelled. Waving at the departing SeaRay, she screeched, "GO GET HIM!"

Davecki grinned. *Happy to oblige you, maam*! and he knocked *Steak Warning* up into gear and pounded the throttles to their max. As *Steak Warning* careened around to the port, he wasn't sure, but to Davecki, it seemed like there might have been a diver popping up in the gloomy wake he left behind.

37

They who lose today may win tomorrow.

—Cervantes
Don Quixote (1605)

ar chases are stupid. Boat chases are REALLY stupid. The SeaRay had a big lead. It was lighter by several tons, had less horsepower by hundreds, but was so far in front of Davecki, all he could do was follow at about the same speed the perp was going.

This is no fun, he thought.

Cops generally don't like high speed chases. Most cops want to go home after their shift and plan their next fishing or hunting expedition, or go work on the book case they're building in their well equipped woodworking shop.

But, then there are the rookies who have a need for speed. And there are the NASCAR driver wannabes. There are a lot of rookies and race car drivers on every force all over the world. Ever see that COPS teaser where the two good old boys are gleefully bragging about their "right" to go 90 mph against traffic on a one-way street? Machismo addicts.

Davecki thought highly of them. As *Steak Warning* droned after the yellow SeaRay in the growing light, he thought, *COPS would never come up here to do video segments on boat chases.*

Davecki locked the helm again and went into the salon. He came out a second later with his cell phone. *I wonder where this guy thinks he's going anyway?*

As he held the phone to his ear, he looked to his left. There, far to the east, just popping up from the watery horizon was the sun, blazing yellow. About halfway from the horizon to his position, Davecki saw the outline of a big old laker heading in to port.

"Yeah, Connie," Davecki yelled. "I know it's hard to hear me. I'm calling from the boat. Yes, I know she called. Say, if you don't mind, could you send a couple of squads down to Barkers? I'm chasing a yellow-hulled SeaRay that was just shooting up the UW-S research vessel."

Davecki listened.

"Yes, you heard me right. Shots were fired."

Listening.

"I don't know which pier. I'll call you back. My low battery warning is beeping. I've got to hang up. I'll call you back when we get into the inner passage. Maybe then I'll know where he's heading."

Davecki punched the power button and stashed the mobile into his pants pocket.

Up ahead the SeaRay darted into the Wisconsin Entry. Davecki followed. The roar of both boat's engines echoing off the concrete breakwaters was loud. When both boats entered the narrow confines of the channel proper, the sound was positively deafening.

Amazing, Davecki thought. *I'm actually gaining on him.* He hadn't noticed it, but, *Steak Warning*, over the course of the last two miles, had closed the gap.

The boats spurted out of the entry channel like two bobbers shooting up from below the surface. To the left, the Clive R. Barker ore carrier was taking on pellets at the BNSF taconite facility.

Thirty seconds later, Davecki yelled out, "What the?" to no one in particular.

Instead of zooming toward Barker's Island as he'd expected, Davecki saw the SeaRay haul hard to port and careen beneath the ancient Great Northern dock.

"Crap!" he yelled.

He picked the cell from his own pocket and hit the speed dial.

"Yeah! Connie!" he yelled. "He's heading into Loon Landing. Send the squads there. And remember, he's armed and dangerous."

Davecki listened.

"No. I don't think so. Only one that I know of..."

Davecki shook the phone. "Damn!" he said.

The battery died just as he attempted to dunk the gunnel into the lake by hauling over hard to port in pursuit.

38

It is morally wrong to allow suckers to keep their money.

—Canada Bill Jones

 evada Henderson knew exactly where he was heading. He too had his cell phone out and was shouting into it. "Yeah. Hi. This is Isak Albertson. I'm going to be coming in in about a half hour or so and was wondering if you could get the SR-20 fueled and warmed up on the apron for me. I'll be in a bit of a rush."

He listened.

"Okay. Fine. No problem. Whatever you want to charge, feel free. I'll be there soon." Henderson stuffed the cell phone into his tan western cut sport jacket pocket and pointed the SeaRay directly at Loon Landing.

Ahead, parked in the growing light was Rental Rod's shiny new V-Rod. It was dripping wet and drying in the early morning light. The owner was nowhere to be seen. Henderson kept the throttles on full. The SeaRay charged up to the inclined boat landing and crashed up onto dry land.

Henderson jumped out of the skidding boat before it stopped grinding the fiberglass keel off on the rough blacktop. He ran like a whitetail up the incline, past the cleaning station and up to the parking lot. As he crested the little rise, there at the back of his S-10 was Rental Rod. He was leaning into the open trunk. Henderson sprinted up, tore off his hat and jerked the driver's door open.

"What's all the commotion?" Rod asked, motioning toward the landing.

"Sort of in a rush, Rod. Got the keys?" Henderson asked.

"Sure do. Right here," Rod said holding up the key fob. "I was just doing as you instructed and checking in the trunk, seeing it's after dawn and all," he said as he tossed Henderson the keys.

"No problem at all, Rod," Henderson said as he caught the keys with his right hand. "Just grab that duffel out of there and close the trunk if you please, 'cause I'm exiting stage left in a hurry."

"Wife didn't care much for your unexpected appearance I take it?" Rod said as he grunted the big green duffel out of the trunk.

"Something like that," Henderson said as he jammed himself into the car.

Rod strolled to the driver's side door.

Henderson powered down the window. "You might want to patch up your friend Garner's feelings about his boat with a little of the fix-em that's in there." He nodded toward the bag.

"Whatever you say, Mr. Dosen. At Rod's Rentals we aim to please."

Henderson started the S-10 and peeled rubber exiting the parking lot.

Rod ambled to his office and went inside for a total of about two minutes. When he exited, without the bag, over the hill of the parking lot, he heard the sound of his motorcycle being started. "What the?" he said just a two white SPD squads screeched into the lot.

39

The art of living lies not in eliminating but in growing with troubles.

—Bernard M. Baruch

ow motorcycle chases, are another thing entirely. Davecki just could not do the type of damage to *Steak Warning* that he saw the SeaRay sustain. He actually slowed down and let his boat coast slowly up to land. In the distance, over the hill, he heard sirens entering the parking lot. As *Steak Warning* nudged up against the shore, Davecki looked past the beached SeaRay and saw a sight sent from heaven. There sitting in the parking lot was Rental Rod's brand new, silver Harley Davidson V-Rod.

"Thank you God! It pays to be a Spirit Detective," Davecki shouted. He reached into the salon, grabbed his Aerostich and jumped overboard. He sprinted as fast as he could toward the bike while stepping into his safety suit. He zipped and tucked and donned the gloves that had stayed stuck in the map pocket.

As he raced toward the bike he prayed, *Come on, Rodney old buddy, stay true to form and let the keys be in the ignition.*

Davecki threw a leg over and thought, *Thank God!* He fired up the Porsche designed engine. Jamming first gear, the rear tire broke loose and smoked up as the bike slued away from the cleaning station and scooted up the hill like a scared rabbit. *This thing passes.*

Over the hill, he saw the squads, squadmen and Rodney. "Which way did he go?" he yelled. Two uniformed arms pointed west. A third held out a helmet from which dangled a curly cord.

Davecki put the helmet on.

"He's driving a red S-10 Blazer," Officer Jimmy Hix yelled.

Rod plugged the phone jack in as Davecki strapped into the helmet. Rod yelled, "Be careful with my bike!"

Davecki answered by burning rubber. The new Hog didn't handle all that well at speed compared to the VFR. But it sure went fast in a straight line. Between Loon Landing and Perkins he kept his eyes on the road ahead and knew only that the speedo was registering in triple digits. He pushed and pulled the heavy bike around cars, campers, pickup trucks and heavy transport trucks like they were pylons at Keith Code's Superbike school in Glendale, California.

Suddenly the helmet phone chirped. He started thumbing buttons until the chirping stopped. "This is Alphonse Dave Davecki. I'm too busy to come to the phone right now. But if you'll...,"

"DAVECKI YOU ASS! Quit playing around! You're the worst cop in the world!"

"I love you too, Chief. As a matter of fact, I'm hardly a cop at all. But, be that as it may, how did you get this number?"

"God dammit Davecki, Connie's getting flooded with calls!"

"Sorry about that, Chief, but I'm trying to catch the bad guy. Seriously, how'd you get this number?"

"And you call yourself a detective? Like that's some big mystery. Jimmy Hix called after you left Loon Landing. Why are you always so, so... theatrical?"

"Just call me King Dramatica, Chief. All I'm trying to do is catch the bad guy."

"Couldn't you catch him a little slower?"

"Hey Chief, you're preaching to the choir. I'll slow down just as soon as the bad guy slows down. I'll chop throttle and pull him over and give him a nice little ticket for murder."

"Wise ass. What's going on?"

"In the cosmic sense, the universe is unfolding as it should oh Great one..."

"DAVECKI!" Callahan's voice screeched in the headset.

"Sorry, Chief. Seriously, I'm after the guy that killed Little Willie. And I won't catch him at all if I don't know which way he went. Is he heading to Duluth or is he staying in Wisconsin?"

"Connie's getting calls from the bridge." Davecki zipped past the exit to Highbridge Boulevard and reefed the handlebar of the Harley around the on-ramp.

Pulling hard up the long bridge incline, Davecki tilted the bike around an emerald green Saturn and wove around a Keselek Koncrete redi-mix truck. As he zoomed under the magnificent arches of the stately bridge, Davecki couldn't resist looking right at the even more magnificent lake stretching off across the planet toward Ontario. There, shining in the sunlight was Gitchi Gummi, blue and monstrous. The only flaw on the turquoise skin was the black blemish of the incoming laker about a half mile offshore. As always, the sight of something so much bigger than himself jolted him, changed his view of the world. He sighed. The huge slice of nature pie made the lunacy matter less. He sighed again and returned to the task at hand. He scanned ahead for a sign of the S-10.

What he saw was a monster Expedition with a red Kojak flashing above the driver's side door.

Davecki flew by the tub-o-guts like it was in reverse. He said into the open mic, "Callahan? You shouldn't be driving that thing backwards in traffic."

"Funny. You shouldn't be going a hundred and fifty on a public roadway."

"Very funny, Chief. Which way did he go?"

"My scanner says Duluth PD's getting calls reporting a speeder on Garfield."

Davecki dove the V-Rod from the left lane hard to the right to catch the off-ramp before it was too late.

"Well Chief, now that we're out of our jurisdiction we'll see how diplomatic you can be. Serves you right for always ragging on me to clean up my social skills."

"Shut up and drive. I can see him up ahead. He's by RMS."

"Good thing you're so high in the air in that car, Chief. I can't see diddly from this thing. It's too low slung."

"He turned right."

"Where the hell is he going?"

"DPD is wondering the same thing."

"I've got a bad feeling about this, Chief."

40

The torment of precautions often exceeds the dangers to be avoided. It is sometimes better to abandon oneself to destiny.

—Napoleon I

Davecki and his boss chased Henderson across Superwood flats along Railroad Street. The S-10 turned right on Canal Street and fled across the Aerial Lift Bridge just after the stop-arm went down. The bridge deck started up to let the incoming lake carrier pass. The bridge operator saw what was happening but was helpless to abort the lift long enough to let the car get safely off the deck.

The Patricia M. Stewart-Cort was coming in and no-way could a thousand foot ship stop just because some lunatic crashed his SUV through gates.

The bridge deck started up. The S-10 sped across the 300 foot long steel grate deck and spit itself off, smashing through the stop-arm on the Park Point side.

Davecki, Callahan and four DPD squads screeched to a halt at the foot of the bridge.

Davecki flipped up the face shield on Rod's helmet. Callahan jumped out of his land yacht. The squadman who had erupted out of his car approached the two and said, "I'm Sergeant O'Kash. What the hell's going on?"

"This is Davecki. I'm Callahan. SPD."

"You're the Chief over there?"

"Right," Callahan said. "We're in pursuit of the nut who killed that biker last week."

Two other Duluth cops trotted up. "This is Officer Scott and Officer DeRosa," O'Kash said. "Callahan and Davecki, SPD," O'Kash said to his co-workers. "They're after the guy that offed that biker."

"The one the Coast Guard found floating in the lake last week?" DeRosa asked.

"The very," Davecki answered. He eyeballed the sky. "You got a chopper that could get me across?"

O'Kash laughed. "What do you think we are? The L.A.P.D. or something? We don't have that kind of money."

"We could call SMDC and ask if their Evac chopper is available," Scott said.

"I'll get on it," DeRosa said sprinting toward his squad.

"I can't believe it. Right here in the Zenith City, there's no police chopper?" Callahan spouted.

"He's getting away!" Davecki said.

"Now calm down, you two," O'Kash said. "Scotty, call the Coast Guard."

"Already done. Dispatch says they're sending a boat right away. It don't matter much anyway. He's trapped out there. There's no way off."

Davecki glared over the gap between the mainland and Park Point.

"Calm down, detective," Callahan said.

"I've got a bad feeling about this. I think he's headed for Sky Harbor and that he has a plane there."

"Take a chill pill, Davecki. The Coast Guard is on its way," Callahan said.

DeRosa ran up. "SMDC's chopper is in Ely medi-vacing a logger who got run over by a skidder."

"You got any squads over there?" Davecki asked.

"Nope. All's we got over there right now in the way of enforcement are two college wildlife interns from UMD who are rounding up rampant bunnies."

"Just frigging great," Davecki shouted. He waved his arm.

"Nice suit," Officer Scott said.

Davecki opened his mouth to speak, but the words were completely obliterated by a tremendous blast from a ship's horn. The obnoxious sound continued for a long interval. This blast was followed by two short burps from the same horn.

Davecki opened his mouth again to restate his drowned out words. Lucky for him B.D. did not hear the words, because the Aerial lift bridge's horn answered with its own deafening blast.

"We'll just have to wait for the Stewart-Cort to pass. By then the Coast Guard can pick you up or you can leave your bike here and we can take after him officially in our squads. Where's he gonna go anyway, Detective? What's your rush? There's no way back except on this bridge. He's as good as caught," O'Kash said.

"Like I said. I think he's headed for the airport. He's gonna take off for Canada and we'll never see him again," Davecki said, staring at the Duluth sergeant. He looked away. To his left, he saw the huge prow of the Stewart-Cort gliding past under the lift bridge. He looked away. He looked down the street. There on the stoop of Grandma's Marketplace, he saw a black-haired man standing. Davecki waved. "Hi, Tom," he shouted.

The man waved back and smiled. *Now there's a can-do guy. He should be a cop*, Davecki thought. *He jumped at the chance to open that store and manage it*, Davecki recalled. "Hey!" Davecki said out loud. "Tom jumped at the chance, so can I."

Callahan, O'Kash, and the uniforms looked at Davecki.

"What?" Callahan asked.

"Hmmmm," O'Kash said. "Maybe we should call the Air National Guard."

Davecki stared at the inbound laker gliding by. "Why is that thing so low. It's gotta be loaded."

"I don't like your look Detective," Callahan said.

"Probably taking a load of Michigan limestone to the Hallet Dock," O'Kash said.

"You must be right," DeRosa said. "Usually the sides are way higher than the road."

"Well isn't that just peachy," Davecki said. He flipped the face shield down. He fired up the V-Rod.

"Davecki stop!" Callahan said. "Even Evel Knievel wouldn't jump the Duluth Ship Canal."

41

Sometimes I go about pitying myself and all the time I am being carried across the sky by beautiful clouds.

—Ojibway Saying

Davecki burned a donut on the pavement and zoomed back down Lake Avenue.

"No way!" O'Kash shouted. He waved his arms to stop Davecki.

Davecki turned in the intersection between Mikey McMurphy's McDeli and the Marketplace.

O'Kash continued waving. He stood, obstructing the path, with feet spread apart.

Manager Tom nodded at Davecki.

Davecki nodded back. He oriented the bike and revved the mill. The engine screamed up to six grand and Davecki burned out again. He clicked into second and the bike stopped sluing beneath him. *This thing is a real dragster*, Davecki thought as the bike accelerated.

Between Davecki and the up-ramp of the bridge, Officers O'Kash, DeRosa and Scott were all waving and forming a human roadblock.

Behind them, Davecki saw Callahan dragging broken pieces of lumber from the stop arm off the roadway. "Good on ya," Davecki said into his helmet.

The V-Rod didn't know what it was doing. It was just supplying the requested amount of power to the rear wheel. Davecki didn't really know what he was doing either. It was all instinct, or insanity. He glanced at the speedo. 85 mph. Not very fast, he thought. He kept the throttle twisted. He pointed the headlight toward the opening between the bridge legs. A prurient thought tried to stomp onto center stage, but Davecki yelled, "No!" His attention focused on the launch ramp, he barely saw the DPD cops scatter as he screamed through their frail human baracade.

The bike shot toward the apex of the approach apron. Davecki looked at the speedo. 115 mph.

Here goes, he thought.

The bike left the ground.

Davecki's hypervigilant mode engaged.

The engine over-revved instantly.

Davecki shut the throttle.

Everything went quiet.

The wind whistled in the helmet.

The phone rang.

"Buzz, buzz, buzz," the sound echoed in his ears.

Davecki considered jabbing the PTT button, but, before he did, he looked down. *That's a hundred feet of open water below me.* Then, into his downward line of sight, the deck of the massive ore carrier hove into view. *I'm sure glad they built the Stewart-Cort a hundred and five feet wide.*

He landed on the deck. Instantly he braked. The bike squatted to a stop at the port side. He revved up again and spun the rear end of the bike around. He shot down the deck dodging tools and bumping over hoses. Ahead, at the base of the superstructure, deckhands started appearing. Up on the flying bridge, a man stood. That man was waving violently. *Everybody's waving at me today.*

Davecki waved back.

Then he got down to business.

He raced to the gathering of men. He flipped up his face shield. "Hi!" he yelled.

Everyone stared except a big man with close-cropped black hair and a barrel chest. That man had "Jim" embroidered over the left pocket of a grease stained work shirt. Jim said, "What in the world's going on?"

Davecki said, "Well, I don't really have time to explain, but, I can tell you I'm a Superior cop and I need to get to Park Point as fast as I can. Could you drop those gunnel chains for me?"

Jim grinned. "Hey, if you're that superior of a cop, I'll do anything to help," he said.

Jim ran to the port side and unsnapped the chain hasp there. The entire length of safety chain sagged to the deck.

Davecki zipped the bike over to the starboard gunnel. He turned and, like Brett Farve calculating the tangent of a pass to Bill Schroeder, Davecki estimated the ratios of westbound to southbound movement and threw in a little fudge factor considering the narrowness of the opening between the bridge's south legs.

Suddenly, he decided to knock off the fudge factor. Something was happening here. It was exactly clear to Davecki in his hyperstate. He suddenly saw it all. He saw the length of the deck. He saw the drop in elevation to the landing zone. He saw the opening of the bridge legs grow wide, wider, widest. He realized anyone in their right mind could fling a speeding bike through such a wide opening. The distance between the bridge's legs suddenly looked like the Grand Canyon.

Jim waved him on.

"Everyone's waving at meeee," Davecki sang the old Glen Campbell song into his helmet. "Can't hear a word they're saying!!!!"

He dumped the clutch. He sped across the deck. The bike resumed its relentless pursuit of perfection in acceleration.

The newest, biggest ore boats are indeed 105 feet wide. At the Soo Locks, they fit in the lock with only a few feet to spare on either side. At the Ship Canal, by comparison, there's ample room to spare. On any given Sunday, on any given passage, there's two hundred feet of excess space between a bulk carrier's hull and the bulwarks of the ship canal. It was this gap that Davecki contended with.

On this day the good Captain of the Patricia M. Stewart-Cort had commenced his turn into the Duluth Ship Basin a little early. The result of that maneuver is always that the big ships shave a few feet off their port clearance.

This was a good thing for Davecki and his soon to be airborne V-Rod.

Another good thing for Davecki was, Jim the chain lowerer was no slouch. With the measured calmness of a man who had been at sea all his life, Jim grabbed a deck hose and bull shipped it in an arc from the flat of the deck into the crease of the weld where the hull sheeting jutted up above the deck steel.

This happened just in time as Davecki accelerated to takeoff. Davecki grinned. *Good old Jim. Jim's da-man*, Davecki thought as the front tire lifted off without the benefit of being blown out by the sharp edge.

The bike did its thing. It shot into midair without hesitation.

Davecki did his thing. Drawing on his enduro riding experience he flung his butt towards the tail light as much as the forward-type controls allowed. He yanked back on the handlebars as hard as he could.

The nose of the heavy bike didn't exactly come up. But it didn't tilt down either. Davecki was satisfied. *Nice old bike. Good boy.* The vision of the front wheel dropping, dropping, dropping... the bike doing a horrible, terrible, crashing, smashing endo vanished.

It was over in a matter of seconds. The bike sailed above the blue choppy water below. Its trajectory carried Davecki right onto the double yellow line painted on the blacktop ramp that was the southern approach of the bridge. The bike swerved a bit upon landing, but... Davecki had nailed it.

Hundreds of people and two Texans had driven thousands of aggregate miles to watch Robbie Knievel jump the Colorado River in his rocket powered "motorcycle." *And they all paid big bucks for the priviledge thereof,* Davecki thought as he scorched the pavement accelerating hard for wherever Nevada Henderson was going. *Maybe I missed my calling.*

42

Few things are impossible to diligence and skill.

—Samuel Johnson, *Rasselas* (1759)

t the Sky Harbor Airport, Henderson parked the red S-10 next to the already unteathered Cirrus SR-20. He took the time to retrieve his Stetson from the back seat. He clambered into the plane, yelled "CLEAR" and started the engine. Without benefit of a preflight checklist, he began his taxi. He steered the aircraft toward the runway. He pointed the nose east, into the wind, and opened the throttle. The prop spun up. The aircraft surged and shuddered. The airplane headed toward 85 miles an hour and lift-off and freedom.

Henderson looked out the left window. Instead of seeing the blur of sand dunes and runway vanishing quickly to his rear, he saw a silver motorcycle pacing him on the runway.

43

Sometimes you knows 'em by the plane of their face.

—Rodriel Heukenlein

s Davecki raced the bike past the chain link gateway into the airport, he saw the SR-20 taxi away. He saw it turn and surge into takeoff. *Too late*, he thought. "The dirty rat!" he yelled out loud.

"No way," he yelled again.

Davecki slalomed the bike through the usual flotsam of a small airport. The odd Piper, the ubiquitous Cessna 185s, the normal Suburbans parked next to the snaked lanyards of absent aircraft that were busy coursing their owners and passengers to very expensive hamburgers in Cable, Ironwood, or Bemidji.

Once through the personal transportation obstacle course, Davecki gassed the V-Rod. *This thing has really got guts!*

It caught the SR-20 easily. He waved the pilot down. It was indeed the same man, for there, on the head looking out from the side window, was the ivory Stetson. Below the broad brimmed hat, a face of rage glared at Davecki.

Geeze. Lighten up fella. Davecki flipped up his helmet. He yelled, "Stop in the name of the LAW!" Davecki cursed himself, *That was lame*. The phone in his ear buzz, buzz, buzzed again. "Not NOW, Kato!" he yelled to the sub-ether. The ringing in his ears stopped.

The plane kept going. In fact, it lifted off the ground.

Davecki knew the jig was about up. The play was about over. The ol' fat lady was about to sing. *Am I ever glad I went to motorcycle training school in Toledo*, he encouraged himself, *otherwise this could be very bad.* And he did the only thing he could do.

He swerved the bike in behind the left wing of the plane and got up close and personal with the fuselage. Without hesitation he grabbed the recessed hand-hold in the fuselage with his right hand

Like magic, Davecki rose from the V-Rod's seat. His head

snapped downward, pulled by the phone connection until the line broke free.

Sorry, Rod. Hope you have insurance.

The bike swooped left once, then right once and then it flipped into the air.

The plane was not high enough to escape the upward trajectory of the Harley. Acting like Michael Jordan reaching for a rising rebound, the Hog soared upward as if in slow motion. It smacked the Cirrus in the underbelly, just below the tail assembly.

All this Davecki observed as he tried to get purchase on the left wing with his boots. He was not successful. His added weight caused the aircraft to settle back to the ground. The tires chirped. Little puffs of smoke erupted from the contact with the concrete runway.

Davecki smelled the smoke and knew something of the tire's temperatures, for, as the aircraft lowered back to earth, so did his feet. Then his legs touched down. Then he started to feel the temperature rise in the knee pads.

All cops cope with stress in their own unique and always creative ways. Many have affairs. It IS the uniform. Lots drink to excess. Bars LOVE off-duty cops on premises. Current circumstances precluded standard coping mechanisms, so, Davecki's left brain sang, *Merrily I skid along, skid along, skid along. Merrily I skid along, my fair Cirrus.*

His right brain put in an order for additional adrenaline.

As the urgent order for additional go-juice was being processed, the left brain added, *So this is what it feels like to be an old muffler dragging under a junker.*

His right brain said, *Better lock and load the helmet.*

Davecki flipped the Duo-Tech closed.

The plane's engine revved higher.

Then all the vibration and skidding sensations ended. Davecki looked down. The ground was falling away very quickly.

"Criminey," Davecki said into the air.

44

When all else fails, try, try again.

enderson banked the Cirrus hard to the left and pulled back on the yoke. "Don't stall on me now baby," he cooed. He looked out the left window. "What a jerk," he said.

When Park Point below turned into blue water, Henderson pushed forward on the yoke and jerked it to the right. "Have a nice ride, asshole," he said as the plane leveled out and banked hard right. A loud thump resounded inside the aircraft.

He looked outside. His passenger had not the decency to fall off. "Take this!" Henderson said. He reefed the yoke left and pushed it forward.

He looked outside and saw the flapping body swing away from the fuselage and crash into the left wing. The man in the red suit outside was thrown far enough onto the wing to wrap an ankle around the leading edge.

"Damn!" Henderson said.

He straightened out his flight. He pointed the nose toward Canada. He reached up and took off his Stetson. He set it on the seat beside him. He reached into the inside pocket of his western cut coat and pulled out the double barrel .25 derringer pocketed there.

"Maybe this'll dislodge you, you jerk," Henderson muttered. He opened the door to shoot a couple of holes into Davecki.

45

It's not about position. It's about your disposition.

—M. Washington

It's a good thing I've been riding motorcycle all these years, Davecki thought. The grip in my right hand is good and strong. But it won't last long.

He looked down. Nothing but blue water. *If I let go now, I'll just go splash and have a nice swim.*

The plane veered and his body crashed into the body of the plane. Then the plane veered left and he was tossed up onto the wing.

Well, isn't that nice, he thought as he caught the edge of the wing with his left boot.

Now all I gotta do is...

"BAM! BAM!"

"Jesus!" Davecki prayed.

"FREEEOOOW," he felt a bullet ricochet off Rod's helmet.

Okay, you bugger. You're getting unreasonable. Davecki humped himself further onto the wing and looked at the man who had decided it was dying time.

"Damn," he said into his helmet. He could see the man was reloading a derringer.

Something will have to be done. Davecki re-gripped the wing with his left arm and let go of the handle that had saved his life thus far. Luckily the Aerostich designers were motorcyclists. They knew how to create an effective map pocket. What they didn't know was they'd also created the perfect pistol pouch. Davecki drew his Glock. He started pumping slugs into the engine cowling.

The plane's engine started sputtering after seven shots. By the thirteenth round, the engine made a sound like two cars crashing and the propeller suddenly appeared, motionless and upright in surprise. Black oil began streaming backward from the engine cowling.

Isn't that sweet, Davecki thought.

The pilot looked out the window. His face was not smiling.

Davecki saluted the man with the muzzle of the Glock.

The man at the controls did not return the courtesy.

Instead, the man pushed the door open wider, the better to shoot the pesky cop.

You just don't get it do you buddy? "Nuh-ahh," Davecki yelled into his helmet. He waggled the Glock in the upright, **don't-do-it** position.

The man's gun hand continued to reach around the door for a shot.

What a jerk, Davecki thought and he leveled his gun. Holding a bead on the man, Davecki prepared to shoot him dead with his two remaining bullets. Just as Davecki squeezed the trigger a loud report sounded. The plane, for all intents and purposes, jerked to a stop in mid-air. Davecki's arm slammed into the wing and the Glock flew off into space.

The airplane's door slammed forward and knocked the derringer from the gunman's hand.

The wind noise subsided exponentially.

Davecki looked up. He saw the contrail of a small rocket curving away into the blue sky. *If an angel was fishing, that would be his monofilament line.* Between the contrail and the plane, a huge parachute was deploying. *Isn't that something?*

The Cirrus' safety chute had deployed. The plane was drifting slowly downward as if it were suspended on a string from a teenager's bedroom ceiling. Compared to the screaming wind, and nearly unbearable forces tearing at him just moments ago, Davecki felt positively at ease.

Until he looked back at the bad man in the cockpit. Davecki saw Nevada Henderson reel in his arm and saw the safety harness fly off. The angular man leaned back and kicked the door with both feet. The door flew open and smacked Davecki right in the helmet.

What is with this guy? Davecki let go of his death grip on the wing and spun around on his back like an up-side-down turtle just as the bad guy crawled out of the cockpit. Holding the wing with both hands, Davecki kicked the door

"Ooofh." The bad guy caught the door in the chest. He staggered around the door while hanging tight. Once clear, he hurled a snakeskin kick of his own.

The blow caught Davecki in the haunch. "Ouch! Would you knock it off?" he said.

"Hah! I'll knock you off!" Henderson yelled. He let go of the door and dove on Davecki.

Davecki had no choice but to let go and defend himself.

The force of Henderson's landing tipped the plane wing ten degrees. It was enough of a dip to let both men slip off into the wild blue yonder.

Is this guy possessed? Davecki thought as Henderson wrapped his knuckly hands around his throat beneath the Duo-Tech helmet.

Henderson was screaming and choking and shaking Davecki.

This is not good. Davecki reached over and grabbed the lapels of Henderson's coat. Waiting for the right timing, Davecki bashed the bad man in the head with his helmet.

The assault stopped. Henderson's grip on Davecki's neck released. Blood spurted from a gash on the bad guy's forehead. Henderson put his hand to his wound and shook his other fist at Davecki. "Serves you right," Davecki said into his helmet as Henderson started drifting away.

46

Do unto others before they do unto you.

—The Golden Rule Revised

he *L.L Bean* was chugging back to port. In the pilot house, Fran Hansen applied a last strip of tape to the white bandage on Don Cameroon's arm. She tossed the tape in the first aid kit and snapped the lid shut. Suddenly a loud explosion in the sky above caused them all to look up.

"Now what?" Cameroon asked.

Simon Jensen, at the wheel of the boat, stuck his head out the port window. "It's a plane in trouble," he answered.

Hansen and Cameroon rushed out the narrow door, looked up.

"No. It's a man!" Fran said.

"No. It's two men!" Cameroon yelled.

The trio watched. The plane swung around like a pendulum under its huge parachute. The men fell.

"If we help those people, the University's going to find us out," Fran said.

"That's nonsense Fran," Cameroon said above the rumble of the big tug. "We ARE the University. Who's going to tell us our business? After Marder, the faculty rules." He held his bandaged arm.

"And how do we explain your gunshot wound?" Fran asked.

"Gunshot wound? Do you see a gunshot wound Simon?"

Jensen said, "All I see is an old guy who cut himself in the garage." He peered out of the window and said, "It looks like they're going to fall over there." He turned the steering wheel hard to port.

"Yes. Yes. Sharpening the lawn mower blade it was," Cameroon said.

Hansen sighed. "Whatever," she said. "But I'd still like to do some research. I'd like a paycheck for another twenty years or so."

"Well, for one, you've got tenure. Two, you can always take early retirement and take a job in the private sector. And three..."

"You could start selling water," Jensen interrupted.

"You'll always have work, Fran," Cameroon said. "Unlike Simon your skills will always be in demand."

"Well, thank you, Don. But, Fran's got a point. There might not be many private firms or Universities interested in hiring a geneticist who's got a proven record of commandeering State-owned dinghies."

"It'll never come to that in a million years. And, even if it did, it would be too much bad publicity. They'd make up a cover story."

"Yeah. Like we were out here on a personal pleasure cruise on this extremely comfortable luxury watercraft," Simon said.

"Or, if they were smart, they'd say we had students and were..."

"Don't even GO there, Don," Fran said.

"Speaking of going there... Look!" Simon said. "That one guy is steering himself in our direction!"

Three heads poked out of the pilot house to watch the aerial display.

"Will you look at that," Fran said.

"They're coming right toward us. This is getting out of hand. The last thing we need now is more visitors. Why all this commotion this morning?" Cameroon said.

"How on earth are they going to survive the fall?" Fran asked.

"It looks like that one guy has on some sort of suit or something. Isn't that a helmet on his head?" Simon asked.

"It sure looks like it. I wonder if it's some sort of publicity stunt?" Cameroon asked.

"For what? A funeral home? Death by skydiving?" Fran asked.

"Who knows and who cares?" Cameroon answered. "All I know is that one guy looks like he's going to smack into us!"

"Oh that'll be fun to clean up," Simon said.

"You are SO disgusting," Fran said.

"Well... It would be a mess," Simon said as he cut the power to the engine. "INCOMING!" he hollered as the man in the red suit splashed down nearby.

"Get below!" Cameroon yelled.

"I'll get the life ring," Fran yelled.

"A gaff might be more appropriate," Simon said.

"Would you SHUT UP!" Fran said.

"Anything you say, Boss," Simon said as he followed the two professors to the lower deck.

47

I like a man with faults, especially when he knows it.
To err is human—I'm uncomfortable around gods.

—Hugh Prather

s he fell, Davecki analyzed what his first move should be upon impact. *Remove helmet? Yeah. That's gotta go first. Then what? Boots? Gotta go. Yep. Then the suit. I don't think Aerostich adds buoyancy compensators as standard equipment.*

Okay, that's it. That's what I've got to do. Provided I'm not killed or knocked unconscious by the impact, Davecki thought. *Oh well. Might as well enjoy the view.*

Davecki looked around. There was Duluth. There was Enger Tower. He twisted in the air. *Hey! There's UW-Superior! I can see the smokestack belching all those environmentally friendly particulants into the air.*

Falling, falling, falling, Davecki enjoyed the view of the bays, the waterfront, the rivers and bridges. *This ain't such an awful terrible way to go, if I'm going,* Davecki reasoned.

Then he saw Henderson and realized the bad guy was maneuvering in the air. Steering his body like a bird, or a plane, or Superman.

What the heck is he up to now? Davecki looked at Henderson. *He's heading toward that boat down there. HEY! That's the L.L. Bean!*

Davecki imitated Henderson and found that he too could steer his body as it fell. He steered himself toward Henderson. *Now this is what I call a high speed chase. And nobody's going to call the Chief and complain!*

Davecki came closer and closer to Henderson. The water was rising fast. *How to land? Feet first? In a ball? No way am I going in head first. Hmmm. Helmet on or off? Definitely on. I like the ball configuration with feet down.* He tucked himself into a ball. *I hope I hit feet first.*

48

If you can't get out of it, get into it.

—Outward Bound Saying

The helmet came off easily. The suit unzipped easily. Shrugging out of the Aerostich went quickly but the left leg hung up on his boot. He thrashed his leg, but couldn't free himself. He sank. He swam upwards. Grateful for its weight and durability while being dragged by the Cirrus, Davecki thought, *I wish this thing wasn't so heavy.* He kicked hard and the suit finally fell off.

Popping to the surface, Davecki gasped for air. He swung his head around. Henderson was treading water on the surface three feet away. The tall cowboy was gagging and choking.

Davecki submerged himself and stroked toward the bad man. He grabbed Henderson by the belt buckle and pulled down. Together they sunk toward the bottom.

Kicks began raining down. The heel of Henderson's boot connected solidly with the top of Davecki's head. *Owww! Man! That hurts. I wish I really had the full story on this big jerk.* Another tremendous kick connected with Davecki's face. *I wonder what really happened at Palisade Head?* A knee connected with Davecki's jaw. He let go of Henderson's belt. He started sinking. *Who does that guy think he is? Why didn't he make a full confession before he killed me? Like they always do in the movies.* The chill of the water faded. He started to feel warm.

I wonder if Clara knows how to swim?

He heard voices. *Is that you, Mom?* Voices above him. *Or is that below?* His arms hung limp. Bubbles blew from his lips. *Not long now.*

His daughter Bethie's round, determined face floated across the inside of his eyelids. *Sorry, Bethie. You'll do great.*

He was sinking. But the voices? Davecki twisted around, looking for the sound. "I was sinking deep in sin, far from the peaceful shore," reverberated in his ears. *Man. I haven't heard that hymn for a long time.* Down, down, down he drifted. "I was sinking deep within, never to smile no more." *Where is that hymn coming from?* "Love lifted me. Love lifted me. When nothing else could help, love lifted me," echoed in his ears.

Davecki spun around in a 360 again. There was no choir anywhere in sight. Yet he could clearly hear the hymn being sung. Then, all of a sudden, Davecki realized, *Hey! That's me singing! So this is what it's like to die.*

"There's a song in my heart and it's glorious," he crooned. *I'll just float down and feed the fishes. That's not such a bad idea.*

As he sang, Davecki perceived a faint roaring sound that seemed to surround him. The sound grew, grew to a deafening din. *That's gotta be Death coming for me. But on a Harley?* The thundering sound hurt his ears. And then the pressure in his chest started to lighten. His descent stopped. He hung suspended in the water. Then his body started upwards. Faster, faster, he shot up. *Is something in the water pushing me up? I must have been a long ways down. Hey! Maybe this is the way to heaven? I won't have to burn, baby, burn up there.*

He continued going up, up, up. *Man, this is a long trip.* It was hours and hours of rising. Then "THUNK!" Davecki fell gracelessly on something hard. *Ow! Man! That's not water.* The impact of his collision caused him to gasp. His water and hymn-filled ears heard screams, shouts, and the roar receding. *Death's heading south.* Then silence.

He took another breath. *I'll be damned.* Davecki opened his eyes. The water looked dusty rose-colored and he could breathe. *Hey, this drowning to death ain't so bad as long as I can breathe underwater.*

49

He sent from on high, He took me; He drew me out of many waters.
He delivered me from my strong enemy, and from those who hated me,
for they were too mighty for me.

—Psalm 18:16-17

Davecki kept his eyes closed. He did, however, remember to keep breathing while, way down, in the deep psychological well of his own personal truth where he knew denial was a good thing for the moment, he erased the actual, factual happenings of the last few minutes.

Hands, watery fingers. Then human hands. Many human fingers, turned him over. He opened his eyes. Looming above, white faces. Don Cameroon and Fran Hansen, from the coffee shop. And a guy in a rubber suit. *Simon the Diver, I presume.* He wanted to say something, but when he opened his mouth, no words came out. He closed his eyes and concentrated on breathing.

Coffee. Davecki opened his eyes. He was in a little room. No, a boat cabin. *Steak Warning?* Fran's pale, worried face hove into view, holding a cup of coffee under his nose. He blinked. He realized he was propped up against a padded bench around a kitchen table, an army blanket was tucked around him.

"I'm a tea-drinker, actually," he croaked.

Hansen said, "I heard you can put ammonia under the nose of an unconscious person. Like smelling salts, you know. But we didn't have any ammonia. So I made coffee."

"You want me to drink ammonia?"

"Just drink the damned coffee, Davecki," Cameroon ordered.

Davecki reached out unsteadily and took the mug. It was warm. "It looks like I'm alive."

"Just barely." Jensen was leaning in the doorway.

Davecki hunched over the warm mug, holding it with both hands. He closed his eyes and sniffed the rich aroma. "What in the world happened?"

Fran sat heavily in the bench across from Davecki and put her head in her hands.

Davecki looked around. "Where's Henderson?"

Blank looks from the three musketeers. "You mean Kevin Halstrom?" Cameroon asked.

"Who in the world is that? What I want to know is, where's the bad guy? Henderson. The guy that was shooting at you earlier. The guy who tried to pick me off the wing of his airplane."

The three looked from one to the other. After a pause, Cameroon said, "Well, I don't know who this Henderson fellow is, but the guy you fell from the sky with, we knew as Kevin Halstrom-Black Bear. And... Well... He's gone."

"Well, you can call him by any name you want. But, the guy you're calling Kevin Hallstrom was really Nevada Henderson and I was after him for killing Little Willie Horton. He got away? How did that happen?"

Fran gasped. "What? HE killed Little Willie. I can't believe it. He was at the FALSIES meeting just last night."

"See? See?" Cameroon said. "I TOLD you that it was him!"

"Well, it was dark. I wasn't looking when the lead started flying," Fran said.

"I KNEW it was Halstrom," Cameroon said. "But NOOOO, you just can't give in and believe in me. Just because I'm old and..."

"All right. All right. Knock it off you two," Jensen said. "It sounds like this Henderson and Kevin Hallstrom are one in the same."

"That's what I was figuring," Davecki said. "Just yesterday I met a girlfriend of Henderson's. What she told me led me to Knute the Fishman. What he said led me to the lake last night. This morning I spotted him out here. He was shooting at you guys. I chased him to Sky Harbor. We fell in the water. He kicked me like a mule a couple of times. I sank. The lake sang hymns to me and now you tell me, after all that, that he got away?"

"Well. That explains it. Hallstrom got Knute to get him in the meeting," Hansen said.

"What it doesn't explain is, why was he shooting at us?" Jensen asked.

"Because his boss, according to the girlfriend, was selling Lake Superior water to the highest bidder through a pipeline," Davecki said. "As unlikely as that seems, something tells me you three know a lot more about that than I do."

The three pipeline pluggers exchanged glances.

Davecki asked, "So what happened to Henderson-Hallstrom? He got away?"

"Not exactly," Hansen said.

"What exactly?" Davecki asked. He looked at Jensen.

Jensen just shrugged his shoulders. "All I know is, when it was obvious you were sinking for good, I dove in to fetch you."

"Thanks a lot," Davecki said.

Cameroon said, "Well, after Simon was under for a minute or so, the lake sort of, hmmm, sort of exploded."

"Exploded?"

"Well, that's the best explanation I can give. The water turned reddish and expanded rapidly."

"Expanded?" Davecki asked.

"It was strange," Hansen said.

"No kidding. Water doesn't explode on a regular basis," Davecki said.

"Not unless there's lots of ammonium nitrate and fuel oil involved," Jensen said grinning.

"What's so funny, Simon?" Cameroon asked.

"Well, when I was down there looking around for you, all hell broke loose. I was swimming and all, but a big huge current came along and dragged me toward the bottom." Jensen stepped up to the table, unzipped his dry suit. He stuck a hand in and fished around. "The cool thing is... when I had been sucked to the bottom, I looked down and there in the sand were these." He pulled his hand out and revealed four twenty-dollar gold pieces.

"What?" Fran shrieked.

"Oh my God," Cameroon blurted.

"What's the deal?" Davecki asked.

Jensen smirked and said, "These, my friend, are gold coins from the wreck of the *Benjamin Noble*."

"Awesome," Davecki said. "But what I want to know is, where's the damn bad guy?"

No one answered.

"What's the problem? Tell me." Davecki looked at Cameroon.

Cameroon rasped the gray stubble on his chin with his fingers. "Wellll..."

"Jensen?" Davecki asked.

"Don't look at me."

"Hansen?"

"All I can figure," Fran said, "is that it was a seiche."

Davecki stared. "A what?"

"A seiche. It's a sudden, brief change in the level of the lake. Usually due to high wind or extreme air pressure. In most cases it's only a matter of a foot or so, but I suppose such an extreme manifestation is possible." Her voice trailed away.

Cameroon said, "I was standing at the railing looking down into the water for Simon to pop up or for dead bodies to surface and all of a sudden it was like an explosion and this thick muscular arm of water shot straight up in the air about ten feet. It was at least six feet in diameter. Maybe it was more like a tongue. You," Cameroon stared at Davecki, "were on top of the wave."

Davecki gulped. "Me?"

"You," Cameroon answered.

"I saw it too," Fran said. "The wave-tongue-thingy..."

"So very scientific," Jensen said.

"Shut up, Simon." Fran smoothed her hair. "The seiche just flicked you off and onto the deck."

"Yeah, like a frog catching a fly, only in reverse," Cameroon said.

"So very sci..."

"SHUT UP, SIMON," Cameroon and Jensen said simultaneously.

"And Henderson?"

Cameroon and Fran glanced at each other. "That was the weird part," Fran said.

Davecki looked at Jensen. "Hey. Don't look at me. I was down below loading my pockets with these." He pulled more gold coins from inside his suit.

Davecki looked at Cameroon. The old professor shrugged. He was without words for once in his life. The shuddering cop looked at Fran. She remained mute. "GIVE!" he used his command voice.

Fran stuttered, "I can hardly believe it, but, right in the middle of the column of water that you were on top of..."

"Was Hallstrom," Cameroon said.

"It was the most unbelievable sight I've ever seen in my life. It was terrible and beautiful at the same time." Cameroon said. "The water had him. It was wrapped around him like a fist."

"And the stranger thing was," Fran pitched in, "he looked like he'd been electrocuted or something. Like he was totally shocked."

"Just like a deer in the headlights," Cameroon added.

"The wave sort of quivered for a second and then it did an abrupt reversal and, SPLASH! It... he... was gone. Sucked down. And he was just...gone. He didn't come back up."

"That's it?" Davecki asked.

"You asked," Simon said.

"I wish I hadn't."

Silence reigned in the cabin for a minute.

"Well, unless we want to do more aquatic research on this trip, may I suggest we make for port?" Simon asked.

"This is all going to be very hard to explain," Davecki said.

"Nothing to it," Simon said. "Davecki caught up to the guy who killed Little Willie. He drowned. Lake Superior doesn't give up its dead, don't you know. We fished the good officer out of the water. End of story."

"No customized zebra mussels?" Fran asked.

"Not unless you want to lose tenure," Cameroon said.

"What's he doing aboard then?" Fran asked nodding at Cameroon.

"Just a little improper ride for a fellow professor," Cameroon said. "Unseemly, but not much more than a minor embarrassment to all."

"Hey, I'm game," Fran said.

"And I'm just here doing my job catching drug running murderers," Davecki said.

"Fire her up, Simon. We're heading for the dock," Hansen said.

Davecki sipped the coffee. "This stuff is going to give me a headache."

50

*Women sometimes forgive a man who forces the opportunity,
but never a man who misses one.*

—Talleyrand-Perigord

Davecki knocked. Almost instantly, Clara opened the door. He walked in.

She took in the sight: Davecki, still wet, pale, bleeding slightly from his cut.

He looked back at her mutely.

"You didn't go to the hospital did you?"

He shook his head, shivering.

"Sit down." Putting her hands on his shoulders, she steered him to a wing back chair. She took a Hudson's Bay blanket from the sofa and covered him with it. "I'm just going to run upstairs and get some bandages and things."

"I'm getting your chair wet."

"Stop talking." She disappeared.

She could have asked if I got him.

He heard foot steps.

A voice said, "What happened to you?"

He opened his eyes. It was Dolly.

"I got in a fight with Henderson," Davecki answered.

"Did you kill the bastard?"

"No," Davecki said.

"What? What happened!"

Davecki sighed. "I don't really know. The lake got him."

"What? Don't talk crazy. I can't take any more crazy talk. What happend?" Dolly asked.

"All I can say is, they're out dragging for him right now. He never came up."

"If he's not dead, I'm not safe," Dolly said.

Clara entered the room with a first-aid kit. "Henderson drowned?"

"That's about it," Davecki said.

"What does that mean? There's more to the story?"

Davecki shrugged. "All I know is I just about drowned and he actually did."

"You're acting strange, detective."

"Like you said, I'm stranger than most."

Dolly laughed. "Ouch! That hurts," she pressed her palm against her swollen face.

"Maybe you should go put an ice pack on your cheek," Clara said.

"Right," Dolly said. She waved her fingers at him. "Bye bye." She breezed out.

Davecki looked at Clara. *Holy mackerel! I gotta get out of here.* "Thanks," he said. "I should go make a report."

"Since when has paperwork been so important to you?" Clara asked.

"Well, once in a while I'm responsible."

She blinked. "Well. You have a big cut on your forehead, Detective."

"Really? I didn't know."

"Can I at least clean it up?"

"Okay."

Clara knelt down. She lifted her hands to the gash on his forehead, frowning slightly.

He watched her work.

"It looks like a surface wound," she muttered.

"What made you call me Alphonse?" he asked.

Her eyes shifted to his. Her hands stilled. "Pardon?"

"On your porch. I was about to strangle Dolly. You called me Alphonse."

"Oh. It just came out. I called you everything else but you weren't listening." She tilted her head, her hands were still on either side of his face. "I wondered about that, later. What made you hear that and not the others?"

He grinned. "No one but my Ma calls me that. So whenever I hear 'Alphonse' I listen."

"Ah." She laughed. She rummaged around in her first aid kit, then swabbed some hydrogen peroxide into his cut.

"Ouch!"

"It doesn't hurt, you big baby. It just bubbles."

"Who's got the cut-open face?"

"You do, Detective." A drop of hydrogen peroxide dripped onto his cheek. She wiped it away with her thumb and tucked the blanket around him more firmly.

He reached up and caught her hand. "Can we be on a first name basis now?"

She looked surprised, but left her hand in his. "Fine by me, Alphonse."

"Call me Dave," he said. He pulled her into his lap and kissed her.

She kissed back.

51

Crime and punishment grow out of one stem.

—Emerson
Compensation, 1841

The great blue lake snuggled in to its basin atop the largest, thickest and oldest slab of solid basalt on the planet. The weight of the water depressed the earth's crust. The depression was purely physical. There was no trace of anxiety or self-hate anywhere in evidence. No, the great lake was satisfied to hunker down in its place and just watch.

There, before the essence of the largest body of fresh water in the world, a man floated, suspended as if in midair, held by the grip of the mighty water. Nevada Henderson's eyes were wide with terror and pain.

Upon that bad man thousands of eager zebra mussels nibbled with minuscule lips of revenge.

Much to the Big Lake's delight.

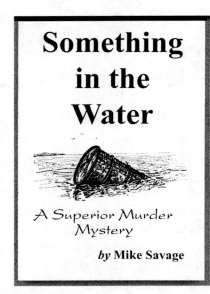

Something in the Water

A Superior Murder Mystery

by Mike Savage

If you haven't read Dave Davecki's first adventure, get your copy of *Something in the Water* as soon a humanly possible.

In this page turner, Davecki "investigates" the death of environmentalist Thurber Gronsby, whose body is found washed up on the sandy shore of Wisconsin Point. In the end the "true" contents of what is in those mysterious barrels dumped in Lake Superior back in the 1950s and '60s is revealed.

Don Boxmeyer of the *St. Paul Pioneer Press* said the book, "Plunges the reader into a real life mystery."

The Superior Daily Telegram said of Something in the water, "Reading Savage is a lot of fun."

Dave Davecki's second adventure involves the rash of arson fires that burned down numerous historic buildings in Superior, Wisconsin. *Burn Baby Burn* isn't quite as innocent as *Something in the Water*, but it does involve a new

partner, and she's a woman. As one reviewer said, "Dave Davecki, the loveless hermit, finds a pal, and she's a gal."

This time Davecki and "Bubba" end up in mortal danger in that most evil of towns, "Murderapolis," where the bad guy provides a scorcher of an ending.

The Duluth News Tribune reviewer said, "A bang-up read whose pages turn themselves."

Kyle Eller of *The Duluth Budgeteer* said, "Mike Savage's new book is good fun."

Other Savage Press Books

BUSINESS

SoundBites by Kathy Kerchner, Second Edition
Dare to Kiss the Frog by vanHauen, Kastberg & Soden

ESSAY

Hint of Frost, Essays on the Earth by Rusty King
Battlenotes: Music of the Vietnam War by Lee Andresen
Hometown Wisconsin by Marshall J. Cook
Potpourri From Kettle Land by Irene I. Luethge

FICTION

Burn Baby Burn by Mike Savage
Keeper of the Town by Don Cameron
Mindset by Enrico Bostone
Something in the Water by Mike Savage
The Year of the Buffalo by Marshall J. Cook
Voices From the North Edge by St. Croix Writers
Walkers in the Mist by Hollis D. Normand

REGIONAL HISTORY, HUMOR MEMOIR

Beyond the Freeway by Peter J. Benzoni
Beyond the Mine by Peter J. Benzoni
Crocodile Tears and Lipstick Smears by Fran Gabino
Fair Game by Fran Gabino
Some Things You Never Forget by Clem Miller
Stop in the Name of the Law by Alex O'Kash
Superior Catholics by Cheney and Meronek
Widow of the Waves by Bev Jamison

OUTDOORS, SPORTS & RECREATION

Curling Superiority! by John Gidley
The Final Buzzer by Chris Russell
The Duluth Tour Book by Jeff Cornelius
Dan's Dirty Dozen by Mike Savage

POETRY

Appalachian Mettle by Paul Bennett
Eraser's Edge by Phil Sneve
Gleanings from the Hillsides by E.M. Johnson
In the Heart of the Forest by Diana Randolph
Moments Beautiful Moments Bright by Brett Bartholomaus
Nameless by Charlie Buckley
Pathways by Mary B. Wadzinski
Philosophical Poems by E.M. Johnson
Poems of Faith and Inspiration by E.M. Johnson
The Morning After the Night She Fell Into the Gorge
by Heidi Howes
Thicker Than Water by Hazel Sangster
Treasured Thoughts by Sierra
Treasures from the Beginning of the World by Jeff Lewis

SOCIAL JUSTICE

Throwaway People: Danger in Paradise by Peter Opack

SPIRITUALITY

The Awakening of the Heart by Jill Downs
The Hillside Story by Pastor Thor Sorenson
Life's Most Relevant Reality by Rod Kissinger, S.J.

OTHER BOOKS AVAILABLE FROM SP

Blueberry Summers by Lawrence Berube
Beyond the Law by Alex O'Kash
Cool Fishing for Kids 8—85
by Frankie Paull and "Jackpine" Bob Cary
Dakota Brave by Howard Johnson
Heart to Heart by Janet Kay
Jackpine Savages by Frank Larson
The Brule River, A Guide's Story by Lawrence Berube
Waterfront by Alex O'Kash

To order additional copies of

LAKE EFFECT

or to receive a copy of the complete
Savage Press Catalog,
contact us at:

Local calls:
(Superior, WI/Duluth, MN area)
715-394-9513

National Voice and FAX orders
1-800-732-3867

E-mail:
mail@savpress.com

Visit on-line at:
www.savpress.com

Visa/MasterCard Accepted

All Savage Press books are available at all chain and
independent bookstores nationwide. Just ask them to
special order if the title is not in stock.